"I want to remind you that this 'marriage' is in name only.

"Any displays of affection will be strictly for the public eye. Agreed?" Caroline asked.

"Absolutely."

"And I sure hope you're not one of those bozos who believes he's a knight in shining armor, because I never believed in fairy tales. Bottom line—I take care of myself."

"Anything else? Good. Now it's my turn," Jeff said. "First, this 'marriage of convenience' is anything but. And second, in deference to all the chivalrous men who still believe that helping a lady is the decent and honorable thing to do…" He offered her a gracefully sweeping bow. "Sir Bozo, at your service."

Dear Reader,

Holiday greetings from all of us at Silhouette Books to all of you. And along with my best wishes, I wanted to give you a present, so I put together six of the best books ever as your holiday surprise. Emilie Richards starts things off with *Woman Without a Name*. I don't want to give away a single one of the fabulous twists and turns packed into this book, but I *can* say this: You've come to expect incredible emotion, riveting characters and compelling storytelling from this award-winning writer, and this book will not disappoint a single one of your high expectations.

And in keeping with the season, here's the next of our HOLIDAY HONEYMOONS, a miniseries shared with Desire and written by Carole Buck and Merline Lovelace. *A Bride for Saint Nick* is Carole's first Intimate Moments novel, but you'll join me in wishing for many more once you've read this tale of a man who thinks he has no hope of love, only to discover—just in time for Christmas—that a wife and a ready-made family are his for the asking.

As for the rest of the month, what could be better than new books from Sally Tyler Hayes and Anita Meyer, along with the contemporary debuts of historical authors Elizabeth Mayne and Cheryl St.John? So sit back, pick up a book and start to enjoy the holiday season. And don't forget to come back next month for some Happy New Year reading right here at Silhouette Intimate Moments, where the best is always waiting to be unwrapped.

Yours,

Leslie Wainger
Senior Editor and Editorial Coordinator

Please address questions and book requests to:
Silhouette Reader Service
U.S.: 3010 Walden Ave., P.O. Box 1325, Buffalo, NY 14269
Canadian: P.O. Box 609, Fort Erie, Ont. L2A 5X3

THE BRIDE
AND THE
BODYGUARD

ANITA MEYER

Published by Silhouette Books
America's Publisher of Contemporary Romance

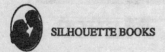

SILHOUETTE BOOKS

ISBN 0-373-07754-8

THE BRIDE AND THE BODYGUARD

This edition published by arrangement with Harlequin Books S.A.

® and TM are trademarks of Harlequin Books S.A., used under license.
Trademarks indicated with ® are registered in the United States Patent
and Trademark Office, the Canadian Trade Marks Office and in other
countries.

Printed in U.S.A.

Books by Anita Meyer

Silhouette Intimate Moments

Chandler's Child #581
The Bride and the Bodyguard #754

ANITA MEYER

lives in Denver, Colorado, with her husband and two children. She devotes her time to her family, writing, tennis and square dancing—in that order. Her passion for writing and her experience as a former teacher led her to establish a publishing center at a local school, where elementary students come to edit, rewrite, illustrate and publish their own stories.

She has won a number of awards (both for writing and tennis!) and she is an active member of several writing organizations. She loves to hear from her readers, who can reach her at: P.O. Box 6074, Denver, Colorado 80206.

For Rick,
my attorney, my planner, my husband, my "Jeff."
Thanks for filling every day with happy surprises.

Prologue

Caroline Southeby glanced around nervously, then jammed the bills from the automated teller machine into her pocket. After punching the buttons one more time, she turned up the collar of her jacket against the cold drizzle and waited for the machine to register another transaction. At a hundred dollars a pop, it had taken most of the night to get the money. Five withdrawals with a guaranteed check card... Hop the subway to the next exit... another five hundred from MasterCard... Find another machine... five more, courtesy of Visa. And now, American Express. A grand total of two thousand dollars. It wasn't much, but you could make it last if you knew what you were doing.

And she did.

Caroline pressed her back against the machine and studied the street in both directions. Nothing. No one.

A gust of wind whipped her hair and sent an icy chill through her body. For once she was glad. This was the kind of weather that kept the indigent huddled in the alleys and the gangs deep in their lairs. Even the police would gravitate to some local hangout on a night like this. Which was just fine with her. The last person she wanted to see right now was a cop.

She stooped down to tie the laces on her running shoe and covertly slipped the five bills under the arch of her foot. Next stop was the New York Port Authority Bus Terminal. She slung the backpack over her shoulder, tucked her chin to her chest, and sloshed along Thirty-seventh Street.

The rain was coming down harder now. Not the warm, gentle shower you expected in early May, but a cold, stinging rain that matched her mood. What she wouldn't give for a cup of Johanna's special-blend coffee and one of her own bakery confections. But The Coffee Café was undoubtedly being watched. She couldn't go near her little shop until this mess was over.

She paid cash for her ticket to Pittsburgh, then climbed aboard the old Greyhound and took a seat in the back. Her denim jacket was soaked and she struggled out of it, then spread it on the seat next to her to dry. As the other passengers boarded the bus, she covertly watched them, taking mental stock. None of them paid her any attention. Finally the driver closed the door, and the bus pulled away from the terminal.

Caroline leaned her head back against the seat and closed her eyes. Almost at once, echoes of her brothers' voices sounded inside her head. *Remember, Caroline. If you're ever in trouble, use cash. Once you hit the road, there can be no credit cards, no checks, no paper trail of any kind.*

"I know, Alden," she whispered.

Move at night. Double back if you have to. You're on your own now, Princess. So remember the stuff we taught you.

"I will, Brian. I won't forget."

No, she would never forget. She would remember everything—all of it—remember the pieces of Alden's boat dragged back to shore, his body lost at sea . . . remember seeing Brian blown away by a single shot . . . remember staring into the cold, hate-filled eyes of Augie Davis. She remembered running to the police, agreeing to testify against the crime boss who had killed her brothers. She remembered being spirited off to a cheap motel, surrounded by detectives who had sworn to protect her—men who passed the time playing cards...reading books...checking their guns.

Caroline shivered reflexively. Somebody, somewhere, had been willing to tell Davis what he needed to know. Like an ugly, monstrous octopus, his tentacles stretched far and deep. Protective custody had lasted only two months. A barrage of gunfire had exploded this morning, shattering the stillness. One cop was killed instantly, two others exchanged fire with the hired assassins, while the fourth jumped out a back window, dragging her with him. She remembered running and stumbling and running again. She remembered the confusion, the sirens, the gathering crowd—and that was when she knew. If she was going to live long enough to put Augie Davis away, she'd have to do it on her own. She bolted into the crowd, and zigzagged her way through stores and shops, until she was sure she had lost the detective.

Caroline looked out the bus window as the cold, gray city began to slip away. She had scribbled a postcard to the D.A.'s office saying she'd be back for Augie Davis's trial. And in the meantime, she'd spend three long months on the road, living out of a backpack, eating at greasy truck stops, always looking over her shoulder. It wouldn't be easy, but it was a whole lot better than the alternative. She couldn't trust the police, and she'd never again agree to being locked up for her own good. She'd do it her way or not at all. And when the time came, she would go back to New York and avenge her beloved brothers.

Raindrops streamed down the window in rivulets, and Caroline watched her reflection cry.

First Alden, then Brian.

And everyone knew bad things always came in threes.

Chapter 1

Jeff McKensie looked from the cashier's check in his hand to the man seated in front of his desk. "Let me get this straight, Arthur. You're offering me twenty-five thousand dollars in cash and a first-class, all-expenses-paid trip to the Virgin Islands."

"That's right."

Jeff rocked back in his tall leather chair and looked skeptically at the old man. Arthur Peterson—Federal Marshal and self-appointed protector of the McKensie clan. Because Jeff's father and Arthur had been best friends, Arthur had been a pseudo member of the family for as long as Jeff could remember. "Uncle" Arthur seemed to think that gave him certain rights—namely, the right to involve Jeff in federal business whenever he needed help. Whatever it was Arthur wanted, it was guaranteed to interrupt, disrupt, and wreak havoc with Jeff's orderly life.

Reluctantly, Jeff studied the old man. His hair was a lot thinner than the last time he had popped into Jeff's life, but his eyebrows were as bushy as ever. To a kid, those brows had been a source of amazement. Especially when Jeff's brother, Mac, persuaded him they were two caterpillars who had taken up permanent residence on Arthur's forehead. But even with those ridiculous brows, Arthur's face was always controlled, exposing only what he wanted you to see.

Today, his face revealed nothing. And he seemed perfectly content to wait for Jeff to take the bait.

Not this time, Arthur.

Knowing the old man was watching every move, Jeff slowly folded the check in half lengthwise. Then he bent back the edges and glanced at Arthur out of the corner of his eye. He certainly had the man's attention. Jeff finished folding the check into a neat little paper airplane and ran his thumb and forefinger along the center crease. He zipped the plane through the air, across the desk, and watched it land, nose first, in Arthur's lap.

"Very amusing," Arthur said, his reserve cracking ever so slightly. "But aren't you even the least bit curious?"

Jeff clasped his hands behind his head and smiled. "Nope."

"You truly don't want to know anything? Her name, her background, her life-threatening situation?"

"Sorry to disappoint you, Arthur, but I'm not interested. If I ask one simple question, I'll be hooked. You'll reel me in faster than a tuna off the back of Mac's boat. Whatever it is, I won't do it. So why don't you leave and let me get back to work?"

Arthur crossed his right leg over his left and settled in the chair. "My dear boy, you wound me. When have I ever had anything but your best interests at heart?"

Jeff threw Arthur a look that would have silenced most men.

Arthur cleared his throat. "Well, be that as it may, I need your help."

"No."

"Jeff, a woman's life is in my hands. At least hear me out." The next word was barely perceptible. "Please."

Jeff looked at the stack of files littering his desk. There were a hundred things he should be doing right now, and listening to some damsel-in-distress story wasn't even in the top fifty. Jeff sighed. The least he could do was to give the old man a sporting chance. "I'm not biting, Arthur," he warned. "But you're welcome to dangle the bait."

Arthur's normally controlled features flooded with relief and he pulled his chair closer to Jeff's desk. "Ever hear of a man named Augie Davis?"

Jeff raised his eyebrows and looked at Arthur curiously. "Every lawyer and lawman in the country has heard of Augie Davis," he answered. "Small-time punk turned syndicated crime boss. He's the biggest success story since Al Capone."

Arthur nodded. "Davis clawed his way to the top, destroying everything and anyone that stood his way. For the last twenty years he's had a very close association with an accountant named Donald Southeby. Rumor has it that Southeby did a lot more than just balance the books. Anyway, Southeby died of a heart attack. Coroner said it was completely legit. The old man's arteries were as hard as cement. But get this—less than a month later, the oldest son, Alden, drowns in a boating 'accident.' And a few weeks after that, the younger son, Brian, is shot to death."

Arthur moved to one of the large windows overlooking downtown San Diego. "Davis is into everything," he continued with his back to Jeff. "And the NYPD has been trying for years to find something that will hold up against him in court. That something turned out to be someone." He turned around and faced Jeff once again. "Caroline Southeby, the last of the family, witnessed her brother's shooting. She's willing to testify against Davis."

"So what's the problem?" Jeff asked. "She testifies. He goes to jail. Case closed."

"*If* she testifies," Arthur corrected. "Davis isn't going to sit around and wait for that to happen...He wants her dead."

Jeff came around to the front of the desk, propped one hip against it, and crossed his arms. "That's why we have cops, Arthur. You put her in a room with someone willing to stare at four walls and order a lot of room service, while the D.A. tries to move up the trial date. Cops do it all the time."

"Thank you, professor, but we tried that—with four men."

"And?" Jeff prompted. The question popped out before he could stop it.

"And something went awry," Arthur admitted slowly. "Two guys stormed the place. When the smoke cleared, one officer and both hit men were dead."

"And the girl?"

Arthur shook his head. "One of the detectives got her out, but she took off and he lost her in the crowd."

"Smart lady," Jeff said. "No offense, Arthur, but I'd split, too, if someone was shooting at me."

Arthur dropped down in the chair with an uncharacteristic resignation. "She was on the road more than three weeks before we caught up with her. She's pretty good. Has a lot of street smarts. But if we can find her, so can Davis, and needless to say, she refuses to have anything more to do with the police."

"I repeat," Jeff said, "smart lady." He pushed himself away from the desk and poured two cups of coffee.

Arthur accepted one of the cups with a grateful nod. "Word on the street is that there are a couple of heavy-duty contracts just waiting to be filled."

"So that's where you come in," Jeff interjected. "You put her in the Witness Protection Program, give her a new name, a new social security number, and dump her in the middle of Iowa."

"Wrong." Arthur took a long, slow breath and swallowed. "That's where *you* come in."

Jeff's cup stalled halfway to his mouth.

"Jeff, I can't 'dump her in the middle of Iowa,' as you so quaintly put it, and leave her alone and unprotected. There's got to be someone with her—someone like you."

"Forget it," Jeff said flatly. "Find someone else."

"There *is* no one else, and I wouldn't be here if I had other options. The raid on the motel leaves little doubt that Davis had a contact inside the department. She doesn't trust the police, so I need a civilian," Arthur said coolly. "Twenty-five to thirty years old, reasonably good-looking—"

Jeff laughed. "I'm flattered."

"He needs the instincts of a cop, the experience of a bodyguard, and the talent of an actor. I say that's you."

"And I say you're crazy. I'm a lawyer now, not a P.I. I shuffle papers for a living. The guy you want has an office three floors down. His name's Bond. James Bond."

Arthur wasn't laughing. "You don't lose the skills just because your license expires. Besides, your new career is perfect. No one will suspect a lawyer of being able to do anything."

"Gee, thanks," Jeff said. "But I'm still not interested in joining your cloak-and-dagger set." He picked up a thick file from his desk and casually opened it. "Good seeing you again, Arthur."

"I'm not going anywhere," Arthur replied. He leaned forward and put his cup on the desk. "Not until I convince you to help."

Jeff clenched his teeth and steeled himself for the oncoming lecture. Any time Arthur really wanted something, he brought out the big guns.

"Jeff, I've been part of your life since the day you were born. Hell, you and Mac were the sons I never had. When your father died, I swore on his grave I'd finish what he started. Fact is, there wasn't much left for me to do. Your brother was already on his own and at twelve years old, you were well on your way. But I was there for you. I made it to football games, band concerts, graduation, the whole works. I helped you get your P.I. license and watched you work your tail off to get through college and law school, and I couldn't have been prouder if you were my own son."

Jeff raked a hand through his hair. Arthur's contributions to the McKensies' success seemed to grow with the passing of time. But it wasn't worth debating. "I know, Arthur."

"And look at you now." Arthur made a great show of admiring the tastefully decorated office with its walnut desk and floor-to-ceiling shelves filled with law books. "Mr. Up-and-Coming Attorney, an associate in a prestigious San Diego law firm. Rumor has it you'll be a full partner in about three years."

"Rumor, huh?" Jeff shook his head. "Then you'll appreciate why I don't want to give this up."

"Which is why you'll be compensated for your inconvenience." Arthur smoothed out the check and put it back on Jeff's desk.

"'Inconvenience'?" Jeff laughed at the absurdity. "Arthur, I make good money sitting behind a desk. I don't need to risk my life to get more. Besides, I seriously doubt the managing partner is going to understand my wanting a two-month vacation in Iowa."

"Au contraire," Arthur said, grinning. "He understands completely. Your job and your clients will be waiting for you when you return."

Jeff blinked. "You already talked to him?"

"Of course, my boy. I would never risk your career."

"No, just my life," Jeff muttered.

"And for the record," Arthur said, ignoring Jeff's comment, "you won't be going anywhere near Iowa. You're getting married."

"Say *what?*"

"It won't be a legitimate ceremony," Arthur amended. "Real license, real chapel, real cake, phony minister. Just enough to persuade people that this is on the up-and-up."

Jeff looked at Arthur as though he were certifiable. "No one is going to believe I woke up this morning and decided to marry the first woman who walked through the door. And stop talking as though I've already agreed to this harebrained scheme."

"Everyone will believe it," Arthur insisted. "She's someone you met while taking the bar review and now she works in northern California. Or maybe she's an old college sweetheart you recently ran into and the passion was rekindled. Be creative. Make something up. And after the wedding, you'll take your new bride on a nice, long, quiet, relaxing honeymoon in the Virgin Islands."

"Spending a couple of months dodging bullets with a total stranger is not my idea of 'quiet and relaxing,'" Jeff countered. "Besides, I can't pull this off by myself. I'll need help, and you don't trust the people in your own department to back me up."

"Then bring Mac in. We'll pay his expenses, too. Tell me what you need, and I'll get it for you. Anything at all." The appeal in Arthur's voice was unmistakable. "Just say yes."

Jeff had a real soft spot where the old man was concerned, and what was worse, Arthur knew it. But this time he had gone too far. Jeff shook his head. "Come on, Arthur, you must know a dozen guys who do this for a living."

"Sure, I know them. But right now, you're the only one I trust." Arthur stood and pulled a photo from the inside pocket of his suit jacket. "I've got a dozen look-alike operatives running across the country trying to divert suspicion from her." He threw the picture on the desk in front of Jeff. "But if you don't help her, she won't live to see her next birthday."

Reluctantly, Jeff glanced at the photo. It was of a woman in her mid- to late-twenties and slender, which gave her a delicate, fragile appearance. Appearances were deceiving, he reminded himself. She had already survived attempted murder and living on the streets. She was probably stronger than he was.

Jeff looked again at the picture. She had an oval face and dark brown hair that brushed the tops of her shoulders and curled in waves around an elegant neck. She was smiling, her lips were full and sensuous, her nose was small and straight. And her eyes . . .

Slowly he picked up the photo. Her eyes were a mesmerizing deep brown. Dark and tempting. Laughing now, but filled with passion. Eyes that touched his soul, stupid as that sounded.

He glanced at Arthur, then looked back at the picture. Once again, those eyes made his stomach knot.

Jeff slowly released the breath he hadn't realized he'd been holding. "You don't play fair, Arthur."

Arthur's expression was a painful mixture of affection and determination. "I can't afford to."

* * *

"Mr. Davis?" The young lady rapped softly on the open door.

"Yes, Susan, what is it?" He beckoned with his hand and she crossed the plush carpet to stand in front of his desk.

"Reports have been coming in all morning from around the country—about the missing woman." Susan offered him a stack of pink message slips.

"Thank you, my dear." He smiled benevolently. "That will be all for now."

One by one, Augie Davis carefully spread out the pieces of paper. Caroline Southeby spotted in Tampa. Southeby woman last seen in Oregon. Southeby reported in New England. Woman matching Southeby's description on the run in Dallas.

Pulling a lined pad from a drawer, he drew up a two-column list—location on the left; operative on the right. He recorded each message, then ran the pink slips through the paper shredder.

And that was exactly what he would do to Caroline Southeby.

Jeff slumped against the inside of the phone booth. It had been less than twenty-four hours since Arthur had talked him into this madness, and already Jeff regretted it. Last night he had flown to Sacramento. This morning he had gone through a rigorous briefing/training session which only served to confirm what a fool he'd been to let Arthur talk him into this assignment. And then this afternoon, he and a policewoman posing as "Caroline Peterson," niece of Federal Marshal Arthur Peterson, went to the Clerk and Recorder's Office and took out a marriage license. Arthur had the real Caroline under lock and key while he prepared the new identity. On the day of the wedding, Arthur would turn her over to Jeff and from then until the trial she was his responsibility.

Jeff pulled a wallet from his back pocket and gently withdrew the photo tucked in the billfold. He had probably looked at that picture a dozen times and every time those eyes hit him in the gut.

He slid the picture back into his wallet and pulled out a telephone calling card. Charging the call to his home number, he drummed his fingers impatiently while he counted the rings.

"'Lo?" The voice on the other end sounded groggy and thick with sleep.

"Mac, is that you?"

"Hey, bro." Mac yawned loudly into the phone. "What d'you want at this hour of the morning?"

"It's the middle of the afternoon, Mac. Open the blinds on that dinghy you sleep in and see for yourself."

The rattle of venetian blinds going up was followed by a loud wince and the crash of the self-same blinds coming down. "You made your point, kid. Now if there's nothing else I'm going to put out an A.P.B. on a bottle of aspirin."

"Wait a minute, Mac. I didn't fly all the way to Sacramento to give you a long-distance wake-up call. We have to talk."

"Sacramento? What are you doing up there?"

Jeff took a deep breath. "I'm getting married next week and I want you to be my best man." The silence on the other end had Jeff convinced Mac had gone off in search of something for his headache. "Mac, you still there?"

"Oh, yeah, I'm here." The sleep had drained from Mac's voice, and, if nothing else, Jeff at least had his brother's full attention. "Kind of sudden, isn't it?" Mac continued.

"Yeah, well, it can't wait."

Mac's epithet was colorful to say the least. "Damn it, Jeff. How could you be so careless? Are you sure it's yours?"

Jeff stared at the phone in disbelief. Yesterday he was sitting in his office, minding his own business, thinking the world was a pretty nice place. Today he had a fiancée who was being chased by members of the New York underworld and a brother who was looking to become an uncle.

"It's not what you think, Mac. I'll explain everything when I get back. Just clear your calendar and start packing. I'll need your help when I get her to the Virgin Islands."

The sounds of someone rummaging through cabinets vanished as Mac's laugh sang across the wires. "Sorry, kid. But I taught you everything I knew when you were thirteen. If you haven't got the hang of it by now, there's nothing more I can do for you." The raucous laughter continued. "On second thought, maybe I should help you out. After all, that's what brothers are for." Jeff listened as Mac drank something, glugging loudly into the phone. "So tell me, what's this lady like?"

Jeff grinned. "How should I know? I haven't met her yet." The sound of choking gave Jeff a satisfying feeling of revenge.

"Is this your idea of a joke?" Mac sputtered.

"Funny, that's exactly what I said to Arthur when he—"

"Arthur's involved in this? No wonder you're not making any sense. How can you even think of hooking up with him again? I haven't forgotten the last mess he coaxed us into. You ended up with cracked ribs and I spent three days in jail."

"This one's different."

"Oh, sure. This time I'll get the cracked ribs and you can sit in jail. Listen, bro. Do yourself a favor. Get on the freeway, skip the San Diego exit, and don't stop until you hit Tijuana."

"I can't do that, Mac. I gave him my word." Jeff listened to the silence on the other end of the line. "So, are you in or out?"

Mac's sigh was loud and long. "I've spent the better part of my life trying to keep you out of trouble. I guess I can do it a little longer."

Jeff stood at the vestry window, looking out over the quiet park. It was a glorious June day—bright and sunny with a soft breeze and a cloudless blue sky. The kind of day that begged you to come outside to listen to the birds and smell the fresh-mowed lawn. Jeff inhaled deeply, but his senses filled with the musty odor of old leather books.

"Are you okay?" asked Mac.

Jeff checked the studs on the front of his shirt and straightened his cummerbund. "I'm fine." Of course, there had been at least three dozen times in the last two days when he had seriously considered getting the hell out of here. But every time he was tempted, he pulled out the photo and those damn eyes drew him back…called to him in a way he hadn't thought possible.

He slipped his hand into his pocket and fingered the picture. He didn't even need to look at it anymore. All he had to do was touch the paper to bring to life every nuance of her smile, the glow in her cheeks, the luster of her hair.

Jeff pulled his hand from his pocket, breaking the spell. He had told no one, not even Mac, about the mesmerizing hold the picture had over him. Soon there would be no need for a picture. The crazy dream was over, and reality had begun.

"You're pacing," Mac said.

Jeff stopped and looked at his brother, reclining in a chair near the window. "Of course I'm pacing. I'm nervous. And I'm going to stay nervous until we get out of this three-ring circus." He rubbed a hand across his eyes. "Arthur has the tickets. Be sure to get yours before you leave the reception. He arranged it so Caroline and I have a long layover in Atlanta. You'll be in St. Croix about three hours ahead of us."

Mac shook his head. "That's not much time. Not if you expect me to find your room, break in, sweep it, *and* check out the guests, personnel, and general surroundings."

"Not to worry," Jeff said. "Arthur took care of that. He promised the owner a lot of future business if this trip goes well. He even offered the services of his very discreet, personal assistant—namely you—to keep an eye on things. Arthur said the owner is expecting you, and will give you carte blanche for anything you need."

"Good ol' Arthur," Mac said. "The man thinks of everything."

"Let's hope so. For all our sakes."

Mac nodded and pushed himself out of the old leather chair. "Well, then, let's get this show on the road."

Fifteen minutes later, Jeff stood at the front of the chapel, looking out over the sea of faces. The tiny church was filled with the fragrance of summer flowers and the soft, low strains of organ music. Sunshine poured in through the stained-glass window above the altar, spilling pools of emerald, ruby and sapphire light across the altar steps. Jeff smiled at his brother, who looked uncomfortable in his formal attire and without his Padres cap.

He watched his grandmother walk down the carpeted aisle and take her place in the wooden pew decorated with a white satin bow. After a moment the maid of honor, dressed in yellow silk, began to glide down the aisle. Jeff nearly choked when she reached the altar and winked at him. It was the same policewoman who had gone with him to get the marriage license.

The music swelled and the familiar strains of the wedding march rose to the vaulted ceiling. In one fluid motion, the congregation stood and turned to face the vestibule.

Jeff's breath caught in his throat as he watched Arthur offer his arm to a vision in white lace. Her bearing was regal. She walked with the grace and elegance of a princess, seeming to float down the aisle. She carried a bouquet of white roses and yellow freesia and wore a crown woven of the same flowers. A gossamer veil, attached to the crown, covered her face.

Jeff watched, spellbound, as the distance closed between them. She lifted her skirts and ascended the stairs to stand next to him.

"We are gathered here today..."

Jeff let the words wash over him as he studied the woman standing by his side. He could the see the outline of her nose, her lips, chin, and swanlike neck, but the veil hid her eyes.

"Who gives this woman in marriage?"

"I do." Arthur lifted the veil from her face and draped it back over the crown of flowers in her hair. He kissed her cheek, then took her right hand and placed it in Jeff's.

Jeff's fingers closed around hers, a symbolic gesture of protection and allegiance. He squeezed her hand and she raised her eyes, large and dark, to meet his.

Chapter 2

"I, Caroline Marie Peterson, take you, Jefferson Paul McKensie, to be my lawfully wedded husband." She paused, giving weight to the words.

Jeff's heart contracted. Nothing could have prepared him for the sound of his name on her lips.

He listened carefully as she recited her vows. There was no hesitancy in her voice. Soft and airy, the words tumbled from her lips, making her sound sure of herself. Already, he liked that about her.

Mac poked his side, pulling Jeff from his reverie. "The ring," Mac whispered. "Take the ring."

With clammy fingers, Jeff picked up the small gold band that lay in the minister's outstretched palm. He held the ring tightly between his thumb and forefinger, determined not to drop it. Taking his bride's left hand in his own, he slipped the ring over her pale polished nail and down to the base of her finger.

"With this ring, I thee wed," he said. The words came easily, with a clarity and depth of feeling he hadn't thought possible. It seemed natural and right, standing here, staring into the eyes of the woman who had haunted him day and night for nearly a week.

Slim, feminine fingers lifted the matching ring and reached for his hand. Her fingertips grazed the underside of his palm, her touch softer than the brush of a dove's wing.

Dove's wing?

Jeff exhaled slightly. He had it bad. Something about that damn picture had turned him into an overnight troubadour, a goner, a sucker, a twentieth-century Sir Walter Raleigh who wanted nothing more than to throw his cloak over every mud puddle in her path.

She slid the golden band gently over his knuckle and clasped his large hand with her much smaller ones. "With this ring, I thee wed," she said gravely.

Compassion squeezed his soul and he looked deeply into her large doe eyes, making her a silent promise—one he meant to keep. He would protect her. He didn't even know her, and yet he knew she was worth protecting, whatever the cost.

"I now pronounce you husband and wife." The minister beamed.

Jeff breathed the fragrance of flowers mingled with perfume. The combination was heady...intoxicating... incredible. He drew a deep breath to steady himself, but the intensity of her scent made his mind go blank.

"You may kiss the bride," the minister prompted.

She bit her lip and Jeff sensed her reluctance. They'd come this far, and for the sake of appearances they had to see it through. He reached out and touched the tendril of hair curled at the base of her neck, wanting to reassure her.

She sighed. His fingers moved over her throat, curving upward to her chin. She was so close. The white lace of her gown came within a breath of touching the satin lapels of his tux. He felt her heat, and felt a corresponding heat climb his own body.

He resisted the urge to pull her closer, satisfied himself instead with cradling her face in his palms. Her skin was smooth, her cheeks flushed. Bending slightly, he pressed his lips to hers. She tasted sweet. Her lips...warm and soft. He couldn't help moving closer, wanting more.

She stiffened. Even over the pounding of his heart, he heard her gasp. Then, suddenly, she relaxed. Her hands gripped his waist, and she offered the shy touch of her tongue.

Blood rushed from his head. He tightened his grip on her, needing to hold on. She responded by melting, weightless, into his arms. He felt himself falling, spinning wildly. Losing the very control he needed to keep her alive.

A thunderous applause startled them apart. Jeff stepped back, swearing silently. Her eyes were dark...smoldering...mesmerizing. She broke contact, looking down at the band of shimmering gold on her finger. When she raised her head again, her face was composed, her eyes shuttered. She offered Jeff a controlled smile and turned to greet the assembly.

The rousing sounds of the recessional erupted in the tiny church. Jeff took a deep breath and offered her his arm. She hesitated only a moment before slipping her hand around the crook of his elbow, her fingers resting lightly on his sleeve. The thickness of his jacket and shirt protected him from her touch, but he felt it anyway. Unbidden, his thoughts flew to her touching him in other, more intimate places.

Dangerous thoughts.

He dismissed the thoughts and escorted her down the aisle past the cheering, laughing crowd. They stopped at the back of the church and waited for his grandmother, Arthur and Mac.

The receiving line went smoothly and Jeff shook hands and hugged a seemingly endless string of well-wishers. Then suddenly the chapel was empty, quiet. Gran and Arthur slipped outside, joining the guests awaiting the newlyweds.

"All clear," Mac said, coming back into the chapel foyer. "The limo's right out front with the door open and the motor running." He clapped Jeff on the shoulder and winked at the bride. "A quick dash through forty pounds of rice and you're home free."

"Birdseed," she corrected.

"What?"

"Birdseed. People don't throw rice anymore. They throw birdseed."

"Since when?" Mac asked.

"Since we started worrying about the environment," Jeff said. "Throwing rice is ecologically unsound because birds and squirrels choke on it. Using birdseed preserves the tradition without endangering the wildlife."

"Well, nobody told me about it," Mac grumbled. He patted his bulging pockets. "What am I supposed to do with all this rice?"

"Make pilaf," Jeff suggested dryly.

Mac made a face. "Give me two minutes to get into position, then come on out." He disappeared out the door.

Jeff looked down at his new bride. As before, those dark eyes spoke volumes—alert, wary, apprehensive. She was skittish; understandably so.

"You'll have to forgive my brother," Jeff said. "He has all the sensitivity of a three-bean salad."

A laugh bubbled forth—a rich, wonderful female laugh tinged with relief.

Jeff smiled into her bright, shining eyes and fingered one of the white roses in her bouquet. "But if things get rough, he'll be there for us."

He wanted to say something more, to promise her that they wouldn't need Mac's help, that everything would be all right. But he knew instinctively she would reject his assurances for what they were—feeble attempts to make her feel better. There were no guarantees, and they both knew it.

Jeff opened the chapel door a crack and peeked outside. A blur of faces lined both sides of the concrete walk. "I hope you're fast. That group out there means business."

She arched an eyebrow. "I'm used to running," she said firmly. "I can handle it."

Jeff didn't miss the double meaning of her words or the careful way she seemed to choose them. "Good," he said, reaching for her hand. "Then let's do it." His fingers closed firmly around hers, offering protection, but giving her the freedom to pull away if she wanted to.

She followed him through the old wooden doors but paused at the top of the stone steps, scanning the faces in the crowd. Jeff shifted uneasily. He didn't like her standing there, out in the open and exposed. But Mac had secured the area, and he trusted his brother's judgment as much as he trusted his own. The time might come when he would give the orders and she would have to take them, but for now he could be patient, and wait until she was ready.

Finally she turned to him and nodded slightly. Taking a deep breath, she lifted her skirts and bolted down the walkway, with Jeff matching her steps, stride for stride. A cascade of sunflower, cracked corn, and millet seeds showered them as they dashed to the waiting limousine.

"Hurry," Jeff said, swiping at the tiny pellets that clung to his clothes and hair. He helped her into the limousine, then jumped in behind her. Even after Mac slammed the door, Jeff could hear the birdseed pinging against the smoky windows of the white Rolls-Royce.

He brushed some of the seeds off his suit and onto the floor, then settled back into the gray leather seat, eyeing his new wife. She flipped open a compartment concealing a fancy stereo system, and pushed the electronic scanner until the mellow sounds of an old Everly Brothers tune filled the car. Then she lowered the partition separating them from the driver.

"Please drive around for a while," she said. "We'll let you know when we're ready to go to the reception." She pushed another button and the divider panel whirred closed. Finally she turned in the seat to face him.

"Mr. McKensie—" she began.

"Jeff," he interrupted gently. "Call me Jeff. No need to stand on formality now that we're married."

"We are *not* married," she stated flatly. "And just for the record, I wanted no part of this ridiculous charade."

Jeff eyed her curiously. "Then why did you agree to it?"

"I didn't," she said. "Peterson gave me a simple choice—either I let him set me up in the Witness Protection Program with a new identity or I could sit in a jail cell from now until the trial. Some choice. No way was I going to be locked up ever again. But I didn't know until last night that my new identity included this trip to the altar. If I had my way, I'd be out on the streets, not on display in a lace straitjacket.''

So Arthur had manipulated her, too. Well, Jeff couldn't blame him for that. Arthur was only trying to keep her safe. Now it was Jeff's turn.

"So, how much am I worth?" she asked.

"What?"

"Money. How much is Arthur paying you to keep me alive?"

Jeff looked at Ms. Caroline Southeby-Peterson-McKensie and blinked. She *looked* like the woman in the photo—all soft and delicate, like some medieval princess—but she sure didn't sound like her, or act like her, either.

And since when did photographs have voices and mannerisms?

Jeff shook his head. Since his elaborate fantasies had taken over and robbed him of his common sense.

"Twenty-five thousand dollars," he answered bluntly, "which I'll split with my brother. Plus all expenses—his, mine, and yours."

Suspicion raised her brows. "That's very charitable of you, considering you could make a lot more working for Augie Davis. I'm worth a half million—dead. And you and your brother are going to keep me alive for only twenty-five grand? Hardly seems fair."

Jeff stared at her. If the lady had any feelings, she sure wasn't showing them. Her voice sounded cool and distant and deathly calm. She talked about her life as though it was the business deal of the week. "There were other considerations," he said slowly.

"Like possible fringe benefits?" she asked. "Well, let's get a few things straight. First of all, I want to remind you that this 'marriage' is in name only. Any displays of affection will be strictly for the public eye. Agreed?"

"Absolutely," Jeff said coolly. His princess had been displaced by an ungrateful wench, and he was more likely to take her across his knee than into his arms.

"Second, there are no seconds. No second chances. If anything goes wrong, I'm out of here. Understood?"

"Fine by me." In fact, as far as he was concerned, she could leave right now. He would be more than happy to refund Arthur's money. With interest.

"And last, I sure hope you're not one of those bozos who believes he's a knight in shining armor, because I never believed in fairy tales. Bottom line—I take care of myself."

The Everly Brothers were done harmonizing, and she reached across the console to turn up the volume on the earthy voices of The Supremes.

"Anything else?" Jeff asked.

She turned to face him again. "No, that about covers it."

"Good. Now it's my turn." He jabbed the tuning button on the radio, cutting off Diana Ross and filling the limo with the unmistakable sounds of a harpsichord. "First of all, I consider this 'marriage of convenience' anything but. Rest assured, I won't have any trouble keeping my hands off you." *Not anymore.*

She blinked but said nothing.

"Second, I don't believe in second chances, either. You get one shot in life. Either you make it, or you blow it. I've got plans for the rest of my life, so I don't intend to blow it. And furthermore, there's something more important at stake than money. It's called honor. I gave Arthur my word. So you're going to do exactly what I tell you, when I tell you, where I tell you, and in return, I'm going to keep you alive. Understood?"

Those damn eyes were the size of saucers, but Jeff couldn't see anything more than shock registered there.

"And finally, in deference to all the chivalrous men who still believe that helping a lady is the decent thing to do..." As gracefully as possible in the low-ceilinged car, he offered her a sweeping bow. "Sir Bozo," he said, "at your service."

Caroline looked skeptically at the figure all but kneeling at her feet. The man was crazy. But then he'd have to be to go along with this half-baked, harebrained, idiotic...

The twanging harpsichord ended abruptly and something akin to the "1812 Overture" exploded into the back of the limousine.

Caroline nearly jumped out of her skin, much to the amusement of her would-be knight. He settled back in the seat and folded his arms across his broad chest, a wry smile tugging at the corners of his mouth. The same mouth that just moments ago had kissed her and stolen her breath away.

She pulled her heart out of the pit of her stomach and tried to shove it back where it belonged. Then, with a flick of her wrist she changed the radio station, exhaling a sigh of relief as The Platters began crooning a familiar song. She leaned her head against the back of the seat and closed her eyes.

"You're really into oldies, aren't you?" he said.

"Not as old as the stuff you seem to like," she muttered.

"Well, you look too young to know about that sock-hop stuff." He punched the selector button back to the discordant music, then turned the volume up another notch. "Tchaikovsky," he said, not bothering to keep the grin off his face. "Powerful stuff."

She bit back a wince as cymbals clashed all around her. "So you only listen to classics."

"That's right," Jeff admitted. "Real music like Debussy, Rachmaninoff, Ravel—"

"Then allow me to return the compliment," Caroline said smoothly. She flipped off the radio and closed the stereo compartment with a well-defined click. "You're very well preserved for man who's been around since Mozart."

His laughter was full and hearty. "Touché," he said. The laughter died as suddenly as it had started. "Ordinarily I like a woman with a quick wit."

Ordinarily I like a man with blue eyes.

"Mr. McKensie....Jeff..." Caroline struggled to find the right words. "It would seem that neither of us is particularly happy with this arrangement. Perhaps it's not too late to get Peterson to change his mind. I can go back underground and you can go back...to wherever you came from," she finished lamely.

"I came from my law office," Jeff said. "And as for Arthur Peterson, forget it. I guarantee, the man won't budge."

Caroline opened her mouth to say something, closed it, then opened it again. "You're a lawyer?" she finally sputtered.

"Corporate securities," Jeff said. He did a double take as she continued to stare at him. "Do you have a problem with that?"

"Problem?" Caroline shook her head in disbelief. "Why should there be a problem? I'm entrusting my life to a legal-beagle paper pusher. Makes perfect sense to me."

A week's worth of tension had built to the point of eruption and Jeff was ready to strangle the very person he had been hired to protect. "Listen, lady, the way I hear it, you set up the rules. No cops, no feds, no P.I.s... What did you think was left?"

"How should I know? A professional bodyguard would have been nice. Or at least somebody with a little experience."

Jeff threw up his arms. "Well, hell, if you wanted references, why didn't you say so? I've got tons of experience. I was hall monitor in the sixth grade, I've rescued at least half a dozen treed cats in my lifetime, *and* I was a school crossing guard for two consecutive years. Never lost a single kid."

"That's it, buster. I don't need you or your sarcasm." Caroline slammed a button on the console and the privacy window began to open. "Stop the car!" she yelled to the driver. "Now!" She threw the bridal bouquet in Jeff's face and ripped open the door, not waiting for the car to stop.

"Oh, no, you don't." Jeff wrapped an arm around her waist and hauled her back, then slammed the door closed with his free hand.

"Let go of me, you...you..." She struggled to break free, but his powerful arm tightened like a vise, crushing her against the hard wall of his chest.

"Take us to the reception," he barked. He hit the console button, closing the glass on the wide-eyed driver.

Caroline continued to struggle, but her efforts were futile. As soon as the car was again under way, Jeff released her and pushed her back into the seat.

"Don't you ever do that again," he warned.

"I was just about to tell you the same thing," she snapped. "That caveman routine may work on some women, but not me. I won't be bullied or manhandled by anyone, especially some hotshot attorney playing James Bond."

"Look, lady, it's your call. We can do this the hard way or the easy way. Baby-sitter, jailer, husband—it's all the same. You're still stuck with me. From now until the trial, I'm going to be your shadow. You won't be able to hiccup without my knowing it. So you might as well get used to it, princess."

"Don't call me that."

"What?"

"Princess. Don't ever call me that again."

He opened his mouth to answer with some fancy quip or ribald comment, but the pain in her eyes stopped him cold. She was serious. Dead serious. And every self-respecting knight knew a battle line when he saw one.

Caroline clenched her fist until her nails bit into the palm of her hand. Damn, why had she agreed to this? It was bad enough going alone. Now she had someone else to worry about—someone who had never lived on the streets in his life. Who was protecting whom in this crazy mess?

"We're almost there," he said, his voice harsh and strained.

"The easy way," she answered. "Since I don't have much choice."

His grin was one the Cheshire cat would envy. "For better or for worse," he quipped.

She shot him a warning look as she straightened the crown of flowers in her hair. "Don't get any ideas, McKensie. This is a temporary truce."

He reached down and retrieved the bouquet of roses and freesia. "Here," he said, offering her the slightly disheveled flowers. "You'd better hang on to these. You'll want to throw them again later." That wicked smile still danced across his face.

She snatched the flowers out of his hand. In the back of her mind a small bell dinged, signaling the end of round one. He might have won this one, but she knew how to go the distance.

"It's show time," he said as the limo stopped. "Ready?"

The car door opened and Caroline smiled at him—not a forced, awkward grimace, but a full-blown, sunlight-bright smile that warmed him all the way to his toes.

"Wow," he whispered. "When you smile like that you really do look like a prin—a lovely medieval maiden." He climbed out, then turned and offered her his hand.

She accepted his help and stepped out of the car, her smile never wavering. "Don't get excited, Sir Bozo," she said, her voice pitched for his ears only. "It's not for you. It's for them." She inclined her head toward the small crowd that waited outside the reception hall.

Jeff waved to the laughing, cheering crowd. Then, without a word of warning, he drew the lady into his arms. One arm slipped around her waist, holding her tight, while his free hand traced the curve of her cheek and jaw, caressed the soft skin of her neck, fingered the silky hair at her nape.

She squirmed but he held fast, and her movements only served to bring her body into closer contact with his. "What do you think you're doing?" she said as he nuzzled the soft skin at her ear.

He raised his head and looked into her dark, smoldering eyes. "Don't worry, sweetheart," he said. "It's not for you." His head dipped again, his mouth zeroing in on her lips. "It's for them."

At the back of the crowd, a man smiled and cheered with the rest. Wedding receptions were such heartwarming events—especially when he would be a cool five thousand dollars richer for making a single phone call.

Chapter 3

Mac tapped his spoon against the crystal glass and a hush fell over the room. He stood and raised his goblet high in the air with one hand while making a Vulcan hand sign with the other. "A toast to Mr. and Mrs. Jefferson McKensie," he said. "May they live long and prosper." A swell of cheers and the clink of glasses echoed as the guests toasted the newlyweds.

Caroline sipped her champagne, then pushed the food around her plate with a fork. No doubt most brides were too nervous or too excited to do more than nibble at the reception. But the happy, laughing pretense was another matter. Small talk was out of the question. It took every effort just to keep a smile fixed rigidly in place, and she had the aching jaw muscles to prove it.

The band of shimmering gold encircling her finger caught the light and she stared at it as though she had never seen it before. The wedding ring was supposed to be a promise of eternal love. Instead it felt cold and heavy. Or maybe it was her heart that felt cold and heavy in the midst of all this gaiety.

"Caroline?"

Jeff's voice was low, close to her ear, and the hair on her neck stood on end. Slowly she turned to face him.

"I spoke to you three times." His voice echoed the concern etched in his deeply tanned face. "Are you all right?"

"I'm fine," she lied. "It's just..." She felt the intensity of his concentration and couldn't remember the last time anyone had listened to her that carefully.

Caroline mentally shook herself. Who was she kidding? She knew exactly the last time someone had listened to her as if what she said really mattered.

Brian had.

And the memory of her brother only served to remind her how very much she had lost.

"It's just what?" Jeff prompted.

"It's just that I would like to get this over with so I can get on with my life," she said irritably.

Or what's left of it.

"Your wish is my command," Jeff replied. He stood and pulled out her chair, bringing her to her feet.

"Now what?" she asked skeptically.

"Dancing, of course," Jeff said. "The sooner we get through these traditions, the sooner we can leave."

The moment Jeff guided her into his arms, Caroline felt as if her entire body had received an electric shock. Her right hand tingled as his fingers wrapped lightly around hers. His right hand burned through the silk and lace of her gown, caressing naked skin at the small of her back. Their bodies were almost touching and the realization ignited a flame in the pit of her stomach.

She closed her eyes and tried to focus her thoughts on something, anything else—the gown and the flowers, the sunlit chapel and the vows she had taken. Simple, powerful phrases of love and devotion...that meant absolutely nothing.

Caroline swallowed around the lump that suddenly stuck in her throat. She had lied when she'd told Jeff she never believed in fairy tales. She had believed...once. But that was a lifetime ago. Now, strangely, in a heart that had been hardened by reality, she felt a yearning for the dreams she had long ago abandoned.

Get real, she warned herself. Even her wildest fantasies had not been of a knight in shining armor, and they certainly never included the total stranger with whom she was dancing.

Not that he couldn't have been a knight.

His skin was bronzed by the sun and his scent was of citrus and spice. His hair was thick and shiny, sun-bleached to the color of golden wheat. He had deep blue eyes with a thick fringe of blond lashes, a strong mouth with a touch of sensuality, prominent cheekbones and a chiseled jaw. And, heaven help her, a slight dimple when he smiled.

Definitely knight material.

And he was definitely smiling.

Jeff felt his chest tighten as he held her. She was exquisite—every inch the beautiful bride. But there was more. An aura of sensuality enveloped her, a radiance that took his breath away.

She wasn't supposed to be this lovely, wasn't supposed to have eyes the color of warm chocolate. She wasn't supposed to be a contradiction of fragile beauty and steely strength. And he sure as hell wasn't supposed to want her. But he did.

Caroline gasped when he pulled her closer. Her trembling hand slid up the rock-hard muscles in his arm to the edge of his broad shoulder, and when she gazed into his smoldering eyes, her mouth went dry. She wet her lips with the tip of her tongue, too late realizing that the innocent gesture only darkened the desire.

A long brown tendril clung to her jawline. He released her hand and curled the hair around his finger, grazing her sensitized skin with the back of his hand. "You're so...soft."

"I'm not soft," she said, her voice sounding far too husky, even to her own ears. "In fact, I'm very strong."

He tightened his hold around her waist. "You can be both, you know."

Her heart pounded uncontrollably and heated blood sang through her veins. What was going on here? This wasn't like her. She was Caroline Southeby. Independent. Self-reliant. Stalwart in the face of mobsters and assassins. Able to deflect police officers at a single glance.

And now she was all weak in the knees because of a reasonably attractive man with bedroom eyes. Another flame, hot and restless, burned deep inside and she was powerless to stop it. Her knees buckled, and she leaned against him for support. His solid torso radiated heat, consuming her from without as swiftly as she burned within. She laid her cheek against the smooth satin lapel.

And then it happened.

Without warning a flash of light exploded, blinding her. Her heart seemed to stop and she clutched at Jeff as she waited for the searing pain that her mind knew would follow.

But it didn't.

And after an eternity passed, she forced her hands to release their death-hold grip.

"It's all right, Caroline," Jeff said softly. "It was only a flashbulb."

"Flashbulb?" Her mind struggled to comprehend.

"From a camera," he explained.

"But…" Her heart lurched as the magnitude of his words sank in. "But there can't be any pictures," she gasped.

"There aren't," Jeff said soothingly. "The photographer is a police officer. He'll be flashing away all afternoon, but there's no film in the camera. Relax. You're safe. I promise you."

Relax? Not a chance. She'd tried that and look what had happened. No, no more. She had to stay alert and focused. She spotted Mac coming toward them.

He cleared his throat with a self-conscious sound. "May I?" he asked, grinning at the dark look that clouded Jeff's face.

"No," Jeff said bluntly. He swung her around and danced her away from his brother.

Mac persisted, trotting along behind Jeff and tapping him once again. "You wouldn't make a scene at your own wedding, would you?"

"Yes. Besides, don't you have some best-man stuff to do?"

"This is it," Mac said. "I'm supposed to dance with the bride and welcome her to the family."

"Says who?"

"Emily Post."

Jeff put his head close to hers. "Pretend you don't see him," he whispered loudly. "Maybe he'll give up and go away." Jeff waved his hand as if swatting an irritating mosquito.

"Bzz," Mac said, following the couple around the dance floor.

"He's... um... still there." Caroline tried unsuccessfully to stifle a laugh.

Jeff sighed loudly. "If you leave I'll give you a dollar."

Mac paused for a moment to consider the offer. "Nah."

"A hundred dollars?"

"Nope."

Jeff stopped dancing and glared at his brother. "How much will it cost to get rid of you?"

Mac grinned. "Bro, there isn't enough money in all the world to pass up an opportunity to dance with this divine creature." He pushed in front of Jeff and danced her away, grinning the whole time.

"Do you always get what you want?" Caroline asked Mac after he had whirled her a safe distance from his brother.

"Not always, but often enough," he admitted.

Caroline looked him over appraisingly. "Honest, but not arrogant. That's good."

Mac grinned. "Then I'm succeeding."

"At what?" she asked skeptically.

"At making you feel warm... welcome..." He paused before adding the final word. "Safe."

The brittleness of her laughter surprised them both. "Safe?" she asked. "You sound like your brother. No offense, but I'm not likely to feel safe until Augie Davis is convicted and put away."

Mac puffed out his chest. "Not even with two big, strong, he-man types to protect you?"

"Oh, no," Caroline groaned. "Not you, too."

"Not 'me too' what?" Mac asked, more than a little confused.

"Mr. McKensie, let me ask you something. Do you have any real experience in witness protection?"

"My father was Mr. McKensie. I'm Mac. And to answer your question—no, I've never actually done this before. But I've been in more than a few tight spots in my day."

Now it was her turn to stare. "Tight spots? Mr. Mc-Kensie, a tight spot is when you've parallel parked and the car in front and the car behind have you blocked in. You'll forgive me if I consider my situation something more than a tight spot."

"My name is Mac, and I'm well aware of your situation. I wouldn't be here if I didn't think I could handle the job."

"Ah, now we get the arrogance."

"Arrogance, my ass. Lady, I know what I'm doing. I've been a marine, a cop, head of security, a—"

"Wait a minute," Caroline interrupted. "If you've had that much experience, why didn't Peterson ask *you* to take this job?"

Mac scowled. "Arthur thinks I'm flighty. He says I've got more exes than Elizabeth Taylor and Mickey Rooney combined."

Caroline shook her head. "What on earth does your marital status have to do with this?"

"Not ex-wives," Mac explained. "Ex-jobs. I'm an *ex*-marine, *ex*-cop, *ex*-P.I., *ex* ... Well, you get the picture. Anyway, Arthur prefers working with more stable people. Like my baby brother, Jeff of Gibraltar."

"Jeff of Gibraltar?" she repeated slowly.

"Yeah. The guy planned out his life when he was in kindergarten and he hasn't missed a step since. College, law school, partnership. And talk about overachiever. He wants to learn karate? He's a fifth-level black belt. Part-time P.I. to pay for school? He builds a full-time practice in one summer. Need to learn about firearms? He could give lessons to Annie Oakley." Mac shook his head. "It's a good thing I'm not the insecure type, or I might have developed a complex."

Caroline smiled. "I don't believe a person's worth is determined solely by his accomplishments."

"Oh, don't get me wrong," Mac said quickly. "Jeff has a lot of good qualities. He's loyal, dependable, trustworthy, protective, true-blue—"

Caroline laughed. "You make him sound like a Saint Bernard."

"Now that you mention it," Mac said, "there are a lot of similarities."

She returned his smile. "But basically, in this very roundabout fashion, you're trying to tell me not to worry because your brother is rock solid, is that it?"

"Are you kidding? His middle name's Prudential."

"Really?" She tried hard to keep a straight face. "I could have sworn the minister said it was Paul."

Mac shook his head solemnly. "It's a source of embarrassment," he confided. "And since this wasn't a real ceremony, Jeff decided to use a more conventional middle name."

"And since we're divulging family secrets," Jeff said, tapping Mac on the shoulder, "why don't you tell the lady *your* real name?"

"Why don't I go check on Gran?" Mac replied, quickly placing Caroline's hand in his brother's.

"Wise choice," Jeff said, slipping his arm around his bride and pulling her close once more.

From the corner of her eye Caroline caught sight of a man standing alone, watching them with an intensity that made her skin crawl. Surely, he was guest, a friend of the McKensies. But he looked out of place, different.

She turned to keep him in view and reflexively her fingers tightened on Jeff's hand and shoulder.

"What's wrong?"

Caroline hesitated. The man was talking and laughing now with several other guests. Maybe she was mistaken. Maybe her imagination was running rampant. It was hard to think straight anymore. She questioned everyone and everything. Augie Davis was so powerful. There was no telling how far his reach extended.

She glanced again at the man in the corner. He was still there, and he was still watching her. Of that much she was certain. She looked up into Jeff's face, a face engraved with real concern, and decided to take a chance. "That man," she said. "The one over there, talking to the lady in the blue dress. He's been staring at me. Do you know him?" She held her breath.

"No," Jeff said. "But I will." Without missing a beat, he waltzed her over to his grandmother's table and offered her a seat. "Smile," he whispered, nuzzling her ear. "I'll be right back."

She never saw him nod or wink or motion to Mac and Arthur, but as Jeff laughed and pumped the stranger's hand, they swooped down and quietly escorted the man out of the reception room. Less than ten minutes later all three were back—minus the guest.

"Who was it?" she asked Jeff when he appeared at her side.

"Tell you later," Jeff said. "Now, let's cut that cake."

Jeff leaned forward and looked past Caroline out the small oval window of the plane. Under the dark cover of night, the plane continued its ascent, and after a few more minutes, clouds completely obscured the twinkling lights of Atlanta.

He ventured a glance at the lady sleeping next to him. She hadn't been on the plane more than two minutes when she had fallen asleep—or rather, collapsed.

He watched the slow rise and fall of her chest, listened to her gentle breathing, noticed the faint circles under her eyes. She was exhausted. The pressure she'd been under the last few weeks was enough to fell a lumberjack.

With hired assassins breathing down her neck and a price on her head, the seriousness of her situation was never far from the surface. Like that guy at the reception. He wasn't a hit man, but he was a known informer. Arthur promised to take care of him, but Jeff wasn't satisfied. He had canceled the plane reservations to St. Croix for Mr. and Mrs. Jefferson McKensie and made other, more circuitous arrangements for Mr. and Mrs. Paul Jefferson.

Jeff let out a deep breath and rubbed the base of his neck. From the moment Arthur had shown him her photo, he'd been flooded with an inexplicable desire to sweep her into his arms and protect her from dangers both real and imagined. He still wanted to protect her, but now he wondered why nobody had tried to protect him from doing something as crazy as marrying a total stranger.

Well, not *really* marrying her. But ever since he had stood at that altar, it sure as hell felt real. It would take constant reminding that the beautiful lady sleeping beside him wasn't really his wife.

And she was beautiful. Hell, any man with eyes could see she was as perfectly made as a woman could be. He let his narrowed gaze travel slowly down the length of her body. She was everything a guy could want. Only trouble was, he didn't know a damn thing about Caroline Southeby McKensie.

She was a mystery, a walking enigma. He could sense a darkness about her, an underlying sorrow that reinforced her beauty with a mantle of steel. In sleep, she opened like a morning glory. The tough, cold, I-can-go-it-alone defense unfurled, giving him a glimpse of the younger, softer, vulnerable woman inside. But he knew she would close up again as soon as she awoke, just like the flower protecting itself from the night.

Earlier, her mass of hair had been twisted into an intricate plait. Now, as she slept, the strands came undone, framing her oval face in a halo of brown curls. The memory of their silkiness against his fingers made him want to touch them again. He sucked in a hard, deep breath. The memory of her softness, her scent, her warmth, made him want to do a lot of other things—things he couldn't allow himself to think about.

She moaned softly and turned toward him in her sleep. Twin crescents of lashes, as rich and dark as the earth, shadowed her cheeks. Her mouth was a pale rose, her lips slightly parted.

He eased his arm around her shoulders, and she curled against him, her head dropping to his chest. Her body was exquisite, the soft linen jacket outlining her full breasts, the curving valley of her waist, the seductive arch of her hip. His arm tightened possessively around her as her silky hair brushed against his throat, its fragrance as sweet as summer rain.

And she slept on, leaving him alone and uncomfortable with his thoughts. No doubt about it, it was going to be a hell of a long two months.

Caroline stood in the baggage claim and tried to stretch the kinks out of her bone-weary body. Her sleep had been haunted by memories of her father and Alden and Brian, and she awoke on a sob as the plane began its descent into St. Croix. The lemony glow of sunrise arched its way across the eastern sky, bathing her in soft, warm light. With practiced care, she'd pushed aside the gut-wrenching fear.

She watched Jeff pluck their suitcases off the conveyor belt. The Alexander Hamilton Airport on St. Croix was a lot different than the international one in Atlanta. The island airport was open, and balmy tropical breezes wafted around her as she followed Jeff outside to a station-wagon taxi. The climate was wonderful, and the humidity surprisingly low. It was probably eighty degrees in the early-morning sun—not much different than it had been in San Diego yesterday afternoon.

Was it only yesterday she had walked down the aisle to wed a complete stranger? Less than a day since she had smiled and danced and tried to act the part of a blushing bride? In some ways it seemed like an eternity. Time was such a strange phenomenon, breathing a different life into everything it touched.

Augie Davis's trial was nearly two months away. Two months of pretending to be gloriously happy. Two months of living side by side, day in and day out, with a man she had met less than twenty-four hours ago. They were to spend the next three weeks on this island—longer, if things went well; a lot less, if they didn't.

Thankfully, Arthur was leaving that up to them. Their tickets were open-ended and the options were plentiful. They could fly to St. Thomas or St. John and start the honeymoon ruse all over again. They could hop a ship at the pier in Frederiksted and cruise the Caribbean. They could hide out in San Juan, or they could head for home. As long as she got to New York in time for the trial.

And she would. No matter what.

The taxi turned into a drive lined with palm trees. All around them were rolling, manicured lawns sprinkled with cottages, shops, and restaurants. And at the top of the hill stood a large, pink stucco hotel. It was breathtaking, resplendent with bright blazes of hibiscus and bougainvillea. Caroline smiled. There was something soothing about this elegant eighteenth-century relic, reminding her of a time when life was far less complicated . . . less sinister.

The taxi stopped in front of the building and Jeff hopped out. Caroline started to slide out after him, but he remained in the doorway, one hand on the window, the other on the roof of the car, his braced stance effectively blocking her way.

"Excuse me," she said, waiting for him to move. But he didn't so much as twitch a muscle. "I said, excuse me," she repeated a little louder. Still nothing.

She tried to push past him, but he grabbed her shoulder and shoved her back into the car, holding her down while he scanned the area in all directions.

And what did he think *she* had been doing all this time—admiring the scenery? She knew how far it was from the hotel to the road. She knew there was minimal cover from the palm trees and flowering plants. But that worked both ways. From the front of the hotel, there was no place for a sniper to hide.

"Do you mind?" she demanded through clenched teeth, struggling to break free of his viselike grip. She looked at the solid wall blocking the way, from chest to knees, and seriously considered jabbing her somewhat bony elbow into a very strategic target.

"I wouldn't do that if I were you," he said, his voice a silky purr.

"Then get out of my way," she purred back.

"Of course, dear. Allow me." He took her arm and helped her to her feet, then dropped his tote bag on the sidewalk before turning to pay the driver who had already lifted their luggage from the back of the wagon.

"Usually there's a doorman here," the driver said as he tucked the bills Jeff gave him into his shirt pocket. "But it's pretty early. Do you want me to take these inside for you?"

"No, thanks," Jeff replied, offering the man his hand. "I think we can handle it. We don't have that much stuff."

"Right," the man said. He hopped back into the taxi and started down the hill.

Caroline slung her purse over her shoulder, picked up the camera bag, and reached for her suitcase.

"I'll carry that," Jeff said, reaching for it at the same time.

"I can manage."

"But I insist." Forcibly Jeff took the suitcase from her and once again Caroline felt like a volcano ready to blow. Apparently he didn't think she could even manage a suitcase. Well, he didn't know squat—not about her, and certainly not about her abilities. But he would. Before this mess was over, he would learn just how good she was. Starting right now.

"That's very kind of you," she said sweetly, her voice dripping honey. She slid her purse off her shoulder and hoisted it onto his. Then she hung the camera bag around his neck. Finally, she nudged his own suitcase and tote bag with her foot. "Don't forget those," she said blithely. With one last smile, she spun on her heel and walked into the hotel, leaving him to struggle with all the bags alone.

She had taken no more than a few steps into the pink building before coming to an abrupt halt and scanning the lobby. It was highly unlikely a professional hit man would make a move in the middle of a posh hotel in broad daylight—or even early morning. But she looked anyway—a safety precaution, an instinctive reaction born of weeks of being on the road.

"May I help you?" A smiling clerk stood behind the registration desk.

Caroline gave him a quick once-over—bald...bespectacled...benign. "Yes," she said, approaching the desk and returning his smile. "We'd like to check in."

"We?" the clerk asked hesitantly, scanning the empty lobby.

"My...husband and I," Caroline said. She turned toward the front door, with what she hoped was a convincingly puzzled look. "I don't understand," she said. "He was right behind me." She stifled a laugh as the door swung open and Jeff staggered in.

The clerk rushed to his rescue. "Oh, sir," he said apologetically. "You shouldn't have brought those in. We *do* have a doorman, you know. Well, actually, the regular doorman is ill and our bellhops are taking turns on the door. Someone obviously misread the schedule. I am so sorry. Please, allow me."

The bags dropped with a dull thud on the marble floor. "No harm done," Jeff replied pleasantly. But the razor-sharp glance he aimed at Caroline clearly said otherwise. He shoved her purse into her hands, then straightened his shoulders and removed the camera bag from around his neck, placing it on the counter.

The clerk cleared his throat. "Well, then," he said. "Perhaps we should start over. How may I help you?"

"We'd like to check in," Jeff said. "Mr. and Mrs. McKensie."

"Ah, yes, Mr. McKensie. Welcome to St. Croix." The clerk tapped a couple of buttons on the keyboard and the computer came to life. Moments later he offered Jeff room keys and a copy of the hotel newsletter.

"Ah, finally," the clerk said. "Here comes the bellhop to take your bags and show you to your room." He frowned in the direction of the tall man who was hurrying toward the registration desk. The man's head was down, and he was frantically buttoning the buttons on the front of his uniform.

"Show Mr. and Mrs. McKensie to Oceanside No. 8," the clerk ordered sharply.

"Yes, sir," said a familiar voice.

Caroline spun around and looked up into the man's grinning face. "Ma—"

Her words were silenced as Jeff's mouth slammed onto hers, knocking the oxygen from her lungs. With one arm he held her tightly around the waist, with his other hand he held the back of her head, so his lips could plunder hers again and again. Finally, his mouth broke free, and they both gulped in air.

Caroline put the palms of her hands on his chest and pushed him away. His shoulders were rigid with tension, his expression determined, his voice grim. "Now, *darling,*" he said, "would you like to go to the room?"

Unflinching, she matched his angry stare. What she would like to do was knock him into the middle of next week. And she would have, too, if she could have come up with just one reasonable explanation to offer the desk clerk. But discretion being the better part of common sense, she nodded, biting her tongue for the umpteenth time.

"Right this way, sir, ma'am." Mac smiled and gathered the bags, then led the way out of the hotel to a deserted parking lot.

"Are you out of your mind?" Caroline asked Jeff as soon as they were clear of the building. "What was that, some feeble imitation of machismo?" She rushed on, not waiting for an answer. "I reluctantly agreed to this... this... dramatic tableau, but I certainly didn't agree to be pawed by you every time I turn around or open my mouth."

"Then maybe you ought to consider keeping your mouth closed," Jeff said sardonically. "And for your information, I'm not in the habit of forcing myself on unwilling, uncooperative, sharp-tongued shrews. It was a last-ditch effort to prevent you from blowing Mac's cover sky-high."

"Look, guys," Mac ventured, leading them toward one of several small resort vehicles, "it's over and don—"

"I wasn't going to say anything," Caroline insisted.

"The hell you weren't."

"He caught me off guard. I turned around and there he was, grinning like a court jester."

Mac looked indignant. "Hey, wait a min—"

"I don't care if he was standing there buck naked," Jeff said. "When you work undercover you've got to be able to react fast—which is exactly what I did."

"Which is exactly why you nearly got your head busted."

Mac dumped the bags in the car, then started walking away.

"Where do you think you're going?" Jeff demanded.

Mac shrugged. "If you two want to stand here and duke it out in front of God and everybody, be my guest. But I've got better things to do." He jammed his hands into his pants pockets and sauntered down one of the paths.

Caroline glanced around nervously. She had spent weeks making herself all but invisible, yet here she was squaring off in the middle of a parking lot, creating a very angry, very *public* scene. What on earth was she thinking of? She offered up a prayer to the powers that be that no one had witnessed their little debacle, then cast a scathing look at the man who was responsible for the confrontation in the first place.

"All right, all right," Jeff called to Mac. "You made your point. Come back and show us where we're supposed to go."

Mac grinned. "Only if you two promise to kiss and make up."

"Don't push it," Caroline warned.

Mac helped them into the car, then ran around to the driver's side and hopped in.

"So what have you found out?" Jeff asked.

Mac took a deep breath. "Well, to begin with, there are a hundred and forty-eight rooms."

Jeff swore. "What in thunder was Arthur thinking of? It'll take a week just to check them all out."

"Not necessarily," Mac said. "The owners have assured me that everyone here, except you two, made their reservations months ago—long before the Augie Davis thing."

"A bellhop talking with the owners? Now there's a convincing cover," Caroline said dryly.

Mac nodded. "Credit Arthur with that one. I'm the son of some very good friends of the owners. I've been sent down here to learn the hotel business from the ground up. I'll be floating in and out of every position imaginable."

"What else?" Jeff asked.

"The rooms are spread all over. The two-story pink building has basic rooms upstairs and luxury suites on the ground level. There are also basic rooms over there," he said, pointing to a band of linking units on the far side of the main hotel. They rounded a curve and began a slow descent down a long drive. "These four buildings on the right are guest cottages, and there are three superdeluxe suites that sit right on Grenville Beach." He turned left onto another long asphalt drive. "You're in one of the Oceanside rooms. They're along the shoreline between two beaches."

Jeff looked around and whistled appreciatively. "Thank you, Arthur."

Mac nodded. "As far as I can tell, the Oceanside is a perfect choice—not crème de la crème, but very nice—and most honeymooners stay there. Once again, it looks as though the old man knew what he was doing."

"Okay," Jeff said, "what else do we need to know?"

Mac took a deep breath. "You name it, this place has it. Three beaches and two swimming pools—one up on the hill by the main building and one at Grenville Beach. There are eight tennis courts around the corner from the cottages. Two of the courts are lighted at night, so . . ." He glanced in Caroline's direction as he let the sentence trail.

"So, I'll need to avoid that area," she finished neatly. "It's all right, Mac. You don't have to tiptoe around me. I know all about sniper fire, and I have no intention of painting a bull's-eye on my forehead. Go on."

"Well, there are three restaurants and a salon in the main building. Oh, yeah, they got this seaweed wrap that is in-

credible. Makes you feel like a new man. You gotta try—"
He stopped short at the look on their faces.

"You? And seaweed wrap? That's a little hard to picture," Caroline said.

"Especially at this hour of the morning," Jeff added. "And why do I have the feeling this isn't a twenty-four-hour salon? I guess we know where you were when you weren't at the front door."

Mac didn't bother to hide his grin. "Yeah, well, somebody had to check things out. Anyway, in addition to the salon, they've got an exercise trail, lots of classes in tennis and scuba diving, and—" he paused dramatically "—an eighteen-hole professional golf course—par seventy-one. Can you imagine that? Face it, bro. This place is paradise and you landed right in her lap." He looked from Jeff to Caroline and back again. "So to speak."

He parked the car in front of one of a half-dozen single-story curved buildings that formed an S, snaking their way along the coastline. Although the buildings were new, their style maintained the feeling of the old sugar plantation.

Mac dropped the bags in front of a door, pulled out a key, and slid it into the lock.

"Wait a minute," Jeff said, slipping his hand into his pants pocket and withdrawing the two keys the clerk had given him. "When did you get that?"

"Last night. How else was I going to sweep the room?" Mac nudged open the door and Jeff started to follow, but Mac turned around in the doorway, blocking it as neatly as Jeff had blocked Caroline from leaving the car. "Uh-uh," Mac said devilishly.

"Now what?" Jeff asked.

"Don't you guys know anything?" Mac sighed audibly. "The groom is supposed to carry the bride over the threshold."

Caroline's mind painted erotic mental pictures at Mac's suggestion and her body reacted accordingly, leaving her overheated, fluttery, nervous. She turned to look at Jeff at the exact moment he turned to look at her.

"Forget it," they said in unison. Caroline swallowed hard. They spoke at the same time, moved at the same time—could their visual images be anything but the same? A warm blush flared upward from her throat.

"Hey, bro, if you can't handle the job, I'll be more than happy to take your place."

"Over my dead body," Jeff said flatly. "Now, move it."

"Not until you do the right thing."

"This is your last warning," Jeff said coolly.

"I'm not going to budge until—"

For the next hundred years it would be an ongoing debate as to whether Jeff's actions were deliberate or accidental. But before Mac could utter another word, Jeff swept Caroline into his arms. She stiffened and he plowed straight into Mac's chest, knocking his brother solidly on his keister.

Chapter 4

"You two ought to be committed. Of all the idiotic, infantile, sophomoric... Put me down!" Caroline snapped.

"Yeah, and help me up," Mac grumbled, untangling his legs and rubbing the spot on his chest where Caroline had rammed into him.

Jeff dumped his "bride" unceremoniously onto a king-size bed. Then he turned and glared at his brother. Mac struggled to his feet, brushing off his uniform as he stood.

"You have all the manners of a goat," Caroline complained. She slid off the bed, trying to straighten her disheveled appearance. She had lost a shoe and her skirt had hiked halfway to her waist.

Jeff pushed past Mac, and stepped outside to retrieve the luggage. A moment later he threw Caroline's suitcase and camera bag on the bed, then went back for another load. Mac met him halfway and Jeff wrenched the bags from Mac's hands and flung them on the bed with the others.

"Look, there's no reason for everyone to be so touchy," Mac said placatingly.

"Speak for yourself," Caroline groused. She pulled off the remaining shoe and tossed it on the floor next to its mate. Then she unzipped her suitcase and threw back the lid. With any luck, her disposition would improve as soon as she got out of her hot linen suit and sticky nylons.

"Hey, come on, guys, lighten up. You're sitting in the middle of paradise. Blue skies, sunshine, a terrific room—"

"Then why don't you take the room?" Caroline said. "I'll take the beach." She frowned at the contents of the suitcase, which, at first glance, didn't look too promising. There was a boatload of silky lace underwear, a breathtaking rose negligee, and a handful of colored string that apparently doubled as a bathing suit. Closer scrutiny revealed an assortment of toiletries—toothbrush, toothpaste, shampoo, comb, hair dryer, even a little box of—

Caroline stared in disbelief at the happy couple walking hand in hand on the front of the small box. It couldn't be. She opened one end and a half-dozen neatly wrapped packets fell into the palm of her hand. It was.

"Ohmygod," she breathed.

"Are you okay?" Jeff turned from the large bay window he had been inspecting. His face revealed nothing more than concern.

"Fine," she muttered, shoving the packets back in the box and stuffing the box under the negligee. This was obviously someone's idea of a practical joke. But she couldn't keep her imagination from running rampant—thoughts of flimsy underwear and negligees and king-size beds and stupid little packets of...

"You sure?" Jeff asked.

"I'm fine, just dandy, couldn't be better." She grabbed something that looked vaguely like shorts and a shirt and dashed into the bathroom, slamming the door behind her.

"What's wrong with her?" Mac asked.

Jeff shrugged. "Your guess is as good as mine." He turned back and checked the lock on the window. "So, you didn't find anything when you swept the room?"

Mac shook his head. "*Nada*. It's squeaky-clean. Including the phone. But I can't keep coming in here to check things out without attracting a lot of attention. From here on, I'll keep tabs on the new tourists and any hired help that suddenly shows up, and you watch the room.''

"Agreed," Jeff said. He hoisted his suitcase onto the luggage rack and unzipped the double tabs with one smooth motion. "I'll keep you posted as best I can, but basically my plan is to stay put. No one's going to think it's strange if we draw the blinds and hide out for a while. If nothing happens after a week, we might loosen up."

The bathroom door opened and Jeff stared as Caroline walked out. She had changed into a pair of light blue cotton shorts—shorts that bared her long, lithe legs—and a matching blue-and-white striped top. Her long dark hair was tied back in a ponytail, making her look cute and sexy all at the same time.

She reached into the closet for a hanger and her top rode up, revealing the inward curve of her waist. She had the kind of body men dreamed about—exciting, ripe, touchable.

He watched in frank admiration as she settled the suit on the hanger and hung it in the closet.

"A-hem," Mac said, elbowing his brother in the ribs.

"Hmm?" Jeff never took his eyes off Caroline as she searched through the suitcase.

"If there's nothing else . . ."

Jeff watched as Caroline triumphantly pulled a pair of sandals from the bottom of the suitcase and slipped them onto her feet. She crossed the room and had her hand on the doorknob before he realized what she was doing.

"Hey," he said, sprinting across the room. His straight arm whizzed past her head and his palm flattened against the door, neatly trapping her in. "Where do you think you're going?"

"Out."

"Out where?"

"Just out." She waved her hand. "Out there. On the beach. In the sand. You know, out."

"No way," Jeff said bluntly. He pushed her aside and hung the Do Not Disturb sign on the front doorknob, then closed the door.

"Excuse me?" Caroline asked, unable to believe what she had just heard.

"I said, you're not going out. That's not the plan."

"What plan?"

"*The* plan, my plan, the plan that's going to keep you alive for the next two months."

Caroline stared at him in disbelief. "You sound like something out of a bad television show. 'The plan, the plan,'" she mimicked. "Well, I've got a news flash for you, McKensie. I never agreed to any of your plans."

Mac cleared his throat. "I hate to break up this little scene, but, um . . ."

Jeff folded his arms across his chest, stubbornness clearly evident in the strong set of his jaw. "You're staying inside, and that's final." He spoke in a voice that offered no hope of argument or persuasion—which made her all the more determined not to listen to him or, worse yet, obey him.

"What are you going to do? Tie me to a chair?"

"If I have to."

"Guess I'll be on my way now," Mac interjected, sidling toward the door. "I've got front-door duty, you know. And we wouldn't want the folks up on the hill to know what's going on down here, now, would we?"

"Look, McKensie, I won't be bullied by you or anyone else."

"Then stop acting like a spoiled princess who's about to throw a temper tantrum because she can't have her own way."

"Don't worry about my tip," Mac said. "You can make it up to me later. 'Bye." He ducked between Jeff and Caroline and was out the door in a flash.

"You agreed never to call me that," she said, her voice deathly calm.

"And you agreed to do this the easy way." Jeff leaned against the doorjamb and pinned her with a piercing stare. "Looks like we both changed our minds."

Caroline paused to consider her options. It didn't take long to figure out that for the moment she didn't have any. She could coax and plead and wheedle and cajole from now until a certain hot spot froze over, and it wouldn't make a bit of difference.

"So," she said finally, "you're going to play sentinel for the rest of day?"

"Nope." Jeff pushed himself away from the door. Lifting the chain in one hand, he positioned it over the latch opening, then slowly slid it into place. With a self-satisfied grin he walked past her to the large windows. He surveyed the outside area in all directions, then closed the curtains—sheer curtains thin enough to let in the light, yet opaque enough to shield them from view. Without another glance in her direction, he turned his attention to the suitcase on the luggage rack and began systematically putting his clothes in the dresser.

Caroline stood less then a few feet from the door. She balanced lightly on the balls of her feet, poised, ready. She watched Jeff deposit another armload of clothes into a drawer, then glanced back at the door—judging the distance, studying the lock, counting the seconds in her mind.

Jeff picked up a shaving kit and a half-dozen other toiletries and headed into the bathroom. She had her hand on the doorknob when he spoke.

"Did I mention I ran track in high school? I was only a mediocre distance man," he called out, "but I was a great sprinter. Took State my senior year."

Caroline's heart sank and she walked back into the bedroom and dropped into a chair. "Am I supposed to care?"

Jeff came out of the bathroom smiling. "Thought you might be interested."

"You thought wrong," she said flatly. She curled up in a comfy wicker chair next to a circular glass-topped table and looked around the room. It was gorgeous—large and bright and breezy, even with the curtains drawn. The ceiling and walls were a pale peach with a white ceiling fan and white tile floor. The king-size bed was a four-poster with a floral-print coverlet in cool peach and mint green that matched the drapes. Local artwork hung on the walls and a huge tropical plant sat in one corner. Overall, the room was a slice of Caribbean luxury.

So why did she feel like a prisoner in a bejeweled cell?

This wasn't anything like the motel she had been locked up in less than twenty-four hours after Brian's shooting. Nothing like the lonely place where she had wept silent tears for the brother whose funeral she couldn't even attend. It wasn't the same place...wasn't the same time.... Wasn't the same protector.

She watched Jeff as he continued unpacking his bag. He didn't look at all like the hard-boiled cops who had tried to protect her in New York—but his methods were the same. Lock 'er up and throw away the key. Maybe if he understood the fear, the panic...

That panic escalated to an all-new high with the next item Jeff pulled from his suitcase. A .38 revolver—or more accurately, pieces of it. He sat down on the bed, spread open a small towel, and fitted the sections together carefully with the speed and confidence of a man who had done the task countless times before. Caroline swallowed and forced herself to look away, trying to forget.

"Put it away," she said, her voice no more than a rasp that scraped along her throat.

"What?" Jeff never looked up from the weapon.

"Put it away."

It wasn't the words as much as the aching whisper that caught his attention. His hands stilled as he looked at her. The color had drained from her face, and her hands gripped the arms of the wicker chair so tightly, her fingers were trembling spasmodically.

"Caroline, it's just a gun—and a necessity in this line of work. You know that." When she didn't answer, he flipped the edge of the towel over the gun. "If it bothers you that much, go in the bathroom. But understand this, I won't risk your safety by avoiding something that needs to be done."

Caroline tried to speak, but her mouth was too dry, her throat too constricted. The memories hammered at her, chiseling away at her resolve. Brian. The cop. Flashes of light. The screams. The odor of seared flesh. And the blood—so much blood.

A shudder ripped through her body. Surging to her feet, she rushed to the door. She had to get out. Now. Had to see the sky and feel the warmth of the sun on her face. Had to be outside. Free. She grabbed the doorknob with both hands, rattling it awkwardly. Finally the door swung open, just a crack, stopped by the chain that tightened and strained but refused to give.

She felt like a hamster in a wheel—always caged, always running in circles. Brian and Davis and the police, and now this. It was too much. More than she could take. She closed her eyes and slumped against the door, hearing it shut with a deathly finality, feeling the click to the depths of her soul.

"Caroline?" Jeff touched her arm and the chill on her skin shocked him. The ceiling fan was on, but the windows were closed. It had to be eighty degrees in the room.

He rubbed his hands up and down her arms, warming her, silently reassuring her. Gently he stroked her cold white cheek, brushing aside a strand of hair, damp with perspiration.

And then she looked up at him, with eyes that would haunt him for the rest of his days. Eyes filled with fear and desolation and unspeakable sorrow. In that moment, he felt a reaction so strong it was almost painful. He wanted desperately to hold her and protect her and comfort her. He wanted to ease the fear and erase the sadness and make her world whole again.

She shuddered and his arms closed protectively around her, but she pushed him away. When he looked again, her eyes were shadowed, betraying none of the feelings he had seen only moments before.

Caroline dropped into a chair and wrapped her arms around her legs, resting her forehead against her knees. She closed her eyes, taking one deep breath after another. That little scene had been too close, had revealed too much, had made her all the more vulnerable. She had always been impulsive. Occasionally even reckless. But never out of control.

It was the memories, the nightmares that were every bit as powerful as the flesh-and-blood mobster. Maybe even more so.

Running helped. Running always helped. She had to get out and run. Just a little. Just enough to exhaust her body and her mind.

"How long?" she asked.

"What?"

"How long do I have to stay in here?"

"For as long as it takes to know you're safe. A few days. A week, max."

"No. I can't do it."

"Caroline, listen to me. Mac is checking things out as fast as he can. But we've got to be sure we weren't followed. If nothing happens in the next few days, then we'll get out—swimming, golf, tennis, whatever you want. I promise. I'm asking for a few days, not an eternity."

"It's the same thing," she said, shaking her head. "I can't stay in here, locked up. I'll go crazy. Please, Jeff, try to understand. I've got to have something to *do.*"

He pointed to her suitcase, which was still on the bed. "Why don't you unpack?"

She opened the dresser drawer, lifted her suitcase off the bed, and turned it upside down over the drawer. Then she tossed the empty suitcase into the closet and slammed the drawer closed. "All done. Now what?"

Jeff sighed. "Didn't you bring a book to read? A deck of cards? Some needlepoint?"

"I'm on my honeymoon," she retorted. "I didn't think I'd need those things."

Jeff rolled his eyes. "Lucky for you I planned ahead." He strode to his suitcase and pulled out several books. "How about something to read?" he asked, dumping the books on the bed.

Caroline glanced at the fat paperbacks. *War and Peace, Anna Karenina,* and *The History of the Decline and Fall of the Roman Empire.* "I'll pass."

"Okay, how about cards?" Jeff reached back into the suitcase and pulled out two brand-new still-sealed decks. "This goes with it," he said, tossing her another book.

"*Three Hundred Ways to Play Solitaire?* No thanks."

"*New York Times* crossword puzzles?" he asked hopefully, dragging yet another tome from the bottomless suitcase.

Caroline sighed loudly. "Jeff, I need something to *do*. You know, as in moving around—not sitting still."

"Exercise," Jeff said, grinning broadly. "I've got just the thing." Once again he plunged into the suitcase, this time coming up with two ankle weights, a coiled spring stretcher, and a set of handgrips.

"What? No NordicTrack?"

"It's a small suitcase."

Caroline smiled and took one of the handgrips, swinging it around by one handle. "Actually, I like these. My brothers had them. Did you know, the key is visualization? Here, let me show you. First, you position the grip comfortably in one hand—"

"I know how to use—"

"Then you visualize that the spring inside is actually someone's neck, someone who is particularly frustrating or annoying. Then you slowly begin to squeeze your fingers together, all the time imagining that your hand is really around his throat."

Jeff watched in amazement as Caroline pulled the handles of the grip closer and closer together.

"Increase your focus as you increase the pressure," she said. "Slowly...carefully...squeezing the life out of—"

Whatever else she intended to say was lost as the grip sprang out of her hand and flew across the room. Jeff ducked, but the metal exerciser glanced off his shoulder. He swore and grabbed the spot with his hand.

"I'm sorry," she said. "I really didn't mean to... I mean, why don't I just take that and—"

"Forget it, lady." Jeff picked the grip up off the floor. "In your hands this thing is a lethal weapon." He stuffed the exercisers back in his suitcase. "You want something to do?

Here," he said, tossing a remote-control unit in her direction, "watch television."

Caroline deftly caught the remote, but set it aside, focusing instead on a radio situated on the nightstand. Sitting on the edge of the bed, she clicked on the radio and slowly turned the selector dial. She slid past the New Age, the country and western, and the reggae until she found what she was looking for.

"Beach Boys." She sighed. She leaned back against the headboard, tapping her foot on the bedspread.

"Not again," Jeff groaned.

"The sun, the surf, the beach... It's the next best thing to being there. Wouldn't you agree?"

"I think it's loud, crude, and tasteless," Jeff muttered. "But if it makes you happy, be my guest."

Caroline grinned and cranked the volume up another notch. She found a perverse pleasure in watching Jeff cringe. He picked up a book, then lowered himself into a chair—as far away from the radio as possible. After a while, Caroline closed her eyes and immersed herself in the music, letting it calm her frazzled nerves.

The next thing she knew, a hand was gently shaking her awake.

"Caroline?"

She jumped and blinked, looking around in startled confusion. The four-poster bed, white-tiled floor... it all came back with astonishing clarity. She rubbed the back of her neck, stiff from where she had been half leaning and half reclining against the headboard. "What time is it?" she asked groggily.

"About one o'clock."

She looked toward the window. The heavier drapes had been drawn tight. "In the a.m. or p.m.?"

Jeff laughed. "The p.m." He pulled on the cord and the drapes flew back, flooding the room with bright sunlight.

Caroline groaned and shielded her eyes against the sudden glare.

"You were sleeping so soundly, I hated to wake you. But I'm starving and I thought you must be, too. Besides, if you sleep all day, you won't be able to sleep tonight. I'm going to order room service and wondered what you'd like."

"What are my choices?" She rotated her head from side to side, wincing at the pain that shot through her neck.

"Anything you want. Arthur's footing the bill, so the sky's the limit."

She stopped massaging her neck and looked him straight in the eye. "Anything at all?"

"Well," Jeff said hesitantly, "anything the chef can prepare."

"In that case, I want a picnic. I don't care what's in the hamper, as long as there's a blanket to sit on and lots of sand." She stood and stretched, a self-satisfied smile on her face.

"Caroline—"

"You promised," she interrupted. "Now deliver."

"Fair enough," Jeff said. He ran his finger down the hotel's list of services, then picked up the phone and dialed the number for room service. "This is Mr. McKensie in Oceanside No. 8. Do you prepare picnic lunches?... You do? Terrific.... Yes, for two people.... What's included in the special?... Fried chicken...potato salad...fresh fruit..." Jeff looked over at Caroline who nodded vigorously. "That sounds great," he said, "...to drink?"

"Iced tea with lemon," she whispered.

"Two iced teas with lemon. Oh, we'll also need a large blanket or something to sit on...and one—no, better make that two—big buckets of sand."

"You creep!" Caroline shouted.

"Forget the sand," Jeff said hurriedly. "Just send the food." He dropped the phone as Caroline grabbed one of the books. "Don't do anything you'll regret," Jeff warned, backing up a step.

"Regret?" she said caustically. "Not likely." She swung the tome over her head, but the knot in her neck twisted and caught. She yelped, dropped the book, and grabbed the back of her neck.

"Here," Jeff said, "let me rub that for you."

"Forget it. I can do it myself."

"It's the least I can do, since I can't let you go to the health salon for a real massage." Ignoring her protests, he put his hands on her shoulders and forced her down on the bed. Sitting behind her, he gently kneaded the contracted muscles, his large hands stroking rhythmically up and down her neck.

She sat there rigidly, enduring the contact partly because she no longer had the strength to go another round, and partly because he was right—it was his fault that she was in this situation.

"Relax," he said, his warm breath tickling her ear. "Your muscles are coiled in knots." His long fingers continued their exploration, massaging her shoulders, her neck, her throat. "Bend your head forward," he commanded, the rich timbre of his voice sending a thrill down her spine, even as his hands gently forced her head to her chest.

A sigh of genuine pleasure escaped from her lips. She closed her eyes and leaned back, surrendering to the warmth of his hands and the relaxing exhilaration that engulfed her.

Another ache made its presence known, this one in the pit of her stomach. The hot churning made her head spin dizzily, and her veins fizz with fire. Her skin prickled where his fingers touched her. Her breath came faster and her cheeks heated.

She jumped up and walked briskly to the far side of the room. He didn't follow her or call her back. But she could feel his eyes upon her, those deep blue eyes that seemed incredibly sexy.

"Thanks," she said, just to break the silence. "The neck's much better now. See?" She rotated her head in a slow circle as if to prove her point. "If you ever decide to give up law and witness protection, you could always become a masseur." The image of his hands on other parts of her body—stroking, teasing, kneading—flashed through her mind—and possibly his—and her cheeks flamed again.

And still his gaze never wavered.

She turned away from him, wrapping her arms tightly around her waist, as if controlling her body would likewise bring under control her stampeding feelings. She inhaled slowly. The calm she sought remained just beyond her grasp.

"I'm sorry about the sand business," Jeff finally said. "I couldn't resist."

"No big deal," she murmured.

Jeff eyed her suspiciously. "No big deal? It seemed like a pretty big deal a few minutes ago when you were ready to take my head off."

She shrugged. "You've got your plans. I understand that. Sort of."

One of Jeff's eyebrows climbed in a skeptical arch. "Why is it I'm not convinced?"

"Look," Caroline said, "it's pretty tough to eat chicken when you're wearing boxing gloves. Why don't we call a temporary truce, just until after lunch. Okay?"

"Sounds like a plan to me."

"And since you've given me a massage and let me have a nap, why don't you do something for yourself?"

"Like—?"

"Like, take a quick shower before lunch. It would be very refreshing, and if room service rings I can sign for it."

Jeff laughed, loud and long. "You never give up, do you? Well, I hate to disappoint you, but I've already had my shower, while you were—how shall I say?—sawing logs. Didn't you notice?" He pirouetted, watching her with an amused expression.

In leaping from a groggy sleep to the anticipation of getting out, she *hadn't* noticed. But she noticed now. He had changed into a knit polo shirt that molded his chest and upper-arm muscles and emphasized his broad, squared shoulders. His torso narrowed in a classic wedge shape to a hard flat belly clearly defined by the snug-fitting shirt. A pair of white tennis shorts revealed heavy tapered thighs and well-shaped calves. His legs were long, powerful, and covered with dark bronze hair. His feet were bare.

Caroline sucked in a quick breath. Witty and charming, she could handle. Sexy was something else altogether.

When she realized she was staring, she cleared her throat with a self-conscious sound. "I'm sorry I slept through it."

She gulped, wrenching her gaze from the smooth, golden skin exposed by the three open buttons of his shirt.

"Don't worry," he said, grinning. "I'm sure you'll get another chance."

She was spared answering by a loud knocking at the door. Instantly the humor drained from Jeff's face. He pushed her in the direction of the bathroom, then flattened himself against the wall by the outside door.

"Who is it?" he called out.

"Room service. I have a picnic lunch for Mr. and Mrs. McKensie."

"Just a minute." Motioning Caroline to stay out of sight, Jeff grabbed a bathrobe from the closet and threw it on over his clothes. He cinched the sash tightly around his waist, tousled his hair with the palms of his hands, and rumpled the bed. Finally, he cracked open the door and squinted at the bellhop. After a moment he closed the door, slid back the chain, then opened the door all the way. "Sorry to keep you waiting," Jeff said, his voice surprisingly deep and husky.

"No problem, sir. I, uh, understand."

Jeff pulled a bill from the pocket of his robe, and handed it to the young man. "Here you go."

"Thank you, sir."

Jeff set the picnic hamper on the floor while he relocked and rechained the door. "Lunch is served," he said, moving the basket to the glass-topped table. He readjusted the bedspread, then shrugged out of the terry robe and tossed it on the foot of the bed.

"Isn't that going a bit far?" Caroline asked, watching as he combed his hair with his fingers.

"It helps maintain the illusion. And maintaining the illusion will help keep you safe." He pulled a half-dozen containers from the basket. "Come on. Let's eat before we both waste away."

Caroline put a small mound of potato salad and a large assortment of fresh fruit on her plate. "I don't suppose a full stomach will make you amenable to leaving this room long enough to get a breath of fresh air."

Jeff smiled and offered her the container of chicken. "Not a chance."

Somehow she managed to survive the rest of the day. She jogged in circles, and paced back and forth like a duck in a shooting gallery. She sang rock-and-roll songs and briefly considered switching to a lullaby in the hopes of putting Jeff to sleep. She even tried to count the "snow" on a vacant television channel. But all she got for her efforts was a headache.

He, on the other hand, seemed perfectly content to sit and read. If her nervous energy bothered him, he didn't show it. He never so much as batted an eye, never nodded off, never even went to the bathroom.

The sun had set some time ago. Not that she'd seen it, of course, but the air had cooled and the light had grown gradually dimmer, until Jeff had to turn on the lamp to continue reading.

About ten o'clock, Caroline yawned and stretched. "I think I'll take a shower," she said, "and then turn in."

"Uh-huh," mumbled Jeff, turning another page of his book.

"Don't you need to stand guard or something?" she asked.

Jeff hooked a thumb in his book and looked up at her. "You planning on running away?"

"First chance I get," she said bluntly.

Jeff bit back a smile. "I appreciate your honesty...and the warning." He turned his attention back to his book.

Caroline whipped open the dresser drawer and rummaged around, looking for something appropriate to wear. Even if she planned to slip away at the first snore, she would still have to pretend to go to bed. The clingy rose negligee was out of the question. So was the hip-length sheer black baby-doll chemise. She groaned. What on earth had Jeff's grandmother been thinking when she packed these ridiculous things?

Finally she discovered something that made sense—an oversize cotton T-shirt in a tropical print. Obviously intended as a swimsuit cover-up, it would do very nicely as a nightshirt. She gathered up the hair dryer, shampoo, and other toiletries and hurried into the bathroom, closing and locking the door behind her.

The bathroom was spacious, with marble-topped double sinks and brass fixtures, and a coral-rock-walled shower. But one glance told her why Jeff wasn't worried about her slipping out the back door—there wasn't one. And furthermore, there wasn't even a window large enough to crawl through.

Anticipation grew as she showered and washed her hair. She breathed deeply, filling her lungs with steam. Soon she'd be breathing in the cool night air. A few more hours of confinement and then she'd be free.

She understood Jeff's concern for her safety and she truly appreciated his zealous dedication. But it was highly unlikely Augie Davis had had time to uncover her whereabouts—yet. Besides, she knew how to be careful. She wouldn't do anything stupid, wouldn't jeopardize the chance of making Davis pay for what he had done to her family. All she asked in return was a few minutes of freedom. A chance to run, stretch her legs, clear the cobwebs from her mind. She would sneak away as soon as Jeff was asleep, and be back before he realized she was gone.

She toweled off, brushed her teeth, and blow-dried her hair. "I suppose you'll want to fix your bed right in front of the door," she said, coming back into the room.

Jeff looked up from his book with a puzzled expression on his face. "Why would I want to do that?"

"So you'll know if anyone tries to sneak in . . . or out."

Jeff shook his head. "No one can get in with the chain on and the door bolted, and besides, the floor is bad for my back."

"Surely you don't expect me to sleep there," she said, lifting her chin.

"Of course not." He pointed to the bed. "There's room enough for both of us."

"I'm not sleeping with you!"

"No one's asking you to—not in the biblical sense, anyway. But be practical. There's only one bed, no couch, a tiled floor, and we both need to stay well rested and healthy for the next few weeks. The bed is huge and there's no reason why we can't share it. You stay on your side, and I'll stay on mine. I'll even let you choose the side."

"How generous," Caroline said. "But no thanks." She picked up a pillow and tossed it to him. "You can take the tub."

"And have you sneak away in the middle of the night? Not a chance." He tossed the pillow back to her, then snagged a piece of clothing from the dresser drawer and disappeared into the bathroom.

A minute and a half later, he was back—dressed only in a pair of pajama bottoms. "I'm sleeping right here," he said, pointing to the bed.

She gulped and tried not to stare at the perfectly proportioned, half-naked body before her—the broad shoulders rippling with muscles, the smooth bronzed chest, the hard taut belly, the fisted hands firmly planted on his hips.

"And what makes you think I won't slip away just because you're sleeping on the bed?" she asked.

"These." He reached into his suitcase and pulled out a pair of handcuffs, dangling them in the air.

Her eyes widened in disbelief. "You've got to be kidding."

"They're standard P.I. issue. Although, I admit, this is the first time I've had to use them on a client."

"You can't chain me to the bed. It's illegal."

"I'm not going to." He held up the key to the cuffs, made sure she saw it, then carefully placed it on top of the television. "I'm going to chain you to me."

"In your dreams," she retorted.

"I assure you, I am a man of honor. I have never violated a woman, or taken advantage of her. And I'm not going to start now."

"You're treating me like a criminal," Caroline protested. "I'm not the enemy."

"Neither am I."

"Could have fooled me." She watched as he opened one of the cuffs and wrapped it around his own right wrist, then clicked the metal shut.

"Oh, no," she said, backing away.

"Oh, yes," he said, stepping toward her. "Right or left, it's your choice."

"What if I have to go to the bathroom?"

"You'll wake me up. We'll climb out of bed, get the key off the television, and unlock you. When you're done, the cuff goes back on."

"It's dehumanizing. It's against the Geneva Convention."

Jeff made a face.

"I don't want to sleep in the same bed with you, let alone chained together. What if I give you my word that I won't try anything?"

"I wouldn't believe you. You already told me you were going outside first chance you got."

"Well, what if I promise? What if I give you my word?"

"Not good enough."

"You don't trust me, do you?"

"Nope."

"Well, then, looks like we have something in common after all." She drew herself up, squared her shoulders and held out her left arm, offering him her wrist. "You'll regret this, McKensie. Mark my words."

He smiled as he clicked the bracelet around her slender wrist. Then he threw back the bedspread and sheet and climbed into bed, taking her with him. "Good night, Caroline. Sweet dreams."

Sunlight streamed through a crack in the curtains and bounced off one side of Jeff's face as he lay on his stomach, his head turned to the window. He squinted and started to roll over onto his back until the tug on his right wrist reminded him his movements weren't entirely his own. Instantly he stilled, not wanting to wake her.

Still facing the window, he let the sunlight slowly wash away the dregs of the best night's sleep he'd had in weeks.

It took two elements to sleep well—an exhausted body and peace of mind. And last night he had both. He was physically spent from the nonstop activity of the past forty-eight hours, and, thanks to the handcuffs, his mind was released from the burden of responsibility for Caroline's safety. She had to stay put for the night, and that fact left his mind completely... unfettered.

He chuckled at his own joke. Heck, he knew how to get the upper hand—or wrist.

He inched his **right** leg under the covers toward her side of the bed. His promise not to take advantage of her vulnerable situation was good—as far as it went. But surely he couldn't be held responsible if his leg casually brushed against hers while in the throes of sleep.

He stretched his leg a little farther, surprised he hadn't connected with her, surprised at how cool the sheets seemed, surprised that his movements hadn't disturbed her slumber.

He tried to sit up, but was abruptly yanked back down on the bed. Squirming onto his left side, he quickly discovered the problem.

One handcuff was still attached to his wrist.

The other was locked around a bedpost.

And Caroline was gone.

Chapter 5

Instantly awake, Jeff stared at the cold, empty place beside him, and his blood froze in his veins. Every single word she had said since they'd arrived at the beach house washed over him like a stinging rain.

She had tried to tell him, tried to explain how she had to get out, how the confines of the room imprisoned her. But he wouldn't listen. He'd pushed her too far, backed her up against some invisible wall.

And now she was gone.

A knife of regret twisted in his gut. A cold knot of fear replaced the anger.

He yanked futilely at the handcuff, glancing at the top of the television. The small metal key was still there, mocking him with its nearness.

Damn! What was she, a female Houdini?

Wrapping both hands around the wooden spindle of the bedstead, he tried to twist it first in one direction, then in the other. The thing solidly refused to budge.

He cursed first his stupidity and then hers. As soon as he caught up with her, he was going to throttle her...

Unless someone else beat him to it.

The sobering thought infused him with renewed energy. He planted his feet against the headboard, grabbed the wooden spindle, and pulled.

Caroline breathed deeply as she jogged along the well-marked trail, filling her lungs with the luscious fragrance of the frangipani. A warm tropical breeze whispered through the palms and hibiscus, bougainvillea and ixora were in full bloom.

Paradise. Pure and simple.

And heaven knew, she needed a piece of paradise.

This was what Arthur Peterson had promised her. A place of tranquillity and beauty. A reasonable-size area to patrol and monitor. Freedom and space to move about.

The cold, stinging rain and harsh memories were back in New York where they belonged. She would return to them soon enough. But for now, for just a little while, she'd pretend that the whole world existed on this little island, where the sun was warm, the air was fragrant, and the breezes were gentle.

A small twinge of guilt rippled through her conscience, but she brushed it aside. With luck she would be back in the room and rehandcuffed to Jeff before he even knew she was gone. And if he did wake— Well, it served him right for having the audacity to treat her like a common thief.

She rounded a turn, jumped over a low-hanging branch of a thick baobab tree and winked at the huge sea gull carved in the wooden sign that marked the trail. Remorse be damned. She couldn't be melancholy on a day like this.

She exhaled on a puff, forcing the cold, stale air out of her lungs and cleansing her mind of the fear that had relentlessly pursued her since the night Brian was shot. Then she inhaled again, more deeply than she would have if she were running on an indoor track, trying to fill every pore with the scented air, letting the sun warm her to her soul.

She ran lightly, easily, pacing herself, running for the sheer joy of it. She had already been twice around the two-mile course, and had yet to encounter another soul. Early morning was always the best time to run. That's how it had been in Europe—all those years in boarding school when she would get up before dawn and run with the wind in her face, racing the sun into the sky. A time when life seemed so...uncomplicated. Lonely, yes. But uncomplicated, guileless, accepting. If she closed her eyes, she could almost recapture those days....

Caroline shivered. A sudden chill enveloped her like an icy mist, belying the tropical heat. Her scalp prickled, and apprehension tingled up her spine and spread along her shoulders. Her ears strained, were greeted only by a deep silence. Even the birds seemed suddenly quiet.

You're being ridiculous, she scolded herself. The trail rose to the top of a small knoll and Caroline paused, jogging in place, as she scanned the trail for signs of a fellow runner. No splash of color...no noise...nothing.

Shaking her head, she turned and continued on, determined to regain some of the serenity that had vanished as quickly as it had appeared. *Two more laps,* she thought. *Just two more and then I'll go back.* She picked up the pace, testing herself, pushing her muscles to the limit.

A twig snapped and every nerve in her body went on instant alert. She stopped and turned. But again there was nothing. No one. The first real tendrils of fear seeped through her.

She started running again, faster than before, and she heard the sound of footsteps pounding the trail behind her. Perhaps she had been hasty in leaving the security of the room, foolish in coming out here alone. Memories chased her and she ran as much to stay ahead of them as any pursuer.

She was at least half a mile from the room—half a world from safety. A coiling, rasping fear sucked the air from her lungs. Her heart thumped painfully against her breastbone, then climbed up into her throat and threatened to close off her breathing. The bitter taste of bile lay against her tongue.

Her boundaries began shrinking—collapsing. She felt trapped, even in the midst of all this openness. She struggled to breathe as invisible walls closed around her.

A sudden breeze, whipped up from the sea, whistled through the trees and she shivered. Alden was dead. So was Brian. Her sanity was threatened by the unspeakable notion that life could be cut short so quickly, so easily.

A scream echoed through her mind. She would stand and fight the way her brothers had—and she would win.

Never breaking stride, she rounded the next turn and ducked under a limb, crouching between the tree and the large wooden sea gull sign. Her view of the trail was severely restricted, but that meant she was equally hidden. With the echo of footsteps pounding in her brain, she held her breath, and waited.

Jeff ran with the determination of a man possessed. He ran along the oceanfront, the sand sucking at his feet. He turned and headed uphill past the vacant tennis courts, past the cottages and the silent shops, past the empty swimming pools. He had never been much of a distance runner and he was uncertain of his stamina. But he had to find her...*would* find her... would die trying.

He had paged Mac as soon as he had gotten out of the damn handcuffs. Mac had assured him no taxis or cars had been to the hotel since about ten the previous evening. Mac was searching indoors—the lobby, the arcade, the restaurants, the salon—while Jeff took the outside. She had to be on the property somewhere... unless she tried to walk all the way to Christiansted... or swim.

Maybe she was at one of the workout stations located along the jogging trail. Then again, maybe she was on the other side of the track. Two miles was a long way and if they ran at the same pace, they could run all day and never find each other.

Jeff stopped at the next workout station. Bending forward, hands on his knees, he panted heavily. He checked his pager, hoping against hope it would reveal a number even though the beeper had not gone off. He and Mac had promised to call each other as soon as she was found, but the LCD display was blank.

Damn, where was she?

Jeff straightened and raised his face to the sky. *Please, God, let me find her. And if I do, I swear it'll be different. We'll work something out.*

A splash of color—a speckled pink—somewhere ahead caught his eye. A flower? A bird? Maybe. Maybe not. It might have been a headband or some article of clothing. Heck, he didn't even know what she was wearing. The last time he'd seen her she was in a printed nightshirt that came midway to her thighs and bared her long, long legs. Not much to go on.

He saw the color again, bobbing up and down, but farther away. It was no bird or flower. Of that much he was sure. That pink whatever-it-was belonged to a human, and even if it wasn't Caroline, it might be someone who had seen her.

Jeff took off, pounding the trail, putting to use all those years of training as a sprinter. He focused on the splash of color, trying to keep it in view, tracking it as it weaved through the trees. He pushed harder and was beginning to close the gap when it suddenly disappeared. Up ahead, the trail rounded a corner and with a final burst of speed, Jeff threw himself into the curve.

Too late he discovered the limb of a large baobab tree that lay across the road. He tried to jump it, but his foot caught in the branch and sent him sprawling facedown on the trail. He got out no more than a grunt when his arm was whipped behind him and a knee was pressed firmly into the small of his back.

"All right, buster. Who are you, and why are you following me?"

"Caroline?" Jeff tried to turn his head around and get a look at his assailant.

"Jeff?" Her grip relaxed a fraction of a second, before she changed her mind and yanked a little harder on his arm.

"What are you trying to do, break my arm?"

"You're lucky I don't break both arms for scaring me half to death. Exactly what were you trying to prove, anyway?"

"I wasn't trying to prove anything. I was trying to *find* you. Guess you were in too much of a hurry to leave a note."

"I thought I'd be back before you woke up."

Jeff twisted uncomfortably on the dirt-packed trail. "Do you mind if we finish this discussion standing up?"

"I don't know," she said slowly. "I rather like it this way—my being in control, for a change."

In one fluid motion, Jeff flipped her onto her back, instantly reversing their positions. He straddled her waist, pinned her wrists over her head with his right hand, then laid his left forearm across her throat. "Don't get too used to it," he growled.

Caroline swallowed against the pressure on her throat. She blinked, but said nothing.

After a moment he stood, pulling her to her feet. "You're lucky it was me. Otherwise you would have looked pretty foolish trying to explain to the management why you attacked an innocent jogger out for a morning run."

She looked down, dusting the dirt from her clothes. Her eyes focused first on the small black revolver lying near his feet, then traveled slowly up the length of his body until she met his steady gaze with one of her own. "I suppose *you'd* like to explain to some passerby why you're running the exercise trail wearing little more than your pajamas and a gun."

Jeff scooped up the revolver, checked the safety, blew away a few specks of dirt, and slipped it into the shoulder holster under his arm. Then he buttoned his short-sleeved shirt, concealing the weapon. "I didn't have a lot of time to spend on my wardrobe," he countered. "I grabbed the gun and my sneakers and took off."

"So I see," she said, eyeing him up and down once more.

"This isn't funny, Caroline. What you did was stupid and reckless. Anything could have happened out here."

"I told you before, I can take care of myself."

"Not from what I see. You're standing out in the middle of nowhere. It's barely dawn. You're alone, and unprotected."

"I'm perfectly safe," she insisted. "We've been here less than twenty-four hours. Davis hasn't had time to find me."

"Maybe. Maybe not. But I'm not willing to take that chance." He raked a hand through his hair in frustration. "Damn it, lady. Didn't it occur to you that someone might worry?"

"Better watch it, McKensie. You sound as though you care."

He took a step closer. "Maybe I do," he said.

"Maybe you shouldn't," she warned, her chin jutting as she stood toe-to-toe with him.

Jeff clenched his fist, resisting the urge to knock some sense into her. "What is it going to take to get through to you?" he demanded. "Look around here. You could have been shot at a dozen different points along this trail."

"By you or the bad guys?"

"What is it with you?" he shouted. He grabbed her arms and shook her roughly. "This whole thing is one big joke to you. Don't you give a damn about your own life?"

Caroline squirmed out of his grasp and pushed him away. For weeks she had teetered on the brink of an emotional precipice, holding on only by the sheer force of her own will. And now the one man who was supposed to save her was about to push her over the edge.

"A joke?" she whispered. "Is that what you think?" She swallowed hard and her voice came out stronger and louder as her words tumbled forth in a rush. "Well, let me tell you something. Let me tell you how funny it is finding out your old man is the accountant for the worst crime syndicate in New York. Or what a laugh you get watching your brother bleed all over the Persian library rug. Or how about this one?—you're sitting in a locked room, surrounded by cops cleaning their guns, when suddenly the whole place goes up like the Fourth of July. Downright hysterical, wouldn't you say?" She swiped angrily at the tears pooling behind her eyelids. "Maybe I do make light of things. Maybe I am too quick with a joke or a retort. But it's the only way I can deal with what's happened. It's the only way I can keep from going crazy, from shattering into a zillion pieces, and ending up like some impossible jigsaw puzzle that just won't fit together. And if you can't handle that, if my behavior offends the delicate sensibilities of the squeaky-clean Yuppie lawyer, then you can take off right now. I don't need you. I don't need anyone."

"Caroline—" Jeff reached for her, but she stumbled back.

"Don't touch me. Don't...don't do anything." She waved her hands uselessly. "Just leave me alone." She turned and fled down the trail.

For a moment Jeff stood there, watching her retreating form. Twice now, he had misunderstood. Twice he had misread the pain and sorrow that haunted her beautiful eyes. He hated himself for hurting her, for adding to her unspoken grief, and he'd give anything to turn back the clock.

But that wasn't possible. So he did the next-best thing. He ran after her. Not fast enough to catch her, but fast enough to keep her in sight, to watch the surrounding area as best he could, to follow at a discreet distance as she finished the course. She never stopped, never paused, never looked around. He watched her disappear into the room and by the time he ran in after her, the bathroom door was closed and he could hear the shower running.

Jeff paged Mac to let him know she had been found. Then he put the gun back in the nightstand, and sat down on the bed to wait.

Caroline threw her head back and let the warm water run down her face. After that miserable little confession to Jeff, the shower felt like a safe haven—no cops, no guns, no bodyguards, no pretend husbands; just a little cocoon that was wet and warm. She would like nothing more than to curl up and stay put for, oh, say, the next two or three years.

Funny how the small enclosure didn't bother her. But then, she had never been claustrophobic. No, what she objected to was being locked in. At least in the shower you could leave whenever you wanted to.

Couldn't you?

Caroline looked at the glass door, knowing full well it was held shut by only a small metal clasp. But the seed of doubt had already been planted in her mind. Her fingers reached for the handle, then stopped in midair.

This is crazy, she told herself. *It's just a shower door. It's not locked. You* know *that. You don't have to test it.*

Her hand stayed where it was, just a few inches from the door, fingers twitching. But there was no way to dispel the doubt... the disquiet... the niggling fear.

She held out for as long as she could, then lunged against the glass door. It flew open on impact, swinging around and bouncing off the wall behind it. Caroline reached into the room, grabbed the chrome handle and yanked the door shut.

She sagged against the wall, feeling stupid and foolish. She could handle real locks—physical ones, the kind you could touch. She'd even picked Jeff's fancy cuffs the way her brothers had taught her. But fear? Caroline shook her head. Her fear trapped her more than any lock ever could.

The open door had left a chill on her skin and she turned up the hot-water knob, wanting to recapture the warmth and solace. A fine spray of hot water hit her full in the face and a cloud of steam enveloped her body.

The feeling of safety and comfort was out there, just beyond her reach. She rotated the knob another quarter inch, then turned her back to the spray, determined to find some semblance of peace, no matter how small. But the feeling of womb-like safety was long gone, and changing the water temperature didn't bring it back. Caroline angrily jerked the knob again, once more increasing the temperature. If she couldn't recapture the sense of safety, maybe she could cauterize the fear. She gritted her teeth against the quill-like sting, and turned the knob higher still. Again and again. Hotter and hotter.

Tears flooded her eyes. Her back was on fire, but it was only a fraction of a pain that went so deep, surely there was no end to it.

The steam was thick and she couldn't see her arm or her hand or the knob that she gripped so tightly it might have shattered. Her body was wrapped in an ethereal cloud that was heavy and choking. Her back went numb and she had the strangest sense that she was melting, her body becoming a small puddle on the shower floor. In her mind she could see herself whirlpooling around and around, growing smaller and smaller as she funneled down the drain.

In a burst of lucidity, she spun the knob in the opposite direction, then sank to the floor as cold water pelted her. Like forging a heated horseshoe and plunging it into a bucket of icy water, she felt her body sizzling, adapting to its new shape. The water swept away the surface pain, and the cold numbed her feelings until the top layer was frozen solid. She no longer felt the emotional current, but she knew it was still there—deep inside, running silently, stealthily, like a winter stream waiting for a spring thaw.

Caroline struggled to her feet and turned off the water. A couple of months. All she had to do was hold it together for a couple more months. She would stay alive long enough to make Augie Davis pay for what he had done to her family. She would harbor her sanity for that reason alone.

She leaned against the shower door, opening it with the weight of her body. She stepped onto the bath mat and gingerly eased the towel around her tender shoulders. Sixty days. And then she could fall apart or melt down the drain or do whatever the hell she wanted—and it wouldn't make a damn bit of difference to anyone.

She dried off and slipped into a comfortable robe, wondering just how long she could hide in the bathroom. The last thing she needed was another confrontation with Jeff. Or worse yet, explain why she had ripped open her soul and given him a firsthand look.

And since when did she owe him an explanation for her behavior? For that matter, who even said he wanted one? She considered the possibility. Maybe she didn't have to hide out in the bathroom. Maybe now that Jeff had seen her other side, the so-called soft and vulnerable side, he'd back off and leave her alone. Most men didn't want anything to do with hysterical females. One glimpse of something emotional, and men turned tail and ran.

That's how it had been with her father. Her mother's body was barely in the grave when he'd shipped his kids off to Europe. Why should Jeff be any different? No doubt he was already trying to figure a way out of this . . . delicate entanglement.

In fact, she'd lay odds that right this very minute he was flat against the wall on the opposite side of the room, as far away from her as possible. She tossed the hairbrush onto the vanity and marched out of the bathroom, nearly colliding with him as he waited for her just outside the bathroom door.

"Caroline, I'm sorry."

"Forget it," she said, rushing past him. *So much for predictability.* She kept her back to him, rearranging the clothes that hung in the closet.

"I can't," he persisted, coming up behind her. "I had no right to pass judgment on you. I really am sorry."

Her glance darted around the large room. There was no escape, no place to hide. She grabbed a large book from the dresser, and curled up in one of the wicker chairs, drawing her legs up under her and tucking the robe around her bare feet.

"It's no big deal," she said. She flipped quickly to the first page.

Jeff followed her across the room. "It *is* a big deal," he said, pulling the other chair closer to hers. He took the book out of her hands and placed it on the table. "You were right about everything. It'll be a lot easier to get through the next few months if you're in one piece. And if that means using humor or sarcasm or cursing me out, well, I understand. And I promise not to give you a hard time about it ever again."

Caroline folded her arms across her chest and looked everywhere but at Jeff. This wasn't going the way she had planned. Not only was he *not* backing off, he actually expected her to talk about it. She squirmed uncomfortably in the chair and picked at a piece of invisible lint. She couldn't do it.

As if reading her mind, Jeff took her hand, stilling it with his own. "Look. I'm no shrink, but I know that sooner or later you're going to have to deal with what happened to you and your family." He paused for a long moment before continuing, forcing her with his silence to meet his penetrating gaze. "But you get to say when."

Caroline looked into eyes as deep and blue as the Caribbean and felt as though she were drowning.

She could protect herself against insult and injury. She even believed she could protect herself from the hired guns of an underworld mobster. But she hadn't a clue how to defend herself against the caring and kindness she saw in his eyes. She looked away, saying nothing.

"If it would make you feel better," he offered, "I'll let you hit me with this book."

She bit the inside of her lip to keep from smiling. "Don't tempt me," she said in as gruff a voice as she could muster. "Just give it back." She reached across the table, but to her surprise, his hands snaked out and captured hers.

"In a minute," he said, toying with her fingers. His thumbs brushed back and forth across her palms and a tiny shiver raced down her spine.

"Caroline, I've had a lot of time to think this morning, and I admit I've been a little... unreasonable."

Her eyebrows soared in a skeptical arch.

"All right," he amended. "A lot unreasonable." He linked their hands, entwining his fingers with hers. "I'd like us to start over."

Her breath caught in her throat and she dropped her head, studying their clasped hands. The contrast was striking, in texture and color and size. Compared to her own small, pale hands, his were large and strong and well tanned. Yet his fingers were tapered and elegant.

He released her hand and cupped her chin, tilting her face so she was forced to look at him. His eyes were dark and intent, and once again she was stunned by the tenderness she saw there.

"We can work this out," Jeff said, "if we both bend a little. For instance, I'll give up the house arrest." He smiled and her heart did a slow roll in her chest. "We can go shopping, have dinner in one of the restaurants, even swim in the pool or the ocean as long as there are lots of people around."

"And in return?" she asked uncertainly.

"In return, I want to know where you are at all times. You won't go anywhere alone, and you won't sneak out in the middle of the night."

"No more handcuffs?"

"No more handcuffs," he promised.

"Does that mean you trust me?"

Jeff shook his head. "I wouldn't go that far," he said slowly. "But frankly, I don't want to have to break another spindle." He gestured with his thumb in the general direction of the bed.

She followed his glance to the headboard and her mouth dropped open. "You broke the bed?"

"I had to," he said. "I couldn't reach the key." He looked at her suspiciously. "Which reminds me, how did you get away?"

She shrugged. "I picked the lock."

"You what? Where did you learn a stunt like that? And how is it you happen to carry a set of lock picks to bed with you?"

Caroline laughed. "My brothers taught me years ago." She looked at Jeff pointedly. "I wasn't born a spoiled little princess, you know."

Jeff made a face, licked the tip of his finger and made a mark in the air.

"And, for your information," she continued, "I don't need a set of lock picks. I can use a hairpin, a safety pin..." She smiled and fingered one dangling pierced earring. "Even a fishhook earring."

Caroline stood thigh-deep in the ocean, slowly dribbling water over her arms.

"I thought you wanted to go swimming," Jeff grumbled.

"Well?"

"Well, you've been out here thirty minutes and you still aren't wet."

"I'm wet," she protested. "Partly."

"Barely." Jeff watched her take two more steps until the waves lapped at her hips, licking skin the color of a pale apricot. His gaze traveled upward, taking in the curve at the slender waist... the long, graceful back... the high breasts filling the bikini top. He drew in a sharp breath as she stirred her hand through the water, stroking and caressing it like a lover. He closed his eyes, but couldn't banish the image from his mind. He dived under the water, careful not to splash her, swam in a large circle around her, then came up beside her. He tossed his head, slinging his hair away from his face.

"I thought you were supposed to be the reckless, impulsive one—the one who jumped in with both feet."

"Not in water," Caroline said. She scooped up a handful of water and dribbled it down first one arm, then the other. "I'll get wet my own way, in my own time."

"Suit yourself," Jeff said. "But at the rate you're going, by the time you get wet, it'll be too dark to swim. You do swim, don't you? Because if you don't, I'll be happy to teach you." He ducked under the water and came up behind her. Slipping one arm around her waist, he grabbed her arm with his other hand and began moving it in a circular motion. "Cup your fingers, grab the water and pull it back, then reach forward and—"

"I know how to swim," Caroline said, struggling out of his arms and pushing him away. She brushed the droplets of water off her neck and chest. "I just like to take my time. Some things I prefer to do slowly, deliberately, savoring the—"

From out of nowhere, the sound of a gunshot split the air, stopping her words in her throat.

Chapter 6

Reflexively, Jeff exploded out of the water like a performing dolphin. For a split second he seemed suspended in the air, towering over her. Then he came down, his hands on her head, pushing her down, down, until she was submerged underwater.

Caroline opened her mouth to protest, but she lost her balance and the sea engulfed her. She struggled to regain her footing, then came up sputtering and gasping for breath. Again, Jeff's hands were on her. Shielding her with his body, he half pushed, half dragged her down. She only had time to grab one quick breath before the water closed over her head once again.

"Damn you," she spat, as she struggled to her feet a second time. "If you wanted to kill me, why didn't you do it in San Diego? You could have saved the taxpayers a lot of money."

"The noise," Jeff said. "It sounded like a gunshot. I thought someone was shooting at you." He scanned the shoreline carefully. "Must have been a car backfiring."

"A car?" she screamed. "You nearly drowned me because of a car? Look at me," she said, trying unsuccessfully to push back her dripping hair from her face. "I'm all wet."

"Caroline," Jeff said with a calmness he didn't feel, "you're standing in the middle of the ocean. You're *supposed* to be wet."

"Not like this," she retorted, pulling the useless clip from her matted curls and squeezing salt water from her hair.

Maybe it was a release of the tension that had wrapped around his heart when he heard the shot. Maybe it was all the wasted adrenaline surging through his bloodstream or the ridiculous sight of her standing in the ocean trying to wipe the water from her hair and face. But whatever the cause, the result was the same. Jeff threw his head back and laughed, loud and long.

"You think it's funny? Well, how would you like it if someone jumped on your head and held you under?" Without giving him a chance to explain, Caroline jumped on his back. With a hand on each shoulder, she threw her weight forward, straight-arming him down into the water, jumping off at the last moment.

He came up choking on seawater, just as she had. "Why, you little witch," he sputtered.

"What's the matter?" she taunted. "You can dish it out, but you can't take it, is that it?"

The look he gave her was blatantly sexual. "I can take anything you have to give—and then some."

"Then take this," she said, "and use it to cool off." She reached back with her arm, then swung it forward, skimming the water, intending to douse him with spray.

But this time he was ready. Using the spray as cover, he dived under and came up between her legs, lifting her out of the water seated on his shoulders.

"Put me down!" she yelled, kicking futilely while he clamped her legs against his chest.

"What did you say?" Jeff asked, calmly ignoring her protests.

She reached down and put one hand under his chin and the other at the back of his head. "I said put me down, or I'll break your neck with my bare hands."

"Yes, ma'am," Jeff answered. In one swift move, he slid his hands down her legs to her ankles, then flipped her in a backward somersault off his shoulders.

He turned around and waited for the splashing to subside so he could watch the fireworks. No doubt about it, when she came up, she would be spitting mad. She would sling her long, sleek hair out of her face and her eyes would flash lightning bolts. *Coup de foudre*—a lightning bolt. That was what she was, and he couldn't wait to see those eyes flash again.

Jeff looked anxiously at the spot where he thought she'd gone under. "Caroline?" He plowed the area in a small circle, heavy water dragging his body, ocean waves breaking against his back. He half expected her to jump out at him, to grab his leg or his arm, but there was nothing—nothing but a huge expanse of water.

"Caroline!" He dived into the water, swimming hard against the incoming tide. How long had she been under? *One-thousand-one, one-thousand-two.* The numbers echoed in his brain, ticking off each second like a sonic boom. *One-thousand-three, one-thousand-four.* She must have hit her head or swallowed too much water. His chest constricted—not because his lungs felt deprived of air, but because of the sudden pain squeezing his heart.

Damn! Where was she?

And then he spotted her, facedown. A large wave pounded her body, tossing her aside like a rag doll.

Jeff reached her in a heartbeat. He flipped her over and into his arms as his legs propelled them toward the shore. Her skin was translucent, and blue tinged her lips. Water and sand grabbed his legs and sucked at his feet as he ran onto the beach.

He laid her down in the sand and knelt beside her. Quickly he checked her mouth for blockage, then tipped her head back, pinched her nose and covered her mouth with his own.

Three times he exhaled deeply into her mouth, forcing her body to accept his breath. He rolled her onto her stomach and pumped her back beneath the rib cage, then turned her over and started the process again. *Come on,* he silently urged. *Breathe, damn it!*

She coughed violently and he pulled her onto her side, pounding firmly between her shoulder blades with the heel of his hand. She coughed again and her eyes fluttered briefly, then closed as she dropped back on the sand.

"Oh, no, you don't." He jerked her neck up with his left hand while closing her nose with his right. Taking a huge breath, he held it for a moment before coming down on her mouth—hard—expelling air into her lungs. He raised his head and drew another breath, then came down again, this time gentling the impact. He felt warmth returning to her cold flesh and he willed the heat of his body into hers as he tried to infuse her with his strength. She shuddered once and his arms tightened protectively around her.

Her breathing came in ragged, choking gasps. Relief swept through him and he sat her up, cradling her in his arms. "Caroline?"

Her head fell back and she looked at him with glazed and unfocused eyes. He touched her cheek. Her skin was warm...and very soft. His fingers rested on the pulse point at the side of her neck and he felt the pulse beat strong and steady.

She watched him now through half-closed lids, her eyes as soft as her skin. She managed an unfocused smile and drew a shaky breath, one that molded the wet bikini top around her full breasts and brushed against his chest. Desire, swift and powerful, thrummed through him. He lowered his head until his lips were no more than a hairbreadth from hers, until their breath mingled and tension crackled between them.

He waited, expecting her to stiffen or pull back. But she did neither. So he touched his lips to hers...gently...testing. She tasted of salt water and smelled of sea air.

He whispered her name against her mouth and a shudder racked her body. With a low groan he tightened his arms around her, crushing her to his chest, pressing her against the long, hard length of his body.

His tongue swept past her lips, invading her mouth. He deepened the kiss—slowly, persuasively—and when she opened for him, he plunged deeper, taking everything she offered.

An answering passion swelled inside her like an ocean wave, and her fingers splayed across the warm expanse of his rock-solid chest. She felt the rapid beating of his heart.

Caroline slid her hands up the taut muscles twitching in his arms, and his shoulders seemed to expand as her arms stole around his neck. She ruffled her fingers through the hair at the nape of his neck—so much thicker and softer than she had imagined.

A low, deep sound of approval vibrated in his throat and her blood raced. A wild pulse thundered in her ears and swirling heat coiled through her.

He pulled back and she raised her eyes to meet his darkened gaze. She was so close she could see herself reflected in the black centers of his hungry, smoldering eyes; feel herself drowning in blue whirlpools of promise.

He eased her onto her back until she felt the warm sand mold itself to the contours of her body. He loomed over her, leaning on his arms, his hips pressed intimately against the cradle of hers. The sea air brushed over her heated skin, a contrast to the heightened waves of urgency pulsing through her body.

Droplets of water clung to his broad chest, his sun-bleached hair, his blond lashes. His skin glistened, making him look more virile and dangerous than any man had the right to look.

A lock of damp hair tumbled across his forehead and magnetically drew her hand upward to brush it from his face. His hair was beginning to dry in the late-afternoon sun. The sea breeze tousled it, and it curled, soft and unruly, against his neck. Of their own volition, her fingers combed through the springy thickness.

He caught her hand, turned it over, and kissed the center of her palm, his lips caressing the sensitive flesh. The simple gesture drew her attention to his firm, wide mouth and she felt her own lips part in expectation.

The tide was coming in, and somewhere, in a distant knowing, she could feel cool water lapping at her feet. But she wasn't cold. She was kept warm by the male heat and swelling masculine power radiating from his large, sexy body.

This man stirred in her a passion she hadn't thought possible. She felt it in her breasts, in the tensed muscles of her thighs, in the throbbing of her very core.

His gaze dropped to her mouth, and when he ran his thumb across her swollen lips, her breath caught in her throat. He leaned forward, his head bending slowly toward hers. He lowered his mouth and their lips touched. His kiss wasn't gentle. Nor was it rough and demanding. It was simply... devastating. Like succumbing to the ocean's undertow, she slipped further and further away, flooded with emotions that could no longer be dammed up.

A shrill whistle blew and they jumped apart like a couple of teenagers caught necking at a high school prom.

"Oops," Mac said, grinning wickedly. "Shooting a remake of *From Here to Eternity?*" He paused as if considering the possibility. "You know, I never thought of you as the Burt Lancaster type—"

"Knock it off, Mac," Jeff warned. He jumped up, then offered a hand to Caroline, helping her to her feet. "What are you doing here, anyway?"

Twirling the nylon cord that hung around his neck, Mac swung the whistle in slow, lazy circles. Then he turned around and pointed to the letters on the back of his baggy sleeveless top.

"You're the lifeguard?" Caroline asked incredulously.

Mac grinned. "For the moment. Some little kid told me he saw a man carrying a dead lady out of the ocean. You guys are lucky that's all he saw." His admiring gaze swept over her scantily clad body. "You look pretty good for a corpse."

Scooping up one of the nearby beach towels, Jeff shook out the sand, then draped the towel around her shoulders, pulling the edges together across her breasts. He knew he was being chauvinistic, but the honest truth was that he didn't want Mac or anyone else seeing her wearing nothing more than a few scraps of cloth. "She had a little accident," Jeff said tersely.

"Accident?" Mac echoed. He looked from his brother to Caroline and back again. "What kind of accident?"

"I was diving," she said. "Backward...and I hit my head. It's no big deal." She glanced at Jeff out of the corner of her eye as she gingerly touched the back of her head. "I'll be more careful next time."

"Man, you'd better be," Mac said. "In fact, maybe you should have your head examined—I mean, looked at— You know what I mean."

Jeff gripped Caroline's arm with one hand while, with the other, he lifted her chin and peered into her eyes. "Mac's right," he said. "Maybe we'd better drive you into Christiansted to see a doctor. You might have a mild concussion."

"Don't be ridiculous," Caroline said. She brushed aside Jeff's hand and knelt to retrieve the rest of her things. "It will only draw more attention to us. And that's the last thing any of us wants."

Jeff watched her as she kicked her feet into a pair of beach thongs. Her color was good and she seemed steady enough. "All right," he reluctantly agreed. "No doctor."

"Good," she said. "Now I'm going back to the room and see if I can't wash off some of this sand and salt water." She slung her tote bag over one shoulder, turned and headed up through the trees that separated the rooms from the secluded beach.

"I have to get back to work," Mac said. "There aren't usually any swimmers this late in the day, but I need to be there just in case." He watched Caroline's retreating form. "Is she going to be all right?"

"I think so," Jeff replied. He slipped his arms into a T-shirt, then pulled it over his head. "I'll wake her up every few hours tonight—just to make sure," he added in response to Mac's highly suggestive expression.

Mac nodded. "Call me if you need anything—anything medical, that is." He turned and sprinted up the beach, disappearing around the cove.

Jeff shot one last glance in Mac's direction, then grabbed his things and hurried up the hill after Caroline. Walking behind her definitely had its advantages. From this position it was easy to admire her long, shapely legs and the inverted heart shape of her bottom just visible below the towel.

Jeff ground his teeth together as he remembered all too clearly the sweet promise of her hips. He clenched his fist around the towel and cursed the Fates that had thrown him together with a woman who tempted him so. She had grace and beauty, wit and charm. Her laughter was like sunshine and her eyes warmed his soul.

He wanted her.

And she wanted him, too.

Her response to his kiss had told him that and more. Never before had he seen such pure desire in a woman's eyes—desire that mirrored his own. Never before had his reaction been so completely overpowering. And if Mac hadn't shown up...

None of this made any sense. He'd known beautiful women before. He'd known women who were smart and sassy and more than willing. But he'd never known anyone who could get to him the way she had.

Maybe it was a natural reaction to the accident. Fear was a powerful aphrodisiac, and just thinking about what might have happened—what still might happen—was enough to send him over the edge. He had been hired to protect her—not seduce her. How could he expect to do his job when his mind was on her? He had no right entertaining such thoughts of her. No rights to her at all.

Kissing her like that had been a mistake—a big one. A mistake he vowed never to repeat. He had slipped once. Held her in his arms, run his hands over her body, kissed her lips, gazed into her incredible eyes.

It was one time too many.

And not nearly enough.

* * *

For the second time that day, Caroline slumped against the coral-rock wall of the shower. This time she was not engulfed by heat and fiery steam. Nor did she feel the sting of ice-cold water. In fact, the water wasn't even on.

Although her hair was caked with sand, and salt water coated her body, she couldn't bear to wash it away. Not yet. For that also meant washing off the feel of his hands and the taste of his kisses—something she wasn't ready to do.

She closed her eyes and touched her hand to her lips, remembering. For a few amazingly wonderful minutes she had felt poised on the edge of an exhilarating discovery. Her body quivered with the shock of real passion, real desire, and a dozen sensations she had never before experienced sprang to life.

It was just a kiss, she reminded herself. Hardly even noteworthy in today's freewheeling sexual society. But it wasn't "just" a kiss. It was a bone-jarring kiss. A soul-wrenching kiss. *His* kiss.

And she had wanted it to go on forever.

Caroline gave herself a mental shake. *Forever* was a word used by children and dreamers and optimists. It hadn't been in her vocabulary for a very long time. So why did it show up now? Now—when "forever" was more remote than at any other time in her life. Now—when the future was so incredibly uncertain. Now—when she was the last surviving member of the Southeby family.

The reality was that Augie Davis could end her life tomorrow... and she was thinking of "forever."

It didn't make sense. But then, neither did the hungry passion that had exploded between them, rocking her to the very core. It was as if Jeff had touched a chord—a chord of physical and emotional need—that continued to sing long after it was played.

A sigh escaped her. She wanted to hear the whole song. She wanted to spend the afternoon in rapturous lovemaking, with the percussion of the pounding waves accompanying the music of their bodies. She was ready to act out sexual fantasies she hadn't even known she had.

And it would have been the biggest mistake of her life.

Casual sex and one-night stands had never been for her. She had to care about someone before she could hand over a part of herself. She had to be able to trust in order to give herself so completely.

She didn't trust this man with her life, let alone her heart. And she certainly didn't care about him. Didn't dare care about him—not with Davis slithering in and out of her life like the viper he was. And yet, all it took was a good healthy dose of lust, and she was ready to surrender... run up the white flag... throw away all her principles.

It was crazy. Sheer madness.

Slowly, reluctantly, Caroline turned the shower knobs and let the water sluice down her body. She washed away the sand and the seawater and every physical trace of their ever having been together.

But she couldn't wash the memory out of her mind.

She dried off and dressed quickly, wrapping a towel, turban-style, around her head. The only way to handle things with Jeff was to keep it light, humorous, funny.

"Your turn," she sang out, as she breezed out of the bathroom—and promptly walked into him... again.

"Caroline, I'm sorry," he said, his large frame all but blocking the doorway.

"Didn't we rehearse this scene this morning?" Taking a deep breath, she forced herself to step around him, careful not to brush against his body. She was absurdly afraid that if she touched him, even casually, there would be no way to prevent the smoldering flame from becoming a raging inferno.

"I mean it. I'm really sorry."

She pinned on a bright, insouciant smile. "About the kiss or the dunking?"

His steady gaze never left her face. "Both. I was unprofessional and totally out of line. I betrayed your trust and took advantage of you. It won't happen again. I promise."

"Look, McKensie. You didn't betray my trust. I told you before, I don't have any. No offense, but that's the way I am. Now go take your shower and I'll call room service and order dinner.''

He gave her a funny look—one she couldn't decipher...or chose not to. Finally he nodded, then pulled a few items of clothing from the drawer. "I won't be long," he said. "And I'll leave the door ajar. If you need anything, yell."

Caroline paced the room, looking out the window, deliberately keeping her back to the open bathroom door. Knowing full well if she stood at just the right angle, the shower with its glass door would be fully visible. It didn't take a quantum leap of imagination to picture him in there—lowering his crossed arms, grabbing the bottom of his T-shirt, pulling it slowly over his head.

It didn't take a visionary to see the wide, well-muscled shoulders that tapered to narrow, equally muscular hips, or the long, powerful legs covered with dark bronze hair. She knew, without looking, that a black Speedo swimsuit, barely wider than her hand, covered his male strength.

Without realizing it, she had narrowed her full-room pacing, and now found herself walking like a sentry just the few feet back and forth in front of the bathroom door. She could hear the water running, and could feel the steam encircling his body.

The mind had the power to play incredible games, and more than once, reality had been a far cry from what she had imagined. Obviously, this was another one of those cases—and one quick peek would put all this nonsense to rest.

Hands planted firmly on her hips, she spun around in front of the bathroom door—and swallowed hard. An arousing glimpse of firm, rounded buttocks and heavy male thighs greeted her. A deep valley ran down his spine, bordered by thick ridges of muscle. He was magnificent...powerful...perfect. His wet body glistened and flexed as he soaped himself, moving the bar with quick, efficient strokes. She watched in fascination as he stepped under the fine spray and rainbow droplets zigzagged down his back.

And then he began to turn around....

Caroline fled, nearly tripping over her own feet in her haste to get away. Trying unsuccessfully to banish the images from her mind, she grabbed the phone and with shaky fingers punched the buttons for room service.

What she needed was a little food and a good night's rest—but she'd settle for one serious piña colada.

Augie Davis smiled into the phone, then placed it in the cradle with a soft click. He opened the middle drawer of his desk and selected a felt-tip marker—black. Lifting the cover of the single file lying in front of him, he scanned the remaining names on his list of suspected Carolines. Slowly, deliberately, he drew a fat line through the one in Missouri. The woman had been a problem.

She wasn't Caroline Southeby, but she would never be a problem for anyone—ever again.

Chapter 7

Caroline stretched out on the chaise longue and felt the sun slide along the length of her body like a lover's caress. After three weeks in this tropical paradise she enjoyed surrendering to the sun and the sand and the cooling trade wind that drifted lazily over the water.

So far, everything had gone according to plan. There was no sign of Augie Davis or any of his men. Nothing strange or unusual had happened with the hotel guests or staff. Even the weather had been absolutely glorious—surrounding them with balmy days and warm, tropical nights. It was almost paradise.

Almost.

There was one glitch in this Garden of Eden.

And his name was Jefferson McKensie.

Caroline scowled as she thought of the change that had come over Jeff since that afternoon on the beach. He had done a complete one-eighty. He was gothic and stoic and all business. He seemed edgy, tense, strung out. Occasionally he was downright hostile. And he avoided her like the plague—which was pretty funny, considering he was rarely more than a few feet away.

Their meals were eaten in silence, he sat up reading most of the night, and when they went swimming, he always made sure they stayed a respectable distance apart.

And why? Because of a few shared kisses?

Caroline shook her head. Not likely. The mouth that had covered hers was sinfully experienced. But when she had tried to talk to him about it, he'd cut her off before she could say more than three words.

"I'm sorry," he had said. "It won't happen again."

Perversely, that was exactly what she wanted.

And the rejection stung more than she cared to admit.

With a small huff, she rolled onto her stomach and rested her head on her folded arms. Why should she waste her time thinking about him? She might as well enjoy the time alone before old Frosty came back with their lemonades and put the deep freeze on everything within a three-mile radius.

Who needs him, anyway? she thought. Certainly not an independent, self-reliant woman like herself. She was going to make the most of this tropical paradise—the sun, the sand, the gentle breeze . . .

A shadow blocked the sun, throwing her body into shade. She turned quickly toward the source, but her eyes were blinded by the glare of white-hot sunshine reflecting off the ocean.

"Hi, Caroline," said a small voice.

Caroline pushed her mirrored sunglasses to the top of her head. "Hi, Alex. What are you up to today?"

The six-year-old held up a bucket and shovel. "Sand castles," he said gravely. "I took a class so now I can build 'em really good. Wanna help?"

Caroline grinned. Alex took great pride in the fact that *he* was the one who spotted her the day she "drownded," and he'd been an almost-constant companion ever since. Jeff wasn't happy about the child's presence, but it didn't take long to check him out. Alex and his parents had come to this resort every summer for the past five years, and as an added precaution, Arthur had unearthed the family's genealogy for four generations. Everyone from Alex to his great-grandparents had checked out clean.

"I'd love to," she said. "But I might not be very good."
She pitched her voice low, even though there was no one
around to overhear them. "I've never done it before," she
confided.

"That's okay," Alex said brightly. "I can teach you." He
grabbed her hand and pulled her toward the wet sand near
the water's edge. "First you have to pick the right spot. You
can't be too close to the water or the waves will mess it up
before you're done. And you can't be too far away or you'll
have to carry lots of water to get it wet." His face pensive,
Alex turned around in a slow circle, surveying the area. "I
think we should build it right . . . here." He broad-jumped
into the sand, planting both feet in the spot where their castle would be built.

"Looks good to me," Caroline said, kneeling in the sand.
"Just tell me what to do."

For nearly two hours, Jeff watched Caroline pack wet
sand into a plastic bucket and turn it upside down on the
beach, making structures that looked vaguely like medieval
turrets. She built up a sand wall, and carved out little windows with the help of a discarded Popsicle stick. With her
bare hands, she dug a moat around the perimeter, and
lugged about two dozen buckets of seawater to fill it.

And he couldn't take his eyes off her.

Three weeks in the sun had driven the pallor from her
features. Her skin was now lightly tanned, and her brown
hair tumbled in waves around her shoulders, glittering in the
sunlight. The breeze blew a few silky wisps across her face,
and she swept them away with the back of her hand as she
worked. He was mesmerized by the sound of soft voices and
quiet laughter.

An inexplicable longing stirred inside him—long-dormant
memories he was powerless to stop. Memories of his parents . . . of himself and Mac as children . . . of being part of
a family.

Most of his life had been lived according to a master
plan—a plan he had conceived and designed while still in
high school. Methodically, he'd mapped out his career—

college, law school, associate, partner. Every stage was carefully charted, complete with short-term and long-term goals all neatly arranged.

He also knew that someday he would marry. Eventually, he would have 2.3 children and a golden retriever, a respectable home in the suburbs and a minivan. But that was still a ways down the road. He had slotted it roughly for the period of time between being an associate and becoming a partner—give or take a year.

And he was right on track, perhaps even a little ahead of schedule. His life was going just the way he wanted it to go. He had allowed nothing to impact his well-laid plans.

Until now.

Now, suddenly, crazily, in the semishade of a Caribbean palm, he was ready to dump his life's blueprint into the nearest trash can . . . because of her.

She was everything he had ever wanted and more. She was bright and witty and passionate. And if her rapport with this child was any indication, she would make one hell of a mom.

He could only begin to imagine what it would be like to wake up every morning to the sound of her laughter, to look into her glorious eyes at the end of each day, to go to bed at night with the taste of her on his lips.

Fate had dealt her a miserable hand, stripping her of everything she held dear, making her tough and distrustful, fighting just to stay alive. She deserved better. She deserved to be loved and cherished, cared for and comforted. She deserved a man whose world revolved around her, a man to sleep beside and a raise a family with, a man who would abandon everything else in life to make her happy.

A gull swooped overhead, casting a sudden shadow on the sand, and Jeff instantly sobered.

These were the kinds of thoughts that could get them all killed. How could he protect her, how could he hope to perform his job, when his mind was light-years away? He needed to keep a clear head. And that had to be his first— his only—priority.

A faint beeping sound drew his attention to the pager hooked at his waist. Alarmed, he pulled it off and examined it closely. A telephone number appeared on the LCD display. Mac's number, to be used only in an emergency.

Jeff took a step toward Caroline, then stopped. His first reaction was to grab her hand and haul her off to someplace safe until he could contact Mac and find out what the hell was going on. But maybe that was exactly what someone would expect him do.

Someone like Augie Davis.

Jeff studied the area. The ocean effectively cut off half the access. There was no way a boat could reach the shore—it would hit the coral reefs long before it hit the beach. And there was nothing unusual going on in the water, just the dozen or so people who had been frolicking there most of the afternoon. Over the ridge was the golf course, with four holes of wide-open grassy lawn and no place to hide. The only possible place for an attack was from the area directly behind Caroline. The area dotted with palm trees and baobabs—the area where he now stood.

For a long moment Jeff wrestled with the options. Yanking her off the beach would arouse a great deal of suspicion, not to mention the job it would do on her sanity. She had calmed down a lot over the past three weeks, and wasn't as jittery or skittish as she had been in the beginning. She was actually starting to relax enough to sleep at night—a fact he could personally attest to, since he spent most of the night watching her. What good would it do to work her into a state of frenzy before he even knew if there was anything to be frenzied about?

None at all.

His fingers twitched as he clutched the pager. Around the corner, not more than fifty yards away, was the lemonade stand...and a telephone. He could go up there, use the phone, and be back in no time.

Jeff looked around once more, convincing himself that no one could get to Caroline without passing him first. Then he turned on silent feet and bolted up the hill.

*   *   *

Caroline gave Alex's shoulders a gentle squeeze as they knelt in the sand, admiring their work. The castle was little more than a lopsided trapezoid, and the turrets bore an amazing resemblance to the Leaning Tower of Pisa, but all in all it wasn't a bad first effort. "What do you think?" she asked her young companion.

Alex laid a small piece of driftwood across the makeshift moat. "It's perfect," he pronounced. "Do you like puppies?"

Caroline blinked. Keeping up with a child's conversation was a lot like trying to catch a zinging racquetball. There was no telling where it would bounce next. "I love puppies," she said.

"Wanna see some?"

"Sure." She stood up and stretched the kinks out of her cramped muscles. Never again would she assume that building a sand castle was child's play—it was hard work. She glanced at her watch as she brushed some of the sand from her arms and legs—and it was time-consuming. She had no idea she'd been at this so long. And where on earth was Jeff?

"What's the matter?" Alex asked, pulling on her hand. "I thought you wanted to see the puppies."

"I do," Caroline said. "But, I need to find my...husband first." She had promised to let Jeff know where she was at all times, and she wasn't going back on her word now. Not when their truce was so fragile. Not when his approval had become so important. "I have to tell him where I'm going," she explained.

The little boy nodded his head knowingly. "Yeah, my mom makes me do that, too. 'Cept here. We come every summer and I know the place real good. They know I can't get lost or nothing. But you can't tell him—he's gone."

"Who's gone?" Caroline asked hesitantly.

"Him. You know, the man you went swimming with. He was standing right over there." Alex pointed to the chaise longue she had been lying on. "But then he left."

"Are you sure? I mean, are you sure it was Jeff? He has blond hair and he's about this tall." She raised her hand some six inches above her head.

Alex nodded. "Yep, it was him, all right."

Caroline stared at the spot, trying to make sense of a situation that defied explanation. This wasn't like Jeff—taking off without telling her, leaving her unattended for the first time in weeks. She shrugged. Maybe he was giving her more freedom, allowing her a little more responsibility for her own safety. She should be elated. Instead, a strange sense of disappointment hovered over her. Okay, so maybe she did protest too much. Maybe she had actually started to enjoy his company—a little.

"Are you coming or not?" Alex asked. His fists were firmly planted on his slender hips and his lower lip stuck out in an unmistakable pout.

"You bet, I'm coming," Caroline said determinedly. If there had been an emergency, Jeff would have said something—warned her. And he obviously wasn't in any trouble himself because Alex said he just left. So, the heck with him.

"Let's go." She grabbed Alex's hand and they took off running, heading for the ridge that overlooked the golf course.

Jeff clenched the receiver. "When did this happen?"

"Twenty... thirty minutes ago," Mac said. "She's a housekeeper. Hasn't missed a single day in the last five years. Today she calls in sick and a replacement is on the way."

Jeff swore.

"Look," Mac said. "I already spoke to Arthur and he's going to run a check. But that could take a while."

"Pack your bags. We're grabbing the next plane out of here."

"Sorry, bro, but Arthur wants you to stay put. A sudden bolt would arouse suspicion. One way or another, he'll call us back in seventy-two hours."

A long sigh escaped Jeff's lips. "Understood. You stay on the newcomer. I'll keep Caroline in the room."

"Right. 'Bye."

Jeff hung up the phone, then leaned back against the side of the kiosk. He should have known something would go wrong. Three weeks in paradise without so much as single rain cloud was more than he had dared hope for in San Diego. But as the days turned into weeks, he had begun to think maybe the apprehension and foreboding were misplaced. Maybe they would get through this ordeal unscathed—physically speaking. Maybe it was all right to start dreaming about the future.

Well, so much for daydreams.

And now he had to tell Caroline.

Jeff cringed at the thought of changing the rules on her. For three weeks she had faithfully lived up to her end of the bargain, and he felt like a heel having to reinstate the house arrest. Maybe she'd understand it was only for three days. And then again, maybe that was another of his fancy pipe dreams.

Three days, and then they'd either go back to the way things were now or hit the road running. Jeff shook his head. Three days of being cooped up with the woman who had haunted him unmercifully from the moment he'd seen her picture. Three days of living side by side, day and night, without so much as an hour off to ease the unbearable tension. Jeff closed his eyes. Waiting for something to blow up or blow over was always the hardest part of this job—and all the signs pointed to a major explosion.

Jeff pushed himself away from the kiosk and jogged back toward the beach. Hot sand burned the soles of his feet as he stopped dead in his tracks.

Caroline was nowhere to be seen.

Chapter 8

"Caroline!" The door bounced off the wall behind it, as Jeff burst into the room.

"I'm right here," she said, coming out of the bathroom and closing the door firmly but quietly—in stark contrast to his blustering. "You don't have to shout."

Jeff raked an angry hand through his hair. His relief at seeing her alive and in one piece was so great, he didn't know whether to hug her or throttle her. "You're lucky I don't skin you alive," he all but snarled. "I've been all over creation looking for you. Where the hell have you been? And what were you thinking, running off like that? We went through this before and you gave me your word—"

"Whoa, buster. Hold it right there." She charged forward until the tips of her sandals bumped against his tennis shoes. Refusing to be intimidated, she jabbed him in the chest with her finger. "You have a lot of nerve lecturing me about *my* promises when you simply up and disappear without so much as a 'See you later.' What was I supposed to do, sit around with sand in my shorts until you decided to grace me with your presence?"

He bent forward until their noses almost touched. "It would have been a damn sight better than taking off the way you did. Scaring me half to death—again."

"Listen here, McKensie. For weeks, I've kept you apprised of every move I made. I told you when I was getting up and when I was going to bed, when I was going out and when I was coming in, when I was going to eat or go swimming or take a shower." She lifted her chin. "And for your information, I looked for you this afternoon. I wanted to tell you where I was going, but *you* weren't around. So, don't go blaming your problems on me."

He'd been so overwhelmed by the mixture of relief and anger surging through his body, that he hadn't realized how close they were standing. So close, he could see the thick fringe of dark lashes framing her remarkable eyes. So close, he could smell her natural scent, clean and fresh and captivating. So close, he could see a light sheen of moisture pearlizing the tiny hollow at the base of her throat.

In the ensuing silence, his heart pounded loudly enough to wake the dead, but if she heard it, she gave no indication. She stood very still. There were no gestures, no shrugs, not even a blink to put an inch or two of welcome space between them. Her eyes stayed level with his, communicating vibrant passion without movement. The same kind of passion he'd seen in her eyes that afternoon on the beach when he'd held her in his arms and kissed her—fierce and ragged and on the edge of control.

He flicked a finger down her hair, then reached up and slowly stroked her cheek. She didn't flinch or pull away and the fire in her eyes was staggering. He bent his head and brushed his lips lightly across hers—a gesture that was more caress than kiss. She tasted sweet, so he sampled her again— drugging, potent, like honeyed whiskey.

And then he heard it—a faint scratching sound on the door, like a lock being picked. Reflexes took over and he pushed her behind him, keeping his body between her and the door.

"What—" Caroline's words died in midair as Jeff's hand clamped across her mouth.

"Shh," he cautioned. His breath fanned the ultrasensitive skin around her ear and her stomach looped into a tight knot. Did the man have any clue what his nearness did to her? Her heart thumped against her ribs as his scent surrounded her. She struggled to concentrate, to block out any sensations that were "him," and focus on what was really happening.

But it was a losing battle. Because what was really happening had nothing to do with external threats and everything to do with internal warnings. Teetering on the edge of an emotional precipice, she knew she would willingly step off—if he was there to catch her.

There was a noise—a rasping against the door—or was it her imagination conjuring up illusory dangers to keep him close?

"I think we've got company," he whispered, his lips tickling her ear. He adjusted his position and his forearm brushed against her breast, sending an erotic shiver down her spine.

Her moan was stifled by the hand across her mouth, and her lips moved wordlessly against the soft underside of his palm. She felt him stiffen, and knew she was the cause. Knew, in that moment, that she affected him as deeply as he affected her.

He backed her up to the far side of the bed and pushed her to the floor. "Stay down," he hissed.

She drew a ragged breath and felt a sudden emptiness as he moved away. Before she could find her voice, he slid open the drawer of the nightstand and slipped out the gun. He moved like liquid mercury toward the door, releasing the safety as he went.

"Jeff, no," she rasped, but he silenced her with a wave of his hand. "You don't understand—" she started again, but his eyebrows drew together in a heavy frown, his eyes narrowed, and his lips formed a thin line as he scowled her into silence.

Fine, she thought. *Be that way.* Kneeling on the floor, with her elbows resting on the bed and her head propped in the heels of her hands, she watched nonchalantly as Jeff slid along the wall to the bathroom.

She'd give him that much—he sure knew what he was doing. He held the cocked revolver high in the air with both hands in classic police fashion. Every inch of his body was braced for combat, from the well-defined muscles of his heavy thighs to the corded biceps straining against his snug-fitting T-shirt. And she was perfectly content to continue the ridiculous charade for the sheer pleasure of admiring his perfect and powerful body.

With his back braced against the wall, Jeff leaned to the side and slowly reached for the doorknob. He threw open the bathroom door and assumed a fighting stance.

"Freeze," he barked . . . and then froze himself as a four-legged ball of fur barked right back.

Caroline laughed so hard her sides ached and tears ran down her cheeks. Jeff slumped against the wall, the gun limp in his hand, adrenaline pumping through his system. "You think this is funny?" he shouted.

"No, I think it's hysterical. You and that . . . that cannon against one poor defenseless little puppy." She collapsed on the bed as another fit of laughter overtook her. "Actually, I think every lady should have a champion—Don Quixote tilting at puppy dogs, St. George the Puppy Slayer . . ." She tapped a finger to her lips. "Or how about—"

"Sir Bozo, knight ridiculaire. I get the general idea." Jeff pushed away from the wall, put the safety on the revolver, and returned it to the drawer. "You might have said something."

"I tried," Caroline said. "Twice. And think about it. There's no window in that bathroom large enough for someone to enter, and you saw me come *out* of the bathroom when you came barging through the front door. It stands to reason there was nothing in there that could hurt us."

"And what the hell is a dog doing in our room, anyway?"

"You're changing the subject," she admonished.

"You're avoiding the question," he charged.

She scooped up the puppy who was pulling a sock out from under the bed. "I'm doing Alex a favor."

Confusion was written all over Jeff's face. "Say what?"

Caroline shook her head. "Alex befriended a hotel employee who was giving away a litter of puppies. This was the last one. Alex desperately wants it, but he hasn't asked his mom yet. So, I agreed to keep the puppy overnight. Okay?"

Jeff scratched the puppy behind his ears. "Fine with me— as long as you're the one who gets up and takes him out in the middle of the night." He scrubbed a hand over his face as another thought occurred to him. "Oh, crud. You can't take him out in the middle of the night and neither can I."

"Why not?"

Jeff struggled to keep his voice quiet and even. "Because one of the housekeepers just called in sick and a so-called 'replacement' is on the way. Until they check her out, Arthur wants us to lie low."

Caroline swallowed the cold knot of fear that suddenly stuck in her throat. "That's why you were so edgy when you came in here...and why you freaked when you heard the scratching on the door. Jeff, I'm sorry. If I had known—"

"I didn't 'freak.' I was being cautious. And you had no way of knowing what was going on. In fact, the only reason I even told you is because we have to go back to the old rules—we're back under house arrest."

"What! Come on, Jeff, you can't do that. We had a deal."

"You broke that deal this afternoon—or have you conveniently forgotten your little disappearing act? The one, I might add, that has probably taken another year off my life."

"I explained all that. I would have told you where I was going, if I could have found you. And did it ever occur to you that your disappearance may have taken a year off *my* life?"

Jeff arched a brow as his eyes locked on to hers. "*You* were worried about *me?*"

"No, I wasn't—but I could have been." She pushed past him, the puppy still in her arms, and sat down on the floor near the window. She took the sock and tied a knot in one end, then swung it back and forth in front of the curious pup.

"You were worried about me." This time it was a statement rather than a question and a smug look crossed his face. He liked that idea—a lot. "Admit it," he challenged.

"I was not worried," Caroline said flatly.

Jeff settled in a chair and began leafing through the latest copy of the resort newsletter. "I say you were."

"And I say you're crazy." She jumped up and snatched the newsletter out of his hands.

"Hey, I was reading that paper."

"Sorry," she replied lightly, "but the puppy needs it more than you do."

A scream tore from her throat as Caroline fought the tangled bedclothes. Blood. She was drowning in a sea of blood. Red and sticky and terrifying. She sucked in air to scream again, but instead a single word emerged—"Brian." His limp body oozing life lay before her while maniacal laughter crackled in her ears. She tried to reach him, to stem the awful flow of blood, but strong arms wound around her, holding her back. They were going to lock her up and she couldn't let that happen. Couldn't live through that again. She fought wildly but viselike hands clamped on to her arms and wouldn't let go.

"Caroline." Jeff shook her, hard. Her scream had stopped his heart and now it hammered painfully against his rib cage. "Caroline, wake up. You're dreaming. Come on, snap out of it."

Fighting him every step of the way, she tried to claw from the murky depths of the dream. Slowly the nightmare faded, and in a final burst of lucidity, she broke through.

"Brian..." Deep sobs racked her body as she fought the anguish that followed her into the present. She pummeled Jeff's chest with her fists, but she hadn't the strength to effect even one glancing blow. "Please," she cried, "not Brian."

Jeff pulled her into his arms and cradled her close. Her body was soaked with sweat and her nightshirt clung to her skin. "It's all right. It was just a dream."

But it wasn't just a dream. It was a flashback that she would probably relive again and again.

"Oh, God." She could feel the walls closing in, trapping her, cutting off her air supply. Her hands tore at the thin-ribbed collar of her nightshirt in a futile attempt to remove the invisible fingers constricting her throat. "I have to get out of here," she gasped. "Please."

Jeff nodded. Wordlessly, he removed the pistol from the nightstand. He ripped the top sheet from the bed and tossed it over his arm, then took her hand and led her to the door.

Whistling for the puppy to follow, Jeff led her around to the back of the bungalow, to the spot where it looked out on the ocean. With his back against the building, he sat down on a stone step, pulling her with him.

In spite of the warm night air, he could feel the chill on her skin. He wrapped the sheet around her shoulders, then pulled her close, trying to comfort her. She had stopped the frantic clawing at her throat, but her breathing still came in long, shaky sobs.

"It's okay," he murmured against her hair. "Let it out."

She collapsed against him then, quivering like a small, frail bird that had fallen from a tree. He rocked her, his hands moving in slow repetitive circles over her back and down her arms. She buried her head against his shoulder, and when he brushed the hair from her face, he found it wet with her silent tears.

It was then that he felt the need. Not desire, or lust, or sexual passion, but real need. The need to hold her and offer her his strength and warmth. The need to give—and receive—comfort and compassion.

A need like he had never known before.

Gently, he stroked her neck and shoulders and back until her trembling stopped and her breathing became more slow and even.

"I'm sorry," she rasped, her throat and mouth as dry as the sand beneath the palms.

"For what?"

"For messing up your plans." She brought her knees up close to her chest and shrugged her shoulders helplessly. "The house arrest and all."

"Oh, that." The smile he offered was warm and friendly. "Well, frankly, Caroline, you've been messing up my plans since the first day I saw your photo, so one more time isn't going to matter." He paused a fraction of a second. When he spoke again, his voice was softer, deeper. "Besides, this was different."

"This was a nightmare." She lifted a limp hand and dragged it through her tangled hair. "People have them all the time. It's no big deal."

"Do you want to talk about it?"

She shook her head, then dropped her chin to her knees. "There's nothing to say."

"I think there is." He put a hand on her shoulder and turned her toward him, gently cupping her cheek so she was forced to look at him. His eyes were dark and intense but contained no pity, just concern. "Tell me what happened to you."

"Why?" She eyed him warily. "Why would you want to know that? What possible difference could it make?" *Why would you care?*

"It can't hurt you, and it might just help. You've been so busy trying to stay alive, I doubt you've had time to grieve, to work through the process." She tried to turn her head away, but he held fast. "Am I right?"

Unblinking, she met his steady gaze. "A lawyer, a bodyguard, and an amateur shrink. Will the real Jefferson McKensie please stand up?"

His smile was as soft as the night air drifting out to sea. "I'd really like to help."

She looked toward the bushes where the puppy sniffed at the ever-blooming hibiscus and ixora. A warm night breeze floated off the waves, ruffling his fur and stirring the flowers so they bobbed and weaved in front of his curious nose.

"What do you want to know?" she asked, never taking her eyes off the inquisitive puppy.

Everything. All of it. Your favorite color and your favorite food. Your earliest memory and your dreams for the future. I want to know about your parents and your brothers and how you came to be in the middle of this sordid mess. I want to know you.

"Whatever you want to tell me," he answered quietly.

"It's a long story," she warned.

"I'm not going anywhere."

"And neither am I, right?"

He smiled, but said nothing.

Caroline took a deep breath and held it as she listened to the incessant whisper of the palm trees. The long fronds brushed against one another as if trading secrets back and forth.

Maybe it was time to let a few of the secrets out. Jeff deserved the truth—to know who he was really getting involved with. Maybe it was time to trust him, just a little, and hope that he and the ageless trees would keep her secrets safe.

"For most of his life," she began slowly, "my father was a bookkeeper, and not a very successful one. He had a few steady clients and he did their books once a month. But it wasn't much, and financially, it wasn't enough. My brothers and I grew up on the streets, learning all sorts of interesting 'survival skills.'"

"Like picking locks?"

Caroline nodded. "Among others. Including some that were a lot more...criminal." She glanced at Jeff from the corner of her eye, not quite knowing what to expect, but steeling herself just in case disgust and repulsion looked back at her. But if her other-side-of-the-tracks upbringing bothered him, he didn't show it. For a split second their eyes met and held. His moonlit face reflected only compassion, encouraging her to continue.

"When I was about eight or nine, my mother became ill," she said. "My father didn't have any medical insurance and it wasn't long before he was heavily in debt. He picked up a second job working in a warehouse, and then a third job as a janitor—but it still wasn't enough. Then one night, he came home with a car filled with groceries and clothes and medicine. It was like Christmas and Thanksgiving and birthdays all rolled into one. He said our troubles were over, thanks to his brand-new 'client.'"

"Augie Davis," Jeff interjected.

She looked away. "Yes. But we didn't know it at the time. Ironically, my mother never had a chance to enjoy my father's newfound success. She died less than six months later. And two weeks after the funeral, my father shipped the three of us off to Europe. Alden and Brian went to a boys' school in England, and I was sent to a school for young ladies in France."

"How old were you?" Jeff asked.

"Ten." Through years of practice, she had mastered the self-control needed to keep her voice flat and even, as though she were reciting historical facts instead of revealing deep personal pain. "Brian was fourteen, Alden sixteen."

Jeff shook his head. Her toneless voice revealed more than any angry outburst. "It must have been incredibly difficult for you—losing both your parents so suddenly."

She shrugged. "Kids are surprisingly adaptable. And, it was a long time ago. In fact," she added, "sometimes it feels like it all happened to someone else, and I just watched from the sidelines." She offered him a faint smile. "Pretty weird, huh?"

Jeff squeezed her hand. "No, I'd say it was pretty normal."

A bird swooped low over the sand, then pulled up sharply and soared back into the sky, until it was little more than a silhouette against the moon.

"Did you see your father very often?"

She shook her head. "Just at Christmas, and even then he couldn't wait to get rid of us. After the first two years, he sent us huge checks and said we ought to use the time off from school to experience other countries and cultures and stuff. Alden was eighteen and had graduated from the prep school. He decided to continue university abroad—not because it was his first choice, but because he wanted to keep the three of us together. He really took care of Brian and me. We were The Three Musketeers—disguised royalty traipsing around Europe. Duke Alden, Lord Brian, and me..."

"The princess," Jeff finished.

Caroline looked at him sideways. "Are you also a psychic? Is there no end to your list of talents?"

Jeff chuckled. "That's not talent. It's elementary deductive reasoning—and it explains why you flew off the handle when I called you that."

"Hold it right there, Sherlock," she said. She struggled out of his arms and turned to face him. "I don't fly off the handle."

One blond eyebrow rose quizzically as he studied her.

"I don't," she protested. "I'm the soul of equanimity." She sounded so affronted that he laughed again.

She drew herself up and tossed one end of the sheet over her shoulder, looking surprisingly dignified for someone dressed in a makeshift toga. "Forget it. Good night."

"Wait." He reached out and caught her hand as she turned to leave. It wasn't so much the restraint on her hand that held her as the look in his eyes. "I didn't mean to imply there was anything funny about what you've gone through. Please, tell me the rest." He made room for her on the stone step between his legs, releasing her hand only when she was within the shelter of his arms. Gently, he pulled her back against his chest, then wrapped his arms around her.

Caroline closed her eyes. Her head rested snugly in the hollow of his shoulder and his nearness infused her with strength and comfort. For the first time in months she felt truly safe. She let the memories—both good and bad—slide to the surface.

"It was the happiest time of my life." She swallowed hard and blinked away the sudden spill of tears. "As kids, we swore nothing would ever come between us—but then we didn't count on growing up. At the university, Alden met a Swiss girl. They fell in love and, since he'd had enough of traveling, they decided to put down roots. He went to work for an American company in Switzerland where they could be close to her family. Brian was just the opposite. He'd been bitten by wanderlust and Europe was simply too small for him. He headed to Asia, eventually made his way to Indonesia, and then Australia. He never stayed long in one place.''

"And you?" Jeff's voice urged her on.

She took a deep breath, filling her lungs with the fragrant scent of frangipani and strong sea air. "Those years abroad were interesting, and I learned a lot. But I never felt like I belonged there. Never quite fit in. I wanted to go home," she said softly. "Not to my father's house—which was hardly a home—but to the States, to New York City, to a place where I was accepted. I enrolled at NYU, rented a little apartment in Brooklyn Heights, got a job, and basically got on with my life."

"Did you keep in touch with your brothers?"

"Always—even with Brian. I have postcards from the four corners of the earth and he would call me at the most ungodly hours. Said he couldn't compute the time change. Every month I'd write a long, chatty letter to Alden and he'd write back or call. And there was another thread that bound us together—our father. And one thing we all agreed on— we hated him."

"Hate is a pretty strong word."

"It's also an accurate one. We needed a father, a parent, but what we got was a check twice a year. We didn't know about Augie Davis or any of his criminal activities. All we knew was that as soon as my father started making big money, he lost interest in us. He didn't even go to Alden's wedding. He sent them a ninety-nine-cent wedding card— and a check for a hundred thousand dollars. Alden sent it back. Then he tried to send Brian money. But Brian was never in one place long enough to get mail. Brian said he enjoyed staying one step ahead of the old man. And when my father found out I was in New York, he offered to buy me my own apartment *and* pay my tuition. Believe me, I wasn't polite like Alden, and I didn't duck it like Brian. I told him exactly what he could do with his money."

"I'm sure you were the soul of equanimity," Jeff teased.

She started to say something, but smiled instead. "Yes, well, maybe I was a tad strong, but he deserved every bit of it."

"You don't have to defend your actions," Jeff said. "I probably would have done the same thing."

A slight breeze blew off the ocean and ruffled one end of the sheet. The puppy growled menacingly, then jumped on it. The section flattened beneath his paws, but bubbled again with the next gust of wind. He grabbed the flap between his teeth and shook it vigorously. After a moment, he dropped it, then poked it several times with his nose. Satisfied it posed no further threat, he stood on his hind legs and tried to climb into Caroline's lap. She offered him a gentle boost and after a moment of circling and sniffing, he curled up and promptly went to sleep.

"It's hard work fighting demons," Jeff said, stroking the puppy in Caroline's lap.

"Even invisible ones?"

"*Especially* invisible ones." He nudged her gently. "Finish your story."

"Not going to let me off the hook, huh?"

"Only if that's what you really want."

She thought about it for a long moment. "No, it's probably better if you know the truth. All of it. At least you'll know what you're really up against." She moved slightly, shifting the puppy's weight to a more comfortable position.

"At college I met a woman named Johanna Gray. We became best friends, then roommates, and finally business partners in The Coffee Café. Johanna is a coffee expert— not just the usual French roast or Kona coffee, but every exotic blend imaginable. She even developed a few of her own. And all those years in France had taught me about the power of the pastry—croissants, éclairs, napoleons, croquembouche—"

"Whoa, stop. Breakfast is still six hours away."

"Not to mention the rest of Europe with its scones, crumpets, strudel, Danish—"

"And you can make all that stuff?"

"Of course. You're not the only one with hidden talents."

"I'm impressed."

"The bank wasn't. It takes a lot of capital to start something even that small. Of course, my father offered to finance the whole thing—"

"But you told him he could jump off the Brooklyn Bridge."

She grinned. "Something like that. Anyway, after months of begging and pleading, we got a bank loan, rented an old storefront on Atlantic Avenue between Brooklyn Heights and Cobble Hill, and opened for business. Coffees and pastries any time of the day. The success rate on this type of venture is minimal, but we did it. Of course, in the beginning we lived on cold coffee and stale pastries, but we paid off the entire loan in eighteen months and have been making a decent profit ever since."

"Is Johanna running the place alone now?"

Caroline shook her head. "Arthur has her in hiding, too. He was afraid Davis might use her to get to me. Heaven knows who's running our shop—probably running it into the ground."

"I doubt that," Jeff said. "Arthur's a good man. He'll take care of it. So what happened next?"

Caroline took a deep breath. "My father died in January. His housekeeper called me. I contacted Alden, and he located Brian. There was lot of work to be done and a lot of stuff to go through. I took care of the funeral arrangements, Brian inventoried the house and its contents, and Alden got the will into probate and started organizing my father's papers. My brothers stayed at the house. I stayed at my apartment. I should have known," she said, her voice barely a whisper.

"Known what?" Jeff prompted.

"I should have known something was wrong. That Brian and Alden were keeping something from me. But I didn't. I didn't have a clue. I was just so happy to have them back in my life again.''

"What happened?'' Jeff insisted. "Tell me what happened to them.''

"My father had a boat that hadn't been used in a long time. We were going to sell it, but Alden insisted on checking it out first. He was an expert sailor and a world-class swimmer, and wouldn't even *give* a boat away if it was in less-than-perfect condition. He went over that thing from stem to stern. Then one afternoon, about a month after the funeral, he took it out for a final run.'' She turned to Jeff, her eyes filled with tears. "The damn thing just . . . blew up. He never had a chance.''

"How did it blow up?''

"I don't know,'' she said, her voice choking on the words. "The police said it was an accident. The fuel pump or gas line or something. But it couldn't have been.'' She grabbed Jeff's arm. "It couldn't have been,'' she repeated. "Alden checked it out. There was nothing wrong with that boat. I swear it.''

Jeff covered her hands with his. "And what about Brian?''

Caroline shook her head, the tears running unchecked down her cheeks. "Brian got weird. Not like I've ever known him. He was silent and withdrawn. I tried to talk to him about the arrangements, about notifying Alden's wife. But he just shut me out. He locked himself in my father's library and told me to leave him alone. He was like that for days. He wouldn't eat, wouldn't talk to me. Nothing. We should have gone through it together. I could have helped him. We could have helped each other. But he wouldn't let me.'' She looked away.

"What about the shooting?''

"It was Wednesday,'' she said woodenly. "Wednesday night.'' She looked up at him, her eyes vacant and staring. "Did you know I was born on a Wednesday? And 'Wednesday's child is full of woe,' '' she quoted.

"Where were you Wednesday?'' Jeff asked.

"I was working at the Café and I got this chill. Johanna gave me her sweater, but I kept shivering. I called the house, but there was no answer. That didn't surprise me. Brian wouldn't have answered anyway. I worked for another hour but I couldn't shake the feeling that he needed me."

"So you went to the house."

She nodded. "It was all dark. Like a tomb. It had been that way since Alden died. I let myself in and headed to the library, where I knew Brian would be. I was going to bust the door down if he wouldn't let me in. But I didn't have to. When I got downstairs, there was a faint light spilling from the library. And there were voices—two of them—Brian's and another man's. They were arguing so loudly I could hear them halfway up the stairs."

"What about?"

"I'm not sure. Brian said something about 'Alden' and 'ledgers.' He was really angry. I'd never heard him like that. I stepped into the room and...and..." She squeezed her eyes shut, blocking out the images, the memory, the pain.

"And what, Caroline?"

"Brian. Oh, God, Brian." She covered her face with her hands and began rocking back and forth.

Jeff slowly, gently pulled her hands away from her face. "Tell me what you saw."

"I can't."

"You've got to. It's the only way you'll ever be free of the nightmares."

She shook her head and continued rocking. The sheet slipped from her shoulders and fell to her waist. The puppy, awakened by the movement, struggled to his feet.

Jeff lifted the puppy to the ground, then held Caroline's face in both his hands, forcing her to look at him. "Caroline, listen to me. I won't let anything happen to you. That's a promise, and I never break a promise. I'll be right here all the time. But you've got to tell me everything."

"It all happened so fast," she said.

"Play it over in your mind," Jeff urged. "Like a movie running in slow motion. What was the first thing you saw?"

She closed her eyes again, but this time she wasn't retreating. She was watching the internal film, the pictures she had avoided for so long. "The look on their faces—all three of them. Shock, disbelief, horror. Especially Brian. He screamed, 'No!' At least it looked like he was screaming. I saw the word on his lips, but I never heard the sound. The older man yelled, 'It's a double cross. Kill them.' The other man pulled out his gun and fired. I heard the shot, and I saw Brian fall. There was blood. So much blood. On his clothes and the carpet and..." The words faded away and the tears began again.

"Don't stop," Jeff whispered. "Finish the story."

"'Run!' he screamed." Her voice was a pale imitation of the brother she loved so dearly. "'Run!' And this time I heard him. There were more shots—two, I think. I started running. And ran and ran until I couldn't remember why I was running. All I could think of was Brian and Alden." Her voice cracked but she went on, the words tumbling faster and faster. "They knew. About my father and the mob. But they never told me. They never told me a damn thing." A sob tore from her throat. "And now they're both dead." The last of her strength slipped away and she crumpled in his arms.

Chapter 9

Jeff drew back the drapes, letting in the pale light of dawn.

Dropping into the rattan chair, he picked up the pen and yellow legal pad lying on the glass-topped table. Hours earlier, he had divided the paper into neat columns headed "Alden," "Brian," "Father," and "Davis." Notes and scribbles and arrows zigzagged back and forth among the four columns. No matter the combination, something didn't add up.

He tossed the pad aside, his gaze drawn to the woman sleeping in the bed. After her long and painful confession, Caroline had fallen into an exhausted sleep, while he had spent the rest of the night pacing.

She lay on her side, her dark hair fanning the pillow. Her eyes—those damned eyes that could flash with anger or burn with passion—had been the first thing to capture his attention. Now they were ringed with dark circles.

Over the last few weeks he had been drawn to her high spirit, her reckless determination, her infuriating stubbornness. And after kissing her on the beach, he had thought about taking Miss Caroline Southeby Peterson McKensie to bed in the real sense of the word. He thought about falling asleep at night with the taste of her kisses on his mouth. Thought about waking the next morning to the sound of her voice.

That was lust. Something he understood.

Something he could control.

Until he had seen her at her most vulnerable. Tonight, for the first time, she had trusted him enough to let him see the depth of her sorrow, to let him share her pain.

She was so totally and completely alone.

He was a man with a family—a brother, a grandmother, even a surrogate father. And while *she* found the courage to fight the mobsters and monsters that dogged her heels, *he* was overcome with an aching loneliness he had never known before.

In the wee hours of dawn he couldn't help but wonder what would happen when all this was over. When her testimony had put Augie Davis away…when she was safe in New York making croissants and Danish for the daily commuters…when he was back in San Diego shuffling papers and filing briefs.

The feeling of emptiness struck again.

Damn. He didn't need this. What was the sense of wondering about the future, when there was no guarantee they would survive the present? And they *wouldn't* survive if he didn't get his head out of the clouds and start using it to figure out this mess.

Arthur wanted him to get close to Caroline. To uncover *why* her brothers had been killed. Well, he'd gotten close, all right. Too close. And he still didn't know any more than he did before.

Jeff scrubbed his face with his hands. Somewhere inside her pretty little head was the answer. He was sure of it.

A soft knock sounded at the door. After a quick check through the peephole, Jeff opened the door, index finger against his mouth. Wordlessly, Mac nodded and offered his brother a large breakfast tray, which he put on the glass-topped table. Then Jeff followed Mac outside, closing the door behind them.

"You look like hell," Mac said. "What happened?"

Jeff slumped against the building. "She told me the whole story last night." He glanced at the sun creeping slowly into the sky. "Or rather, at two this morning."

"And?" Mac prompted.

"And nothing. She opened up just enough to give me the gut-wrenching version of what we already knew—that both her brothers were murdered. We didn't get to the 'why.'"

"Are you going to keep digging?"

Jeff nodded. "I have to. I only hope we come up with something. Something that will make sense of this mess."

Mac inclined his head toward the door. "She okay?"

Jeff shrugged. "She's been out cold for hours." He leaned his head against the wall and knuckled his eyes with his fingers. "Any word on the housekeeper?"

"Not yet, but it's still early. Arthur said to give him three days." Mac sucked in a long, deep breath, then quickly blew it out. "But I can't shake the feeling that this is it."

That simple statement made Jeff's hackles rise. He knew better than to discount his brother's intuition. More often than not, Mac was dead-on. "Why?" Jeff asked slowly.

Mac shook his head. "Because everything around here is picture perfect. I've been a doorman, a bellhop, a lifeguard, and a telephone operator. I've checked the guests, the regular staff, a dozen taxi drivers, and the people who deliver the laundry and the groceries. There's nothing."

"And that bothers you?"

"Yeah, it bothers me. Life isn't perfect. It doesn't work that way. There's always something or someone to make me suspicious. And the fact that there hasn't been is what's making me really suspicious."

Jeff scowled as he tried to follow Mac's convoluted logic. Today it was even worse than usual.

"You hear that?" Mac asked.

Jeff listened. All he heard was scratching against the door. He stifled a yawn. "Better let him out."

"Let who out?"

"The dog."

"What dog?"

"The one in the room."

Mac yanked open the door and a bundle of black-and-brown fur rolled onto the asphalt path. The puppy struggled to its feet and shook itself from head to toe. Then it high-hurdled a bed of azaleas and bounded into the grass. Jeff pushed himself away from the wall and followed the puppy.

"Dumb question," Mac said, hurrying after his brother. "But don't you have enough to do without picking up stray dogs in a first-class resort in the middle of the Virgin Islands?"

"He's not a stray, and he's not mine," Jeff replied. "Caroline's keeping him for Alex."

Mac did a double take. "The kid on the beach—"

"Whose parents have vacationed here every summer for the last five years," Jeff finished. "That's the one."

Mac watched the puppy leap into the air in fruitless pursuit of a butterfly. "I don't like it," he muttered.

"You already said that."

"I'm serious, Jeff. Think about it. Out of nowhere, she gets a dog on the exact same day one of the housekeepers calls in sick."

"It's a coincidence."

"I don't believe in coincidence. Never have, never will. I say the dog's a plant."

Jeff gave his brother a quelling look. "It's a puppy, Mac. No hidden microphones in the collar, no coded messages in the dog food, and no bombs in the chew toy. I checked him out. He's clean. Okay?" He whistled and the puppy obligingly returned, tail wagging vigorously. Jeff sat down on a stone step in front of the bungalow and scratched the puppy behind his ears. "Besides, he'll be gone by the end of the day."

"I don't believe that, either." Mac sat down next to his brother and the dog immediately tried to climb into Mac's lap. Mac pushed him away. "Dogs are a lot like chewing gum," he said. "Sooner or later you get stuck with them." The puppy grabbed one of Mac's shoelaces and pulled the bow into a tight knot.

Jeff scooped up the puppy and tucked it under his arm. "I'd better get back inside. I want to be there when she wakes up."

Mac instantly sobered. "Look, Jeff, I'm sorry. I wish there was something more I could do."

"Nobody should have to go through that kind of hell," Jeff said, with more force than he intended.

"Except Augie Davis."

"Yeah," he echoed. "Except Augie Davis." Once again he felt the anger burning deep inside. The same anger he had felt last night when he'd held Caroline's shaking, sobbing form in his arms. He took a deep breath and let it out slowly.

"Are you going to be all right?" Mac asked.

Jeff offered him a tight smile. "You know, Mac, I saw a lot of gruesome stuff when I was a P.I. But last night, listening to what she said about her brothers—it was different. I wasn't even there, and yet it seemed more...real. I kept imagining what it must have been like for her...watching her brother get shot." He looked out at the ocean and let the morning sun flood him full in the face. "I couldn't help wondering..." He shrugged. "If I saw you go down..." He turned and reached for the doorknob.

Mac grabbed his shoulder and squeezed it hard. "It's not going to happen, bro. So stop thinking about it. I plan to be around a long, long time. After all, someone's got to keep you out of trouble."

Jeff swallowed a lump the size of Gibraltar.

Mac yanked on the bottom of his fitted uniform jacket, straightening it out. "I've gotta get back. Call if you need me." He headed down the asphalt path.

"Mac?"

Mac spun around. "Yeah?"

"Thanks."

Mac saluted, then turned and sprinted down the pathway. Jeff watched until he rounded the corner and disappeared from view.

"Okay, buster," Jeff said, addressing the puppy. "I guess it's time to get to work." He slipped back into the room as quietly as he had slipped out, and deposited the puppy into

the open suitcase Caroline had designated as a makeshift
dog bed.

Of course, the puppy wasn't about to stay put. In less
than a minute, he had climbed out and was busy gnawing on
the strap.

Caroline was still asleep, still in the same position. In fact,
she hadn't moved since she'd crashed. Jeff stood at the side
of the bed watching her. He knew all too well of her restless, fitful nights...of the constant tossing and turning. And
he could only imagine the distorted, terrifying dreams that
haunted her. More than anything else, he wanted to rip those
memories from her so they could never torment her again.

The tones of a Motown group sifted from the radio on the
bedside table. She had fallen asleep listening to those ridiculous oldies—the Beatles and Beach Boys and others he
didn't know. It wasn't easy trying to think with that stuff in
the background, but he didn't change the station. He
couldn't deny her that small measure of comfort.

But now it was morning. He had to wake her.

Had to stick with the plan.

With a flick of his wrist, he turned off the radio. It was
best to keep pushing. Right now while the wound was still
fresh, the memory still sharp. Maybe this morning she'd remember something—some little tidbit she'd overlooked,
something that would provide an answer to all his questions.

He picked up the tray from the table and returned to the
bed. "Rise and shine, Bright Eyes. Breakfast is served."

A muffled groan was her only response.

"C'mon, lady. We've got things to do, people to meet,
puppies to play with."

Caroline pulled the pillow over her head. "I hate morning people," she muttered.

"I thought you got up at the crack of dawn to greet the
early-morning commuters, then send them off with coffee,
doughnuts, and a smile."

"Coffee and doughnuts, yes. Smile, not a chance. Besides, most of them come stumbling in looking and feeling

like I do." She glared at him through half-open eyes. "I kick the cheerful ones."

Jeff grinned. "Even when they bring you breakfast?"

She struggled to a sitting position, leaned back against the headboard, and eyed the silver tray skeptically. "Depends on what they bring."

"Let's see," Jeff said, lifting the cover with a flourish. "We have croissants, éclairs, napoleons, scones, crumpets, strudel, Danish... and one pot of java."

Caroline looked from the huge tray of pastries to his tousled hair and unshaven face. "What? No croquembouche?"

"Hey, I tried," Jeff insisted, pouring the coffee into two cups. "But do you know what the chef said when I asked him if he would whip some up?"

Caroline shook her head and gratefully accepted the cup he offered her.

"Well, neither do I. He said it in French. But I don't think it was repeatable in polite company."

She nearly choked on the coffee. "Jeff, do you even know what croquembouche is?"

"Not exactly," Jeff admitted.

"Believe me, it's not something you 'whip up.' It takes all day to make a good croquembouche. Which is fine, because it's also something you would *not* eat for breakfast." She wrapped her hands around the steaming cup and took a long, slow sip. "When we get back to New York, I'll make you one—for dessert."

It was an innocent remark. But the implication had his heart doing a slow roll inside his chest. She was talking about the future. About a time when crime bosses and hit men and court testimony would all be a distant memory. When there would be nothing preventing them from pursuing a different kind of... friendship.

Jeff studied her over the rim of the china cup. There was no indication her statement should be taken at anything other than face value.

"I'm going to hold you to that," he said lightly. "You owe me one croquembouche—whatever it is."

She smiled and his heart dipped again. "Literally it means 'cracks in the mouth.' You'd better hope you like it."

Somehow he had the feeling it could crack like old shoe leather and he would still love every bite. He snagged a croissant. "We need to talk."

She was instantly wary. Her eyes flashed open, and then, just as quickly, a thin veil dropped over them, hiding her emotions. "About last night?" Her voice was even, a perfectly controlled monotone.

Damn, she was good.

He nodded.

"Look, Jeff, I'm sorry I fell apart. But it's not your job to put me back together like some messed-up Humpty Dumpty."

She turned on the radio and cranked up the volume full blast, but Jeff reached over and snapped it off. He couldn't let her escape into the music.

"I'm not a bit sorry," he said. "I'm glad you told me. Now, maybe I can help you. Maybe we can help each other."

The veil lifted, and the look of caution and suspicion was back in her eyes. "How?"

Jeff took a deep breath, stalling for time. He had to phrase his questions...his doubts...delicately, or she'd clam up and he'd lose whatever ground he'd gained. He held her hand in both of his.

"I have some questions about your story. About what happened to your brothers." Anguish clouded her beautiful eyes as she snatched her hand away. Jeff could see her retreating, emotionally as well as physically. He wanted to pull her close, but forced himself not to touch her. "There are some things I don't understand," he said softly. "Things that don't make sense."

She folded her arms across her chest. "Like what?"

Jeff took another deep breath. "Like why your brothers were killed."

"I don't know," she said harshly, throwing back the sheet and hopping from the bed. "And I don't want to talk about it."

He caught her before she had gone two steps. "You have to, Caroline. It's the only way you'll ever know the truth."

She spun in his arms, then pushed him away. The grief in her eyes turned to anger. "The truth? I told you the truth. All of it. And telling you again isn't going to bring them back. Can't you understand? I just want to forget. I want to sleep at night without seeing their faces. I want to walk down the street without hearing their voices. Is that too much to ask? Is it?"

"Of course not. But do you really think that can happen when there's so much you still don't know? Caroline, look at me." He caught her chin and forced her to face him. "I'm not deliberately trying to hurt you. God knows, the last thing on earth I want is to cause you more pain. But we can't just drop it. The pain won't go away until you've resolved all the issues."

She didn't move. Didn't answer. Didn't even look away.

His frustration grew and he wanted to shake her. "You want me to leave it alone? Fine. Just explain to me why Alden and Brian are dead, and I swear I'll never bring up the subject again."

She struggled to hold it together, but he could see the fight in her slipping away. She looked up at him with eyes that didn't try to conceal her pain. "What do you want from me?"

"I want some answers."

"I don't *have* any answers," she sobbed. "I told you everything I know."

Jeff rubbed his hands up and down her arms. "Maybe not," he said quietly. "Maybe you can still help me sort this thing out."

After a long moment, she nodded. He guided her back to the bed and made her sit down. Then he turned on the radio, keeping the music low enough that they could still talk, but hoping the oldies would offer her some comfort.

"Let's start with Alden," Jeff said. He paused before asking the question. "Are you sure his death wasn't an accident?"

Her eyes and voice were filled with weariness. "Yes, I'm sure. I told you, my brother was an expert seaman. He had been over that boat with a fine-tooth comb. He wouldn't have taken it out if he'd thought there was something wrong."

"Okay," Jeff said slowly. "If it wasn't mechanical, then what about the weather? Bad winds, choppy waves, anything like that?"

She shook her head. "That day the weather was crystal clear. The water was calm and there wasn't a cloud in the sky. There was no reason whatsoever for that boat to blow." She picked up her coffee cup and stared into the swirling blackness. "I don't care what the police report says, I know it wasn't an accident."

Jeff rubbed his hand across the stubble on his chin. "Let's assume you're right and someone deliberately sabotaged your father's boat. What if they weren't after Alden? Maybe it was meant for your father."

Again she shook her head. "My father hadn't used the boat in years. That's one of the reasons why Alden went over it so carefully. If someone wanted my father dead, wouldn't it make more sense to rig his car or his office? Why rig a boat he never used? Besides, Alden would have found the problem before he ever put the thing in the water."

"Had Alden taken it out before the day it blew?"

Caroline nodded. "Several times. He'd take it out in the morning, come back and tinker with it in the afternoon, make a few adjustments, and then take it out again the next morning."

Jeff's brows knit together and he spoke more to himself than to her. "So if someone knew Alden's pattern, they could sabotage the boat in the middle of the night, and Alden wouldn't find it until it was too la—" He stopped. "Okay," he said, continuing his oral decoding, "so who wanted to get rid of Alden?"

"Davis," she answered, without a second's hesitation.

"Why?"

"Because—" She stopped short, unable to answer the simple question. "Just because."

"Just because?" Jeff shook his head. "Crazy lunatics may go around killing people 'just because,' but Davis is a businessman. Granted, he's a cold-blooded piece of slime, but he's also a businessman. He wouldn't act impulsively or emotionally. If he killed Alden, it was for a reason—a damn good reason." Jeff sat quietly, letting the silence drive home the importance of what he was saying. "Tell me about Alden. You said he was married and lived in Switzerland, but what was he like?"

Caroline released a long sigh. "He was wonderful—everything you could want in a brother. He was someone you could lean on, someone who would listen, someone you could trust. He was very protective, hardworking—driven, actually. He was passionately in love with his wife, and he would have made a great father. He didn't have many faults, except maybe that he was overly conscientious. Like the thing with the boat. A real 'detail' person. The kind of guy who has to dot all the *i*'s and cross all the *t*'s. Do you know what I mean?"

Of course he knew. The man she was describing could have been his twin. "What did he do for a living?"

"He had a degree in international finance. He worked for an American company with a lot of European markets. I don't know all of it, but part of his job had to do with arranging loans from foreign bankers, investing idle cash, and hedging against currency fluctuations. He had connections with all the Swiss banks, and for that matter, banks all over the world." Her mouth dropped open and she grabbed Jeff's arm. "That's it, isn't it? Augie Davis must have known about Alden's connections and was trying to strong-arm him into working for the organization."

"And when Alden refused, Davis had him killed?"

She nodded excitedly. "That must be it."

Jeff shook his head. "I'm sorry, but that just doesn't add up. Sure, Alden had some special skills, but so do a hundred other guys. If Alden turned him down, Davis could easily have found someone else. Guys like Davis buy and sell people like shares in the stock market. If he wanted entrée into the European market, he wouldn't have had to kill Alden to get it. And from what I've heard about Davis, he already has his fingers in a lot of international pies."

She hung her head. "So we're right back where we started."

"Not necessarily. Every time we talk, I learn something I didn't know before. Sooner or later we'll be able to piece this thing together. It's just a matter of time." Jeff squeezed her hand. "Tell me about Brian."

Caroline stared at the ceiling fan. "I think Brian was absent the day God handed out conformity. Alden was a rock—solid and dependable. But Brian was like water—always in motion. He was the original free spirit. He hated school—it was too structured, too regimented. But he learned real fast." She looked at Jeff and grinned. "Especially things like picking locks and hot-wiring cars. He could move like a shadow, and most of the time you'd never know he was there." She leaned back to watch the ceiling fan again. "He would have made a great cat burglar," she said softly. "Just like Robert Wagner or Cary Grant."

Jeff waited patiently, watching the joy and sorrow flicker across her face, biding his time until the rush of emotion had passed. "Did Brian have any special friends?" he asked gently. "A girlfriend, maybe?"

She shook her head. "Not that he talked about. He was a real loner."

"If you're sure he didn't accept help from your father—"

"He didn't," Caroline interrupted. "He hated the old man as much as the rest of us."

"Let me rephrase that," Jeff said smoothly. "Since he didn't accept any help from your father, how did he earn a living? What did he do to make money?"

"Having money was never important to Brian. If he found a quarter on the way to school, he'd give it to a kid on the playground. From what he said in his letters, he worked only when he needed food or clothes or a place to stay."

"What did he do?"

"Whatever was available. I know he did some sheepshearing in Australia, worked on a vineyard in France, hauled beer kegs in Germany." Caroline shrugged. "Nothing high-tech. It was all manual labor."

"Nothing wrong with that," Jeff said.

"I guess," she said slowly. "But he could have done so much more with his life."

"Was he happy?" Jeff asked.

Caroline nodded. "He seemed to be."

"Then maybe that's all that matters."

She eyed him suspiciously. "That doesn't sound like Mr. Hotshot Gung-ho Go-get-'em Lawyer. You sure you're feeling all right?"

Jeff grinned. "Maybe I'm changing. Maybe I'm beginning to realize there's more to life than chasing the almighty dollar."

"Because it could all be over at any time."

"Yeah," Jeff said quietly. A silence enveloped them, but it wasn't awkward or disquieting. To the contrary, Jeff found it surprisingly comforting. There was a pervasive feeling of "rightness," a sense that this was meant to be, that they were supposed to be together, that things would somehow work out.

He turned to her and their gazes met and held. She felt it, too; he was sure of it. He could see it in her eyes. Gone was the curtain that she used so effectively to hide her emotions.

Spellbound, he watched her reach out, then felt her stroke the rough stubble on his cheek. His blood raced and he closed his eyes, giving in to the gentle caress of her fingers. He clenched his teeth to keep from turning his head and kissing the soft flesh of her palm. He was her protector and her friend.

He could not be her lover.

Her hand dropped away and when he opened his eyes, a sad smile graced her features. "Thank you," she said softly.

"For what?" He resisted the urge to clear his throat.

"For caring enough to see me through this."

"Don't thank me yet. You may decide I was part of the Spanish Inquisition before we're through. Tell me more about Brian."

"There's nothing more to tell."

"All right, then tell me everything you remember about the argument you overheard in the library."

Caroline started to protest, then changed her mind. Like it or not, Jeff was right about several things. First, they still didn't know why Davis wanted her brothers dead. Second, maybe talking would help them figure it out. And third, Jeff really wanted to help her. That was the reason that got to her. The one that meant the most.

She wrapped her arms around her legs and rested her chin on her knees. Staring at the printed bedspread she studied the peach-colored flowers and mint-green leaves. "I only heard two voices," she said slowly. "One was Brian's. He was very angry and very loud. I heard him say 'Alden' and 'my old man' and 'ledgers.'"

"What about the other voice?"

"I didn't know it at the time, but it was Davis. He spoke very softly and calmly. The exact opposite of Brian."

"Could you hear what he said?"

Caroline shook her head. "All I heard was a murmur, more like a purr." Her forehead wrinkled as she struggled to remember. "I can't recall a single word, I'm sorry."

"It's okay," Jeff said soothingly. "What can you tell me about these ledgers?"

She sighed, more in frustration with herself than with Jeff's question. "I haven't a clue what he was talking about."

Jeff raked a hand through his hair. "Well, did you find any ledgers in your father's estate?"

"*I* didn't," Caroline said, "but then I didn't go through his office stuff. Alden did that. I went through the clothes and jewelry and personal effects. But remember, my father was a bookkeeper. It would be strange if he *didn't* keep records."

"Brian didn't say 'records,'" Jeff argued. "He said 'ledgers.' Nobody uses ledgers anymore. At least not since the advent of computers. Recording information by hand is too time-consuming and there's too much margin for error."

"You didn't know my father. He may have been a whiz when it came to juggling numbers, but he was something of a computer phobic. He was always afraid the computer would swallow his records instead of spitting them out. And he liked his numbers in black and white, right where he could see them. It doesn't surprise me that he kept hard copies, but what I don't understand is why he'd keep the information in the house instead of at his office. You don't keep client records in your home, do you?"

"No," Jeff admitted. "But then I don't have any clients like Augie Davis." He shook his head in disbelief. "What I can't figure out is why Davis would work with someone who didn't like computers. I mean, have you ever seen old business ledgers?"

Caroline shook her head.

"Gran still has some of my grandfather's. They're big old brown things, about yea big." He spread his hands about two and a half feet apart. "Real bulky and a nuisance to carry around. My grandfather's smell like old leather—"

She bolted off the bed. "I saw them, Jeff. Two of them."

"What?"

"In the library. There were two old books, real wide, just like you described, on the desk."

"When?"

"That night. The night Brian was shot. I'm sure they weren't there the week before. I'd been in that library a hundred times cleaning out stuff. I would have noticed them."

Jeff grabbed her upper arms and held her still. "What happened to those books?"

She looked up at him, her eyes wide. "I—I'm not sure."

"Come on, Caroline. Think. You saw Brian get shot, you ran to the police. What happened next?"

She took a deep breath. "They called for a squad car and an ambulance. Then a detective took my statement. Before we'd finished, he got a call saying there was no..." She swallowed hard. "The officers didn't find Brian's body, but there was a lot of blood on the library rug. The detective sent a forensics team to the house to investigate or take samples or whatever it is they do, and then he set me up with a police artist. From my descriptions, they were able to identify the two men as Davis and his bodyguard."

She paused to catch her breath and Jeff had to fight to keep from hurrying her along.

"After I finished with the sketch artist, the detective took me back to the house. I couldn't believe it. The place was a mess. The library had been turned upside down. Drawers were torn from the cabinets, files were strewn from one end of the room to the other."

"And the ledgers?" Jeff asked.

Caroline closed her eyes, visualizing the room. When she opened them again, she shook her head. "They were gone."

Chapter 10

"Are you sure?"

Caroline slumped into the rattan chair. "I'm sure. Since the house had been ransacked, I had to go through and make a list of everything that was missing. When I got to the library, I started picking up some of the papers and putting them on the desk—until the police stopped me and told me not to touch anything at the crime scene—and I *know* the ledgers weren't on the desk then. Davis must have taken them."

"Probably," Jeff said, "although it's possible that..."

"That what?"

Jeff watched her face, trying to decide exactly how much to tell her. It took less time than a heartbeat to make up his mind. She had been honest enough to tell him all she knew about the situation; she deserved the same. "Arthur told me your protective custody was..." He paused in search of the right word. "Compromised. Since we know Davis owns someone on the force, it's also possible the ledgers were taken by one of the officers who first arrived on the scene."

Her face went white, and for a moment, Jeff regretted his decision to tell her.

"But frankly, Caroline, that's a real long shot." He took the pot of coffee and refilled her empty cup. "I think it's safe to assume the ledgers belonged to your father and contained information about Davis. It doesn't make sense that Davis would leave them there."

"I guess so." She sipped the coffee, feeling the caffeine stimulate her brain cells. For weeks she had been operating on automatic pilot, fueled only by her own emotional energy. In the aftermath of last night's apocalypse, the overwhelming pain and torment had subsided. In the bright morning sun, she was beginning to think again, beginning to see all the gaps and holes in this damnable puzzle. And she didn't like what she was beginning to see. "What was Brian doing with the ledgers?" she asked Jeff. "And why was he meeting with Davis?"

Jeff busied himself with the tray of pastries. He had hoped she wouldn't be asking those questions until he had some satisfactory answers. "The truth?" he asked. "I don't know."

"But you have a few ideas, right?"

"I'm considering the possibilities." He pushed himself away from the table and moved to the large bank of plate-glass windows. The sun was well into the sky now, and the blue-green ocean shimmered and glistened with reflected light.

He felt, more than heard, her cross the room. She laid her hand on his arm, branding his skin with her touch. "Jeff."

Reluctantly, he turned to face her.

"Please tell me what you're thinking."

"Caroline, half the time I think like a P.I. and the other half, I think like an attorney. Either way, my approach tends to be criminal and cynical. I didn't know your brothers, but because of my background, I'm likely to suspect the worse. For *your* sake, I think it would be best if I keep my opinions to myself." He tried to step around her, but she moved in front of him, neatly trapping him between the window and her own immovable form.

"You told me last night and again this morning that if I'm ever going to find peace, I have to face the truth. I can't do that if you keep it from me."

"Caroline, I—"

She held up her hand. "You also said that every time we talk, you learn something new. Well, every time we talk *I* learn something new, too. I'm not going to hit you, or fall apart in your arms, so please, let's finish it. Right now."

Jeff looked at the long expanse of beach outside the window. She was a lot like that ocean. On the surface, she was buoyant and sparkling. But hidden deep within her was a powerful emotional undertow.

Today, there was a cloudless blue sky and the water was calm. He took that as a sign.

"What do you think was in those two ledgers?" he asked, his eyes never leaving the window.

She thought about it for a moment. "They were probably Davis's business records, maybe a list of everything he was involved in."

"Illegal?"

She nodded at Jeff's broad back. "I would think so, yes."

"What would you do if you were going through your father's things and found a book of criminal activities?"

"I'd take it to the police."

"And if you thought the police might be on Davis's side?"

"Then . . . I'd . . . take it to the D.A. or a lawyer. Someone I trusted. I'd bring it to you," Caroline announced, interjecting a little levity into Jeff's grave-sounding questions.

He spun around and looked at her without flinching. "Brian didn't do that, did he?"

"Well, no—"

"And neither did Alden."

"I'm sure there was a reason—"

"Like maybe they didn't want you to find out about your father, who he was and what he really did for a living."

"Sure, they would do tha—"

"Tell me, Caroline, if you found evidence that could hurt someone—someone you dearly wanted to protect—what would you do with it?"

"I—I don't know."

"Would you contact the criminal and set up a meeting to discuss it?"

"No, of course not—"

Jeff took her by the arms. His voice was barely a whisper. "But that's what Brian did."

She swallowed hard. She had wanted to know what Jeff thought. Now she knew. "Why?" she asked. Her calm demeanor betrayed not one drop of the nervous fear roiling through her stomach. "Why do you think he did that and what did he hope to accomplish?"

Jeff eyed her curiously. This was not the reaction he expected.

"Well?" she prompted.

"The obvious answer would be blackmail," he said.

She considered this, then shook her head. "Brian didn't need money from Davis. My father was a wealthy man. His will had already gone into probate, and we all knew the estate would be split into three equal shares. Brian may have craved excitement, but he was too smart to blackmail an underworld mobster. Not when he already had more money than he knew what to do with."

"Money is only one object of blackmail," Jeff cautioned. "There are plenty of others."

Caroline returned to one of the rattan chairs. "Such as?"

Jeff exhaled a long breath. "Power. Maybe Brian wanted to cut himself in on Davis's organization."

"Never," she said. "Not in a million years."

"I know you don't want to believe it—"

"Tell me, Jeff. If you were trying to blackmail a criminal would you be angry with him?"

Jeff stared at her blankly. "What?"

"Would you raise your voice and shout at him?"

"Of course not, but—"

"Would you yell things about your brother and your father?"

Jeff sat back in stunned silence.

"Would you wave your trump card—that is, the led-gers—under his nose? After all," she said, with a dramatic pause, "that's what Brian did."

Jeff folded his arms across his chest and looked at her with grudging admiration. "Lady, you would make a hell of a lawyer."

Caroline smiled. "I believe it's called reasonable doubt. And I think it's therefore reasonable to assume that Brian was *not* trying to blackmail his way into Davis's good graces." The smile slipped. "But that still doesn't tell us what he *was* doing. What are some of the other reasons for blackmailing?"

"Well, there's revenge, information—"

Her eyes widened. "Information about—"

"Alden," Jeff finished.

"If Brian thought Davis knew something about Alden's death, he might use the ledgers to get Davis to talk."

Jeff nodded. "Maybe."

She propped her elbows on the table and rested her head in her hands. "But it still doesn't tell us anything about Al-den."

Jeff pushed himself away from the table and stretched. "I say we give it a rest. We'll have more luck if we come back to it when we're fresh." He scrubbed a hand across his cheek. "I need to get cleaned up and you need to eat some-thing. You can't think on just coffee. I'll leave the door ajar. If you need anything—"

"Just holler," Caroline finished. "I know, I know."

Jeff looked affronted. "Am I that predictable?"

"You? Predictable?" She made a face. "Just because you've said the same exact thing every day for the past three weeks..."

He grinned. "Hey, I don't have to take this. I'm outta here." He grabbed some clothes from the dresser drawer and disappeared into the bathroom.

Caroline turned her chair so it faced the window and her back was to the bathroom. After three weeks, he knew full well she wasn't going to run away, so why didn't he just close the damn door and be done with it? She heard the rush of water and steadfastly stared at a palm tree outside the window.

But instead of a scaly light-brown trunk, she saw a smooth, broad back, bronzed by the sun. Instead of swirling green fronds, she saw clouds of billowing steam wrapped around a firm, lean torso. She gripped the armrests and stared straight ahead.

They had started out polar opposites. Then he'd become a friend, someone she could tease and laugh with, someone whose company she truly enjoyed. And last night she had offered him something she hadn't given anyone in a long, long time—her trust. He'd taken it and held it. Held it as tenderly as he had held her when she'd finally given in to her grief. Not all men were like her father. There was one who was the best of Alden and Brian combined.

Caroline closed her eyes. Maybe that's all it was. Maybe in a desperate need to cling to her brothers, she had recreated them in the form of Jefferson McKensie.

Maybe.

But she really didn't think so. The deepest grief, the heaviest sorrow, the longest mourning, wouldn't explain the desire that raged through her bloodstream every time their eyes met, their hands touched, their bodies...

She breathed a sigh of relief when the water was finally turned off and she heard the soft click of the shower door open and close. Soon it would be safe to turn around again.

"Everything okay out there?" he asked a few minutes later.

"Just dandy," Caroline muttered. "Fine," she said aloud. She pushed herself out of the chair and crossed the room to stand in the doorway.

He was dressed in a pair of tan chinos, his feet and chest bare. He rubbed his head vigorously with a towel, then tossed it over one shoulder. She watched, fascinated, as he took a can of shaving cream from one of the drawers and squirted a liberal amount into the palm of his hand.

Their eyes met in the wall-to-wall mirror behind the sink. "What are you staring at?" he asked.

"You." Her throat was so dry, the word nearly stuck there.

Jeff spread the white foam over his face and neck, then rinsed his hands. "Haven't you ever seen a man shave before?"

She hoisted herself onto the top of the marble vanity next to the sink and dangled her legs over the side. "Sure, lots of times. But nowadays men use electric razors." She looked at the long handle with a blade folded inside. "Most men don't have the time or the patience to use a safety razor, let alone a straight edge."

Jeff's hands stilled inside the towel and his eyebrows rose. "Really? And is that observation based on your vast experience with men or are you just a self-professed authority on shaving?"

Caroline shrugged. "Authority may be a bit strong. How about—" she pursed her lips "—an aesthete?"

Jeff laughed and flipped open the razor, rinsing it under the faucet.

"You don't believe me?" she asked.

"Of course I believe you. I've just never thought of shaving as a fine art."

"Oh, it's definitely an art," Caroline said. She took the razor from his hand and checked the blade. "Here, I'll show you." She reached up, but he grabbed her wrist and held it tight.

"What do you think you're doing?"

"I'm going to shave you."

"Is that so? And have you ever shaved a man before?"

"No, but I used to watch my brothers all the time."

Jeff laughed. "Honey, watching and doing are two entirely different things. I watch Olympic ski jumping. That doesn't mean I'm fool enough to try it."

Caroline made a face. "You can hardly equate ski jumping with shaving. After all, what's the worst that could happen?"

"I could look like van Gogh," Jeff said, tightening his hold on her wrist.

"Ah," she replied. "So what you're really saying is that you don't trust me."

Jeff stilled. There was that word again. *Trust.* For a long time he stared into her eyes, their faces close, only the sharp edge of the razor between them. Just a few short hours ago he had begged her to trust him. What good were all his fancy words and promises if he wouldn't offer her the same thing?

The moment stretched out between them and then suddenly he released her hand. He positioned himself between her legs, gripped the edge of the marble vanity and held himself rigidly still. "Go ahead," he said calmly.

Caroline stroked the handle of the razor with her thumb and swallowed hard. Once again her actions had been foolish and impulsive. Once again she found herself trapped between a rock and a hard place. Either she made some feeble excuse and politely backed down, or she went for it.

A few weeks ago she would have gone for it—straight for his jugular. But that was a few weeks ago—a lifetime ago. Now the air crackled with tension and there was enough chemistry between them to blow up a science lab.

She was acutely aware of the powerful legs brushing against the insides of her thighs, the strong hands placed flat on the counter on either side of her legs, the handsome face just scant inches from her own.

No, she had no desire to slit his throat or any other part of his anatomy. But she wasn't at all sure she could help it. Not the way her hands, and in fact, her whole insides, were shaking.

She looked into his eyes, so clear and blue they rivaled the sparkling waters of the Caribbean. There was no challenge written there. No "I dare you." Only a complete and utter confidence that took her breath away. He believed in her. He *trusted* her. And that was all the encouragement she needed.

"Turn your head," she said softly.

Obligingly, Jeff turned his head to the right and closed his eyes. Gingerly, she reached out with her fingers and touched his left cheekbone. Pulling the skin tight, she placed the blade against his cheek in front of his ear. With a sure slow stroke, she cut a swath in the white foam, from ear to chin.

Filling the sink with warm water, she rinsed the blade, and repeated the process. Finally she wiped her fingers on the towel draped over his shoulder.

"Other side," she commanded, her voice still little more than a whisper.

He turned again, never looking at her, never wavering. Since she wasn't ambidextrous, the right side of his face was harder. She had to keep her elbow in the air to maintain the all-important angle with the blade. The razor moved again and again across his cheek, leaving nothing but smooth, soft skin in its wake.

Caroline dunked the razor in the sink and took a deep breath before beginning again. She turned his head so he faced her, then tipped it back so the skin on his neck was taut. Starting at base of the neck, she slowly moved the blade upward, always with slow, even strokes. She moved carefully over the Adam's apple, half-afraid he would swallow. But he never moved. Not even a fraction of an inch. It was as though his entire body had turned to stone.

With much of the shaving cream gone, it was easier to see his face. She put the razor on the vanity and used the towel to wipe his neck. So far, so good. Not a single nick or scratch. But then the hardest part was yet to come. She still had to shave his chin, under his nose, and around his mouth.

She wet her lips and picked up the razor once more. "Go like this," she said, stretching her top lip down over her teeth.

The statue came to life. His eyes flashed open and met hers, then quickly closed again. But in that split second she saw the passion, the need, raw and explosive. And it rocked her to her core.

The razor shook as she moved closer—so close she could trace the outline of his lips. So close she could hear his ragged breathing. So close she could smell the minty toothpaste on his breath.

Acutely aware of the intimacy of her actions, she touched his face with trembling fingers. The razor moved with short, feathery strokes as she shaved the tender skin around his upper lip, mindful of the hollow just beneath his nose. She swished the blade in the water and continued working around his mouth, over his chin, and along the jawline. She focused solely on the act, on the small quill-like bristles and the scalpel-sharp blade. But her heart belied her mind's effort, taunting her with his scent, the feel of his skin, and the memory of his kiss.

Somehow she finished the job. "There," she squeaked. She wiped the last of the shaving cream from his face with one end of the towel, then flipped it over her own shoulder. "All done."

Placing her hands flat against his bare chest, she pushed him away and hopped off the vanity, anxious now to put a little distance between his towering form and her overly stimulated libido.

Jeff leaned forward and looked in the mirror, rubbing his hand over his cheek, chin, and neck. "Not bad," he said. "In fact, it's perfect. If you ever decide to give up baking you can always open a barbershop." The look he gave her was overtly sexual. "I guarantee I'll be the first one in line."

She drained the water from the sink, washed and dried the razor blade, and folded it into the handle. "Sorry," she said, wadding up the wet towel and tossing it against his chest, "but someone's got to make the croquembouche."

"What do you mean you didn't ask her?" Caroline planted her hands on her hips and frowned at the little boy who stood in the middle of the room clutching the puppy. He had taken the dog less than an hour ago and she hadn't expected to see either one of them this soon. "Alex, we had a deal. I promised to keep the puppy for one night and you promised to talk to your mom."

The little boy shifted nervously from foot to foot. "Um, I don't think this is a good time." He put the squirming puppy down on the floor. "But it's okay," he added hastily. "I have a *plan*."

Something about that word set her teeth on edge.

"Terrific," she muttered as she looked from Jeff to Mac to Alex and back again. Here was another one. Brian's plan had gotten him killed. Arthur Peterson's plan had put her through an entire wedding ceremony and reception. Jeff's plan translated into house arrest. Mac's plan meant he was continually popping up and barging in as some ridiculously disguised employee—today, a supposed tennis pro.

And now this six-year-old child. Why was it men always had a plan? And why did those plans inevitably mean trouble for her?

"Well, now, Alex," Jeff said, squatting down so they were at eye level. "Is it a good plan? Did you look at it from every angle? Consider all the options?"

Alex nodded solemnly. "It's gonna work," he said. "It's got to."

"I believe you," Jeff replied. "And I'll tell you what. I think we can, uh—" he lowered his voice conspiratorially "—I think we can manage the puppy for another day or two."

"Aw-right!" Alex whooped. He jumped into the air and slapped Jeff's hand in a high five. Then he gave the dog one last hug and skipped out the door.

Jeff looked at Caroline who stood tapping her foot, her arms folded across her chest.

"He got to you, too, didn't he?" she said.

"I don't know what you're talking about," Jeff answered. He gestured to Mac who dug a fuzzy green ball out of a tennis bag and tossed it to him. Jeff rolled the ball across the floor and watched the puppy scamper after it.

"Oh, you don't, do you? Those great big eyes and that angelic little face." She shook her head in disbelief. "At least he only conned me into keeping the puppy one night. You just promised to keep him for several days."

"I said a day or two," Jeff corrected.

Mac snorted. "A day or two, a week or two—do you think a kid knows the difference? I tried to warn you, but you wouldn't listen. Brother, you were had. Hoodwinked. Suckered. Bamboozled—"

"I was helping a poor kid out of a tight spot. After all, we men are *supposed* to stick together. Remember?" Jeff gave Mac a withering look.

The puppy chased the ball until it disappeared under the bed. Caroline retrieved it and rolled it back to him. "Jeff, I'm not upset that you offered to keep this guy a little longer. I think he's adorable. But we can't keep him cooped up in here, and we can't take him outside to play." She paused as the gravity of her words hit home. "Not yet, anyway."

Once again their eyes met. But this time they smiled and in tandem, slowly turned to look at Mac.

Mac grabbed his tennis bag and started backing toward the door. "Don't look at me," he warned. "I'm not taking that mutt and that's final."

"It'll only be for a day," Jeff said.

"Two at the most," Caroline echoed. She picked up the puppy and held him out at arm's length in Mac's direction.

"Uh-uh, no way, not a chance, forget it. I'm not going to baby-sit a dog. If I touch him once, I'll be stuck with him forever."

"It's a dog, Mac," Jeff said. "Not leprosy."

"Sorry," Mac replied, opening the door behind him. "Not interested."

"Fine," Jeff said with mock resignation. "I'll just send Caroline and the poor puppy out on that long, lonely stretch of beach. Or maybe I'll take him out and leave her here, all alone and unprotected...."

Mac swore. "I'll come by every few hours and walk him. But that's it, and that's final." He was gone before either of them could say another word.

Caroline smiled and put the dog back on the floor. "What do we do in the meantime?"

Wordlessly, Jeff picked up the phone. "This is Mr. McKensie in Oceanside No. 8. We need six more copies of the morning paper."

Augie Davis studied his collection of markers. Red. Definitely red. He selected the deepest, darkest red and closed the drawer. The list of names lay before him. Only one name and one location remained.

Caroline Peterson McKensie.

St. Croix.

He pulled the top off the pen and circled the words. Then he held the pad at arm's length, admiring his work. The bloodred color accentuated the name so nicely.

He recapped the pen and put away the file. This called for a celebration. Slowly, he crossed the room. There was no need to hurry. Time was on his side now, and he wanted to savor the moment. He stopped in front of a credenza and withdrew a box of Cuban cigars. Exquisite. Against doctor's orders—but he'd allow this one exception.

Augie Davis rolled the cigar between his thumb and forefinger and inhaled its aromatic scent. Then he picked up the gold-handled cigar trimmer and clipped off the end in one . . . quick . . . snip.

Chapter 11

"**I**rritation," Caroline mumbled, chewing on the end of her pen.

"What?" Jeff glanced up from his book.

She tapped the crossword puzzle resting in her lap. "I need a long synonym for 'irritation.'"

"Exasperation."

Caroline counted the little squares, then shook her head. "Too long."

"Okay," Jeff said. "How about bother...problem... nuisance...pest...vexation...annoyance?"

She tried the words, one after the other. "All too short," she said. "I need something with nine letters."

A soft knock sounded at the door and Jeff jumped to answer it. He looked through the peephole, then shook his head. "How about *M-y b-r-o-t-h-e-r?*" He opened the door and Mac breezed in, wearing strange-looking coveralls.

"I'll bite," Caroline said. "Who are you this time?"

"Assistant groundskeeper...and messenger boy." He grinned. "I've got good news."

Jeff and Caroline exchanged looks. "Arthur cleared the new housekeeper?" Jeff asked.

Mac nodded. "Sure did. The background check was spotless. They traced her history back to kindergarten. She's everything she says she is. And the maid she replaced—flat on her back in the hospital, recovering from an emergency appendectomy. It's completely legit."

"Yes!" Caroline threw on a pair of socks and laced up her running shoes. "Come on, dog. We're out of here."

"Not so fast," Mac said. "We need to talk about him."

Jeff scowled. "Don't start in, Mac. I already I told you he'll be gone in a few days."

"I don't think so. It's already been a few days and besides, the kid and his parents just checked out of the hotel. They left this." He held up a folded piece of paper.

Jeff grabbed the note from Mac's hand. Childish letters covered the hotel stationery: "iknt hvappy bkzmiddhz alrgz. plz fndhma gdhm. Lov, Alex."

"What's it say?" Caroline asked, coming up behind him.

Jeff shrugged. "Beats me. I think it's in code."

She studied the carefully made letters. "I can't have a puppy because midday...my day...my dad has...something or other. Please found...find him a good home. Love, Alex." Caroline looked pointedly at Jeff. "Terrific," she said. "Another great plan bites the dust."

Caroline bent forward, hands on her knees, her chest heaving. "Lord, that feels good," she said, panting.

Gasping for breath, Jeff sagged against the wooden sea gull while the puppy collapsed at his feet. "That's a matter of opinion," he rasped.

Caroline grinned. "Don't you just love it out here?" She spread her arms wide and tipped her head back. "The warm sun on your face, the wind in your hair." She breathed in deeply. "The fragrance and beauty of all these flowers. C'mon, what do you say? Once more around the trail." She smiled at him mischievously. "It'll do you good."

Jeff looked into her eyes, as dark and rich as the earth itself. Filled with excitement and pure joy. She was wearing plain running shorts and a baggy tank top. Her ponytail had slipped to one side and beads of sweat ran down her neck.

And his gut tightened just looking at her.

"I'd love to," he said, enjoying her look of surprise. "But you're forgetting about our friend." He pointed to the puppy still sprawled on the ground. "I've already carried him twice around the trail. It's not comfortable for him, but he's too small to run more than a hundred yards at a time. We'll have to go back."

"Because of the dog."

"Absolutely," Jeff said. "Hey, if it were up to me, I'd run all day."

Caroline nodded thoughtfully. "Good," she said. "Then we'll do this again tomorrow morning. First thing. Maybe we'll even watch the sun come up." She scooped up the puppy and headed back toward the bungalow.

"How's this for a plan?" Jeff said, falling into step beside her. "We'll celebrate our newfound freedom by going to the Sea Breeze tonight for dinner and then catch the live band. Dinner and dancing under the stars." He draped an arm casually around her shoulders. "What do you say, Mrs. McKensie?"

The bright sun glistening on the ocean didn't come close to the sparkle that danced in her eyes. "That's the best plan I've heard in a long, long time," she said. "Thank you."

"Of course, if we're out late tonight, we'll have to sleep in tomorrow. It'll mean missing the early-morning jog and skipping that stuff about watching the sun come up." He ducked as she playfully swatted at his head.

"Or," she said, rubbing the puppy under his chin, "you and old fuzzy face can take a nap this afternoon so you'll have plenty of energy. That way we can do both."

Jeff groaned. "And what exactly will you be doing all afternoon while I'm recharging my battery?"

"I think I'll treat myself with a visit to the health spa. I might even try one of those seaweed wraps Mac talked about." She slowed as they reached the room. "That's not a problem, is it?"

"Not as long as I walk you over there." Jeff fished the key out of his pocket and unlocked the door. "*And* you promise not to leave until I come back and get you. Call me when you're ready. Agreed?''

''Agreed,'' she said eagerly.

Some three hours later she had cleansed her pores with a sauna, relaxed her muscles with a body massage, and rejuvenated her skin with a seaweed wrap. She was now nestled in a thick terry robe, her hair in a turban, while an attendant applied a thick green substance to her face.

''There you are, Mrs. McKensie,'' the woman said. ''That needs to set for about fifteen minutes, so relax and I'll be back shortly.''

Caroline closed her eyes. *Mrs. McKensie.* She was becoming surprisingly comfortable with that name. The hotel employees called her that. Jeff had called her Mrs. McKensie when they were jogging. It felt...natural...and nice.

A soft sigh escaped her.

''You all right?'' a voice asked from off to her left.

Caroline sat bolt upright in the chair. She knew that voice. It was a voice that had coughed or whistled or intruded in a dozen different ways during the past few weeks. Cautiously, she glanced around.

Some six or seven people lay stretched out in chairs, their faces slathered with goo, their eyes closed or covered with cucumbers.

''Now I know why women like to come here,'' the voice said. ''It's very calming, and I rather like being pampered.''

Slowly, Caroline turned and looked at the body lying in the next chair. Like her, its hair was wrapped in a turban. A red mask and cucumbers covered its face, while the rest of its body was hidden by a white terry robe—all except the legs that stuck out from about the knees down. Large, hairy legs.

Caroline suppressed a laugh. It was too ridiculous to even consider.

''I especially like the cucumbers. If you get hungry, you can always stop wearing them and start eating them.'' The figure carefully lifted one cucumber and winked. ''But if they were really smart, they'd make this facial goop out of ranch dressing." He dipped the cucumber in the air. "Just think of the possibilities."

It was too much. Caroline doubled over in a fit of muffled laughter. "You're certifiable, Mac. Totally, completely, unequivocally certifiable."

"Hey, what are you talking about? I'm being paid to keep an eye on you, remember?"

Caroline chuckled. "Somehow I don't think this—" she waved her hand to encompass his strange attire "—was what Arthur had in mind. So, tell me. Did Jeff put you up to it?"

Mac shook his head. "Nope. He told me you were going to spend the afternoon here, and the rest was my idea. I actually wanted to try my hand as a masseur—no pun intended. But something told me you wouldn't approve."

Caroline's eyes narrowed. "You got that right."

"So here I am."

Caroline propped herself up on one elbow. "Look, Mac. I appreciate your dedication. I really do. But I give you my word I will not go anywhere or do anything outside these four walls."

"I know that."

"And you've undoubtedly already checked out every employee and patron in the salon. There's nothing here that can harm me."

"I know that, too."

"So why don't you leave?"

Mac shrugged. "Frankly, I kind of like it here." He held up one hand and peered intently at his nails. "I think I need a manicure. My cuticles are a mess."

"You're going to spend the rest of the afternoon following me around this salon like a puppy, aren't you?" She giggled at the unintentional joke.

Mac scowled. "I'll ignore the reference to four-legged furballs, but yes, that's the basic idea." He lay back, readjusted the cucumber slices, then folded his arms across his chest.

Caroline smiled knowingly. "Okay, pal," she warned. "But I sure hope you know what you're in for."

* * *

"So what's the occasion?" Mac asked Jeff, watching his brother shrug into a lightweight dinner jacket.

"Nothing special," Jeff answered. "We're celebrating our freedom and the fact that we are on the downhill side of this little adventure. The trial is exactly three weeks from today."

Mac nodded. "Are you sure that's all there is to it?"

Jeff ran his fingers through his hair, then checked the result in the mirror. "Of course, I'm sure. Why?"

Mac shrugged. "Seems to me the two of you are going to an awful lot of trouble just to have dinner." He picked up a knotted sock and dangled it in front of the puppy.

Jeff watched as Mac and the puppy tugged on the sock. "I thought you didn't like dogs."

"I love dogs. I just don't like to walk them, feed them, brush them, and clean up after them. They're just like kids. As long as they belong to someone else, they're fine." The puppy growled and Mac growled right back. "So, what are you going to do with this mutt?"

Jeff shrugged. "We posted a sign on the community bulletin board. Hopefully someone will give us a call." He crossed the room and rapped on the bathroom door. "Caroline, our reservations are for eight o'clock." He pushed back the cuff of his left sleeve and glanced at his watch. "You've got fifteen minutes."

"Be right there," came the muffled reply.

"I'd better get going," Mac said. "Sea Breeze, right?"

Jeff nodded.

"I'll go over now and check on your table—make sure you get a good one."

Jeff walked him to the door. "Semisecluded would be nice. With a wall on one side, so I don't have to spend the night watching our backs."

Mac paused, his brow furrowed. "You sure there's nothing else—" He wiggled his hand back and forth aimlessly. "Nothing else you want to tell me?"

Jeff clapped his brother on the back. "There's nothing going on, if that's what you're asking. We're supposed to be honeymooners and it's perfectly normal for a husband to take his new bride dining and dancing. Role-playing. That's all it is.''

Mac nodded, unconvinced. ''Whatever you say, bro. See you over there.'' And without another word he was gone.

Jeff closed the door and returned to the mirror. He unbuttoned two of the buttons on his shirt, and spread the collar out over the lapels of his jacket. They really were just acting the part, regardless of what Mac thought.

So why are you undoing your clothes halfway to your navel?

Hastily he rebuttoned the shirt. ''Get a grip,'' he muttered aloud. ''It's just dinner.'' A little dinner, a little dancing. No more, no less.

Uh-huh, and that explains why you're combing your hair—again.

Jeff stopped running his hands through his hair. Hell of a time for his conscience to prick. Especially when he hadn't even done anything to deserve it.

Yet.

He pulled open the nightstand drawer, taking mental stock as he stuffed the items into his pockets—room key, wallet, handkerchief...gun. Cursing Arthur and Davis and the world in general, Jeff ripped off his jacket and buckled on the shoulder holster. The gun fit snugly under his left arm and with a little luck she wouldn't even know it was there. He slipped back into the jacket.

''Jeff?''

He spun around at the sound of his name—the sound of his name on her lips. The sight that greeted him took his breath away.

She was wearing a halter dress of shimmering coral that looked as soft as satin. It hugged her breasts and molded her hips, then flared slightly to just above the knees. A fine gold chain lay against the hollow of her throat, and her dark brown hair tumbled in loose curls over her bare shoulders.

''Are you all right?'' she asked when a full minute had passed without him saying a single word.

The breath he exhaled could be heard all the way to the sea.

"Just stunned," he finally managed. "You look beautiful."

Pink highlighted her cheeks. "Thank you," she said simply. "I'm glad you like it."

"Like" was an understatement bordering on absurdity. Lust, passion, need, or any one of a thousand other words immediately sprang to mind.

"Are you ready to go?" she asked quietly.

"Absolutely," he said, jumping to open the door. He intended only to be gallant, and to usher her out. But when his hand touched her bare back, desire rocked his sanity. Giving in to the temptation, he savored the touch of her cool, smooth skin. The firm muscles shifted as she walked, subtly caressing his palm, igniting a fire that raced up his arm, then shot due south. It would be so easy, so natural to slide his hand lower, to stroke the small of her back, to follow the curve of her—

He snatched his hand away and curled his burning fingers into a tight fist. At this rate it was going to be one hell of a long night.

Caroline's heart soared as she walked with Jeff from the bungalow to the Sea Breeze. It was a perfect evening. A plump moon sat like a king on a throne of black velvet, while rays of moonlight danced across the water. Silver-capped waves whispered along the beach, answering the murmur of the ancient palms.

As they moved away from the sea, the scent of frangipani and hibiscus grew stronger. Bougainvillea dripped from the terraces like crimson lace, while katydids and cicadas strummed love songs for any who cared to listen.

Jeff looked resplendent in his tan suit with the crisp white shirt. The jacket was tailored to fit his broad shoulders and lean body, and the trousers emphasized more than hid his long legs and narrow hips. Resplendent, indeed.

She followed the line of his shirt to where it opened at the neck, the white a stark contrast to the deep bronze of his skin. Another flash of white caught her eye, the flash of white teeth against a tanned face. His smile was wicked and wonderful. A roguish twinkle danced in his eyes and she knew at once she had been caught staring.

He stroked his thumb against the palm of her hand and her stomach tightened in response.

"Happy?" he asked.

"Happy" didn't come close to describing the way she felt—the way she felt about him. "How could you tell?"

"Your eyes," he said. "They give you away every time."

"I'll have to work on that."

"Don't," he admonished. "I like knowing what you're thinking . . . and feeling."

Caroline lowered her gaze. It was more than a little disconcerting to know he could read her mind. Especially when she herself was just beginning to realize what was there.

They stood in the shadows below the terrace. Above them, soft music mingled with tinkling laughter and the murmur of voices. It would be so easy to toss out some feeble excuse, then bolt up the stairs to the safety of the patio restaurant. But in truth, she was already within arm's reach of all the safety she could ever need. She trusted Jeff with her life. She trusted him with her secrets. Maybe it was time to trust him with her heart.

She turned to face him in the moonlight, hiding nothing. The passion and hunger that had smoldered for weeks was now a roaring conflagration, burning on her face for all the world to see.

For a moment he seemed paralyzed, stunned. Then, with slow-motion clarity she watched him reach out and gently run one finger along the line of her cheek. Their chemistry ignited, and his touch sent a shudder through her body. Leaning forward, he cupped her face between his hands, his gaze traveling slowly over her before meeting her unblinking stare. He didn't speak. He just held her and watched her searchingly, with smoky desire blazing in his deep blue eyes.

She held her breath for fear of breaking the enchanted spell. She *wanted* him to kiss her, wanted to recapture the explosive magic of his lips on hers. She wanted to be pulled into his arms and pressed tightly against him. She wanted to lie with him, body to body, skin to skin, as they had on the beach.

He paused another instant to look at her, and anticipation became the sweetest form of torture. Then he lowered his head until his mouth almost brushed her lips and she felt the rush of his breath. His kiss, when it finally came, was slow and deliberate. He lingered over her lips with a velvet touch that sent her swirling into the night.

Her knees weakened, and with a smothered moan, she wrapped her arms around his waist and melted against him. She could feel the hard muscles of his chest and the rapid pounding of his heart. Or was that the sound of her own pulse hammering in her ears while the distant moon shattered into a million sparkling starbursts?

His hands slid to her shoulders, and gently but firmly he pushed her away, putting an arm's length between them. He cleared his throat before speaking. "I think we should go up to the restaurant. I don't know how long they'll hold the table for us."

His voice sounded huskier than usual, or maybe it was just her fevered imagination and wishful thinking. Wordlessly, she nodded.

Jeff led her to the stairs dotted with lanterns swaying gently in the warm summer breeze. He felt her tremble when he took her arm and a jagged flash of desire shot through him. *Coup de foudre*. The lightning bolt. He had seen it in her eyes. Now he felt it.

At the top of the steps, a smiling maître d' showed them to their seats and offered them menus. It took Jeff less than a split second to assess their location. It was perfect. The round linen-covered table was located in a corner between two sections of an L-shaped stone wall that rose about eight feet high. With their backs to the wall, the rest of the terrace spread out before them. Some twenty tables were scattered across the patio, and beyond those, far beyond the confines of the balcony, lay the Caribbean Sea, dazzling in the moonlight. Jeff picked up a snow-white napkin and draped it across his lap. The restaurant embraced Old World charm, elegance . . . romance.

Romance? Or seduction?

Had that been his intent in bringing her here? Jeff shook his head. This afternoon, he would have sworn on a stack of Bibles that his motives were completely honorable.

Now he wasn't so sure.

The single candle on the table flickered, alternately revealing then shadowing Caroline's features. But he didn't need candlelight to tell him what she looked like. Every detail was permanently etched in his mind.

The candle flared again, softly illuminating her skin. His gaze roamed over her, drinking in the sight of her as a thirsty man gulps water. Her lips were full and moist and slightly swollen from his kiss. Her checks were flushed the color of a dusty rose, and he knew instinctively that he was the cause of it. Her eyes drew him in—fringed pools of dark liquid that beckoned him closer.

As he stared, the warm night breeze fanned the curls framing her graceful throat. The memory of their silkiness brushing the backs of his hands made him want to thread his fingers through those strands and hold her head captive while he kissed her again.

Her scent, her warmth, her softness made him want to do a lot of other things, as well—things he wasn't supposed to think about.

But, damn, he wanted her. Wanted her with an urgency that was becoming physical pain. No woman had ever impacted him the way she did. Her strength and courage touched his heart. Her reckless, impulsive nature made him crazy. And the look in her eyes drove him wild.

That was what had happened earlier.

Almost happened, he corrected himself.

He gripped the menu with enough force to crease it as he studied the entrées. The time *was* coming. A time when they wouldn't be shackled by fear or responsibility. Then nothing would stop them. He would take her into his arms, look deep into her eyes, and whisper in her ear—

"Would *madame* care for an aperitif?"

Chapter 12

"Huh?" The fantasy cracked and Jeff snapped his head up to face the intruder. "What?"

"I said, would you care for an aperitif...a cocktail...something to drink." Mac spoke slowly, carefully and deliberately enunciating each word.

"What are you doing here?" Jeff asked.

"I'm the sommelier," Mac explained, fingering the small gold key dangling from a chain around his neck. He raised his chin and looked down the end of his nose. "The wine steward."

"I know what it is," Jeff countered. "I just can't figure out why you're doing it. It's like having the cat guard the canary."

Mac smiled graciously at Caroline, then threw Jeff a pointed look. "Curious. That's the same thought I just had about you." His unwavering gaze lingered over her, and Jeff was sorely tempted to hit him in the gut with the menu.

"I'll have a Kir Royale," Caroline said, returning Mac's smile.

"Excellent choice. And you, sir?"

"A sparkling water with a twist of lime. Sorry," Jeff said in response to her questioning look. "But just because we're out of house arrest, doesn't mean I'm off duty."

"Oh." The single word spoke volumes. "Maybe you'd be more comfortable if I didn't drink, either."

"Absolutely not," Jeff insisted. "This is your special night and I want you to enjoy it. I promise I'll join you in a glass of wine with dinner. Bring the lady her drink," he said to Mac, dismissing him with a wave of his hand.

Mac did as he was told, returning a few moments later with their drinks.

"May I ask you a question?" Caroline asked Jeff after the waiter had taken their order.

"I think you just did." He watched as the moon and the candle jockeyed for the right to dance golden highlights across her hair. "But if there's something on your mind, ask away."

She raised the fluted glass to her lips and tipped her head back ever so slightly. The coral-colored silk drew tight over her full breasts, confirming his suspicion that she wore nothing underneath. He downed half the glass of Perrier in one gulp.

"What's the connection between you and Arthur Peterson?"

"My dad and Arthur were best friends. They met at the police academy."

"Your dad was a cop?"

Jeff nodded. "For nineteen years. Arthur continued his upward climb into the Federal Marshal's office. But they always remained friends. In fact, Arthur was best man at my parents' wedding."

"I know your parents are deceased. Was your dad ki— I mean, was he working on a case...?"

Jeff shook his head. "Nothing so dramatic. My dad died of a massive heart attack when he was forty-four. I was twelve."

"I'm sorry," she said.

As she reached forward to take his hands, the dress gaped slightly, revealing the swell of her breasts. His blood began to race. And when she drew her fingertips across his knuckles and the back of his hand, he felt it again—a lightning bolt that rocked his senses.

He was in way over his head—and he had absolutely no desire to do anything about it.

The waiter cleared his throat, and Jeff jumped like a kid caught with his hand in the cookie jar, instead of between her soft palms.

A heavenly aroma wafted up from her plate, and Caroline cut off a small slice of fish with her fork. It tasted even better than it smelled. "Mmm." She sighed. "This is incredible." She lifted her wineglass but Jeff stopped her.

"A toast," he said. He lifted his water glass and held it toward hers.

"To what?"

Jeff thought for a long moment. "To the future," he said softly.

She studied him over the rim of her glass. "So you think there will be one?"

"I'll make sure of it."

She smiled—a real smile that shone from the inside out, a smile like he hadn't ever seen before. "To the future," she said, and clinked her glass against his.

The meal passed in amiable conversation. He shared a few stories about some of his more entertaining clients and listened as she revealed how more than one of her culinary creations had gone awry.

But even though the conversation was pleasant and light, Jeff felt the emotionally-charged undercurrent surging beneath the surface. Her laughter sparkled like fine wine. Her hair glistened in the moonlight. And her eyes held a promise of things to come.

Somehow he managed to make it through dinner, but when the plates were cleared and the coffee served, they seemed suddenly to run out of things to say. Jeff sipped his coffee, watching her over the rim of his cup. She was looking out toward the sea, her body swaying in time to the soft music.

"Would you like to dance?" he offered.

She smiled and he led her to the far side of the patio where a live band had been playing all evening. "Wait here." Leaving her stranded alone in the middle of the dance floor, he walked over to the lead singer. With fascination and more than a little curiosity, she watched him say something to the singer, clap the man on the back, and press something into his hand.

The band immediately struck up a familiar refrain and Caroline smiled. "Oldies." She sighed,

"May I?" Jeff asked. With a satisfied grin, he guided her into his arms and held her firmly against him, her thighs pressed intimately against his. And when his hand settled on her bare back, her heart careened out of control.

She could feel each fingertip pressing her skin, slowly mapping the contours of her back, leaving a trail of fire in their wake. His fingers were gentle yet skillful, possessive, drawing her closer to the heat of his body. He cradled her hand against his chest and stepped forward in time to the music.

"I love The Four Seasons," she said. "They're one of my favorites."

"Personally, I prefer Vivaldi's." He tried to look innocent, but the gleam in his eye gave him away.

She felt his gaze caressing her face, his attention focused on her as intently now as it had been during dinner. The music swelled, and she felt graceful and willowy in his arms. They were natural partners, their bodies moving as one. Harmonious. Fluid. Dancing as though they had been together all their lives.

The tempo picked up and he moved into a swing, whirling her around faster and faster. The satiny dress seemed to carry her along until she felt as though she were flying, her feet barely skimming the floor.

Eventually the music changed, slowing long enough for them to catch their breath. Jeff stepped closer, admiring the soft swell of her lower lip and the sweep of dark lashes against her cheeks. The lashes fluttered open and she looked up at him, her eyes dark and mesmerizing, reminding him of the woman he had first seen in the photo. The woman he had sworn to protect.

He pulled her tightly to him and his body instantly responded to his powerful need. She was as light as summer in his arms, and he wanted to hold her forever.

But he wasn't paid to think about "forever." He was paid to think about the next minute and the next hour and the next day. He was paid to keep her safe, not to make her more vulnerable.

He stepped back and dropped her hand. "Are you ready to go?" he asked, more gruffly than he intended.

She shrugged. "Actually, I could dance all night."

"You and Audrey Hepburn," he mumbled. "Never mind," he said in answer to her confused look. "But I think we'd better leave. It's getting late and we'll be safer inside."

Is that a fact? his conscience nagged.

Reluctantly, Caroline nodded. "Whatever you say."

Jeff was different on the walk back to the room. There was tension between them—not sexual tension—or at least it didn't feel like any sexual tension she had ever felt before. But it was definitely tension. And she didn't have a clue where it came from. One minute they were dancing and the next . . .

"Is something wrong?" she asked as she waited for Jeff to unlock the door to their room.

"No, nothing's wrong," he said tersely. "I'm just tired. I think we need to get some sleep."

Sleep?

She shook her head, trying to clear it. Either she had been out of circulation way too long, or something didn't add up. Dinner, dancing under the stars, heated kisses, passionate embrace—and sleep?

In confused silence she watched Jeff push open the door and motion her inside. The puppy jumped around as though they had been gone for a few weeks instead of a few hours, but Jeff ignored him. He closed and locked the door, then grabbed a book and slumped down in a corner chair.

"What are you staring at?" he growled, moments later.

Caroline swallowed. "Nothing. I . . . Nothing."

He returned to his book and she looked away. Whatever else happened, she'd be damned if she'd let him see how much his coldness hurt. Maybe she had misread him. Maybe she wanted more from him than he was willing to give. Maybe she was simply a damned fool.

This last thought ousted her from her emotional stupor. Resisting the urge to throw her purse at his head, she threw it on the bed instead. She reached behind her neck to unclasp the gold chain, but the thing stubbornly refused to budge. She twisted it slightly but only managed to entangle it in her hair.

"Hold still, I'll do it."

She hadn't heard him cross the room, but she felt his fingers entwine in her hair as he struggled to separate the strands from the necklace. She closed her eyes and bit her lip as hot sparks danced everywhere he touched.

Obeying his unspoken command, she bent her head, baring the nape of her neck. With a final gentle tug, he freed the chain. "There," he said, brushing the hair to one side. His breath fanned her ultrasensitive skin and she bit down harder.

Holding her hair out of the way with the side of his hand, he fumbled with the clasp. The constant brush of his fingers created a heat that found its match deep in her belly. And when his hands slid the ends of the chain around her throat, she couldn't control the long shiver that chased down her spine. She reached up to catch the sliding chain and caught his hands instead. Another quiver ripped through her body.

With a curse, he spun her around and hauled her to him. His mouth slammed onto hers, the forgotten chain slipping to the floor. His tongue dived deep, and he tightened one arm around her waist, grinding his lower body against hers. She melted against him, accepting his searing kiss; inviting, welcoming, demanding more.

His tongue stroked deep one last time, then he tore his mouth away. Shifting his hands to her upper arms, he held her away from him. He wanted her, he needed her, he might even love her, but the job came first. "No," he said. "We can't do this."

"Wanna bet?" Reaching out, she stroked his jawline with her fingers, traced his lips with her thumb, until he caught her hand and stilled it, pressing a quick kiss into her palm.

"Caroline, listen," he said hoarsely. He backed away from her. "Arthur is paying me to protect you. Becoming involved like this is not part of the plan."

"The plan?" She ran a hand through her tangled hair. "If you say that P-word one more time, I'm going to scream. Forget the damn plan," she croaked. "Life wasn't meant to be planned. You don't schedule sex in your Day-Timer. It just happens. It could be happening right now." Another thought occurred to her, and her heart squeezed painfully. "Unless..." She blinked once, twice. "Unless you don't want me."

"Don't want you?" Now it was his turn to look incredulous. "Lady, you smile and I want you, you speak and I want you, you look at me with those damn tempting eyes and it's all I can do to keep my hands off you." He glanced about the room helplessly. "I've got to get out of here."

"Jeff, wait."

"No, *you* wait. I'm taking the dog out. I'll be back in a few minutes." He whistled for the dog and slammed the door behind them.

Once again Caroline stood in the middle of the room, feeling heat and desire course through her body with no place to go. And she wasn't the only one. After that bone-jarring kiss, his breathing had been ragged and too fast. Color heightened his face and she had seen something raw and primitive in his eyes.

She slipped her watch off her wrist and set it on the nightstand. Oh, she would wait, all right—all of about ten minutes. She placed a quick call to room service, dug through the dresser drawer until she found the blue satin chemise, then disappeared into the bathroom.

Jeff circled the bungalow six times, hoping the cool night air and a little exercise would work as well as a cold shower.

It didn't come close.

Just thinking about her, all soft and dewy-eyed, sent heat pooling in his groin.

Again.

"Damn." There was nothing worse than doing the right thing for all the wrong reasons. Or was this the wrong thing for all the right reasons? He shook his head. Either way, it looked as though he would spend the night sleeping in a chair.

With the puppy at his heels, he returned to the room. The bathroom door was closed and he could hear water running in the sink. "I'm back," he shouted. Slipping out of his suit jacket, he removed the gun and shoulder holster, then stripped to the waist. He was rummaging through the dresser drawer when the knock sounded on the front door.

He scooped up the gun and pointed it toward the ceiling, close to his face. "Yes?"

"Room service," the voice answered.

Jeff ventured a quick look through the peephole. Sure enough, the young man was wearing a hotel uniform, but it wasn't Mac. "Who are your looking for?" Jeff asked.

"McKensie, Oceanside No. 8," the kid replied.

Jeff waited a heartbeat, then two.

"Is something wrong, sir?"

Stuffing the gun inside the waistband at the small of his back, Jeff reluctantly opened the door. "I didn't order anything," he said tersely.

"I did."

Jeff spun around at the sound of her voice—her soft, whiskeyed voice, sounding for all the world like a young Lauren Bacall. If it had only been the voice, he might have handled it, but it was what she was wearing that did him in.

She was dressed in a satin nightie the color of sapphires. Suspended from the slimmest straps, the front hugged her breasts, while the flared skirt showed to every advantage her long, shapely legs. The gown revealed absolutely nothing—but hinted of hidden promises that had his imagination working overtime. She smiled and he staggered back, banging into the door and knocking it wide open.

"Wow," the kid breathed.

"One brandy, two glasses. Just what I ordered." She took them from the wide-eyed kid and winked. "Give him a big tip, will you?"

Coming to his senses, Jeff stuffed a couple of bills into the kid's hand and slammed the door in his face. "This isn't funny, Caroline," he said, swallowing hard.

She shrugged her shoulders in a whisper of satin and perfume. "I'm not laughing."

"I mean it. This isn't going to work."

"What isn't?" she asked innocently.

"This whole seduction thing. I'm on to you, kid." Great. Now he sounded like Bogart. All he needed was a cigarette, a two-day-old beard, and the Vichy government to complete the scene.

"It's no big deal, Jeff. All I'm offering is an after-dinner drink. What are you afraid of?"

Myself, he thought. "I'm on duty," he said aloud.

Caroline shook her head. "You promised me one drink."

"I had one at dinner." He opened the drawer of the nightstand and put the gun safely inside.

She shook her head again. "That little-bitty wine you had wouldn't fill an eyedropper. You still owe me."

His head snapped at the double meaning of her words, but she met his narrow stare with a wide, clear-eyed look. He watched, uncertainly, as she poured the amber liquid into a brandy snifter and set the bottle on the table. She curled her hands around the glass and swirled it slowly.

"It won't take long to warm it up," she said, walking toward him. She stopped directly in front of him, the glass still cupped in her palms. She swirled the brandy around and around, with hypnotizing effect.

Jeff stared at the swirling liquid, at the dark-haired beauty dressed in sapphire, and his head spun. Their eyes met and held, more intoxicating than the liquor that sloshed up the sides of the glass and down again.

He could have stood there until daybreak, mesmerized, drunk without ever taking a sip. But the brandy swirled once too often, once too fast, once too high, dousing him with a dozen amber droplets.

"Oh, dear," Caroline tsked. She put the glass down and stared at the golden droplets scattered across the broad expanse of his chest. There was one tiny drop about three inches below his throat. "I'll take care of it," she said. Slowly she pressed her lips against the tanned skin, and heard the quick intake of his breath as she tasted the single drop of brandy.

"Lady, you've got exactly thirty seconds to get out of here. I suggest the bathroom—with the door locked."

"Here's another," she said, moving to a spot just beneath his left nipple.

"Twenty-five," he growled.

"And another." She ducked her head, her tongue catching a third taste of the beguiling liquid.

"Twenty." The word died in his throat as her lips moved over his stomach. "That's it," he said. And before she knew what was happening, he'd lifted her into the air, into his arms, and deposited her on the bed.

"I still have fifteen seconds," Caroline said.

"Not anymore." His body covered hers with fierce determination. His mouth plundered hers in a shattering kiss that was demanding and urgent. She tasted hot and honeyed like the fine brandy she had spilled—drugging, sweet and potent. He could gorge himself on her forever and never be filled. His tongue stroked her bottom lip, then plunged into her mouth, exploring every crevice, coaxing her into joining him in a sensual battle. She needed no persuasion. Her lips moved hungrily against his, kindling the desire that flamed between them.

His hand swept along her thigh, over her hip, up her side, and closed around her breast. He felt a surge of satisfaction as the nipple stabbed through the satin into his palm.

He dragged his mouth roughly across her cheek, kissing her jaw, her throat, her shoulder. The narrow straps slipped away, inch by seductive inch, exposing skin as smooth and soft as the satin chemise.

She stripped him of his sanity even as he stripped her of the gown. Her lips, her hands were everywhere, kneading, stroking, caressing, driving him out of his mind.

"You're so beautiful," he whispered in a thick voice when she lay naked before his admiring gaze. He cupped her breasts, drawing his thumbs across the quivering tips, then feasted on the warm, scented flesh. His tongue teased a nipple and her long, throaty moan drove him on.

Her nails raked his bare back and his shoulders seemed to swell beneath her fingertips. She plunged her hands into his hair, so much thicker and softer than she remembered.

His hand slid up the inside of her thigh, between her legs, finding the protected warmth, and she felt the throb of her own desire in his passionate touch. A whimper caught in her throat as pleasure jolted through her.

His hands roved her body, caressing, arousing, filling her with raw desire, making her quiver. Tension wound her stomach into coils, and tremors rocked her body. "Jeff, please!" She reached for him, trying to draw him to her, but he held back, his lips tasting and teasing the secret places his hand had explored just moments before.

She arched beneath him, lifting to his mouth and fingers. Streaks of fire shot through her limbs, melting her body, until she no longer had the power to move or think. Emotions, raw and primitive, drenched her like ocean waves pounding the beach. Whitecapped swells of passion, unbearable pleasure, exquisite pain, crested and broke, over and over again.

It was wonderful, incredible, but it wasn't enough. She wanted more. Wanted him. She pulled him to her and, cursing fingers that wouldn't work, she fumbled with the belt and the button on his trousers.

A harsh groan tore from his throat and he rolled off her, breathing hard. His body ached, and he longed to plunge inside her, to sheathe himself in her sweet fire. But it wouldn't happen. Not tonight.

"Caroline, I'm sorry. But that's it. No more."

"I swear, McKensie," she gasped, "if you say that P-word, I'm going to hit you. Hard. In a place where it will really, really hurt."

He hadn't thought it possible to laugh at a time like this. Especially with the throbbing pain that was ripping through the lower forty, but the expression on her face was priceless. A chuckle rumbled from his chest and he held up his hands in defeat. "That's not what I meant. At least not *that* P-word. I meant the other P-word."

Her lovely brow furrowed as she glanced at the obvious bulge in his trousers.

"Not that one, either," he said, playfully swatting her backside. "Protection." He planted a kiss on her right breast. "I didn't come prepared for this, Bright Eyes. It wasn't part of the pl—you know what I mean."

Her grin was wicked and wonderful. She bounced off the bed, returning a moment later with a box of individually wrapped packets.

Jeff fingered one skeptically. "You make a habit of carrying around a whole box of these?"

"Not me," she replied blithely. "I found them in the suitcase when I unpacked. Arthur's idea of a joke."

Jeff shook his head. "Not his style."

"Your grandmother?"

Jeff made a face. "Not likely."

He smiled at her and she returned his grin. "Mac," they said in unison.

Jeff stripped off the rest of his clothes and pulled her into his arms, covering her face with kisses. "Remind me to thank him in the morning."

She had been in the midst of a lovely dream she couldn't quite remember when she heard the ringing. She wasn't ready for reality. She wanted to slip back into the dream where she felt safe, sated . . . loved.

But the pale light of dawn crept into the room and the persistent ringing echoed inside her head. Extending one bare arm, she grappled for the receiver, then dragged it into the bed. The warmth of Jeff's body beckoned and she snuggled closer.

"'Lo?"

"Caroline?"

"Hmm?"

"Hey, Princess. Is that you?"

Sleep drained away as she struggled to sit up. "Brian?" Her voice choked on the word. "Oh, my God, Brian," she sobbed. "I can't believe it's y—"

A loud click sounded on the other end of the line, and the phone went dead in her hands.

"Brian? Answer me!" she cried. "Brian!"

Chapter 13

Jeff's arms came around her. "Honey, wake up. You're dreaming."

"No," she said, waving the phone. "It's not a dream. He called me."

Jeff brushed a lock of hair from her face. "Who called you?"

"Brian." She dropped the receiver and grabbed his arms. "He's alive, Jeff. He's alive! He called me Caroline and Princess and then we got disconnected...."

Jeff's expletive was short and to the point as he bolted from the bed. "Get dressed," he snapped. He pulled on a pair of briefs and jeans, zipping them one-handed as he grabbed the receiver and punched Mac's beeper number.

She sat in the bed, heedless of the sheet that had slipped to her waist.

"Caroline, get dressed," Jeff barked. "Now!" When she didn't respond, didn't even move, he tipped her head up to face him. Her eyes were distant, hollow, as though she had slipped into another world, another place. He squeezed her hands, stunned at their icy chill. He wanted to slap her, shake her—something to jolt her out of this lethargy. Instead, he forced her to meet his gaze. "I'm sorry, honey, but Brian is dead."

She shook her head in vigorous denial. "He's alive, Jeff. He called me. He called me Princess."

"Caroline, listen to me." Jeff turned a drawer full of clothes upside down over the bed, then tossed the drawer on the floor. Grabbing a T-shirt from the pile, he pulled it on over her head. "It was a trick," he said, forcing her arms through the short sleeves. "Davis found us. We've got to get out of here. Right now." She shook her head, but offered no resistance as he helped her into underwear and slacks.

He didn't have time to curse himself. The helpless look in her eyes was torment enough. A thousand regrets hovered at the edge of his consciousness. If he hadn't given in. If they hadn't made love. If he'd answered the phone the way he always had. It would be a long, long time before he forgave himself. If ever.

"I always wondered..." Caroline said. Her voice was barely audible. Jeff tossed her a pair of socks, but they bounced off her arm and dropped on top of the rumpled sheets. "When they didn't find his body, I wondered if maybe he survived. Now I know."

Jeff laced his sneakers, then strapped on the shoulder holster. "Then why did he hang up on you?" His voice was cruel, but he didn't care. He had to make her see the truth.

"He didn't hang up," she explained. "We were cut off. He'll call back. You'll see."

As if on cue, the phone rang, shocking them both into silence. Caroline lunged for it, but Jeff was faster.

"Hello?"

"What happened?" Mac asked.

"Let me talk to him," she said.

Jeff shook his head. "It's Mac." He turned back to the phone. "Someone called the room about three minutes ago. They know who she is."

Mac swore. "I'll try to find out where the call came from. At least whether it was island or international."

Caroline tugged on Jeff's arm. "Please, Jeff, he's *my* brother."

Jeff shook her off. "We don't have time. I want her off this island now. Go directly to Plan B."

She tried to wrest the phone from Jeff's hand. "Brian?" she shouted. "Brian, I'm here!"

"What the hell's going on?"

Jeff gave up the struggle and let her have the phone.

"Brian, where are you? Are you hurt?"

The silence was palpable. "Uh, Caroline, this is Mac. Are you okay?"

"Oh." She handed the phone to Jeff with an odd half smile that sent a chill racing down his spine.

"Look, bro," Mac said. "She doesn't sound too good. Maybe I should come to the bungalow."

Wedging the phone between his shoulder and ear, Jeff pushed Caroline onto the bed and knelt on the floor, stuffing her feet into socks and sneakers. "No, I can handle it. Just meet me."

"If you're not there in fifteen minutes," Mac said, "I'll come looking."

"Right." Jeff hung up the phone, checked his gun, then slipped a jacket over the holster. When he turned to Caroline, he found her sitting on the floor holding the puppy. She looked up, and the feeling of dread settled around him once again. The vacant look in her eyes was more pronounced, the mind behind them more withdrawn. He squatted down on the floor in front of her. "Honey, think about this. Maybe Brian did survive the shooting. Maybe he is still alive. But he doesn't have the means to track us down. Davis does. I think Davis used Brian's voice to verify you were Caroline. He *knew* it would freak you out. You can't let Davis win. You've got to fight him."

Her brow furrowed and in her eyes Jeff saw the ongoing struggle between what she knew and what she desperately wanted to believe.

"But what if—"

Her voice cracked. She was perilously close to tears. A good sign. Better to have her emotions out in the open, instead of buried deep inside some catatonic state. "I swear to you, Bright Eyes," Jeff said, "when the trial is over, I'll do everything in my power to find out what happened to Brian. I'll get Arthur to help, and Mac, too. It may take some time, but we won't give up. One way or another, we'll try to get some closure on this. Okay?''

Caroline looked at him through eyes clouded with unshed tears. He cared. He really, truly cared. She had been alone and on the run for so long, she had nearly forgotten what it felt like to have someone care for her as much as Jeff did. With tears spilling down her cheeks, she nodded.

''Good. Now let's get the hell out of here.''

She tossed him her wallet and passport, which he stuffed into a small knapsack. Then she hooked the Walkman onto her belt, draped the headphones around her neck, slipped into a nylon warm-up jacket, and picked up the puppy.

''We can't take him,'' Jeff said.

''I'm not leaving without him,'' Caroline countered. ''Alex trusted me to find him a good home, and I will. So we can either stand here and argue, or we can start running.''

No doubt about it, she was back to her old self. With a scowl, Jeff opened the door to the bungalow and searched the horizon. ''Let's go,'' he said, motioning with his arm. He grabbed her hand and they set off at a dead run. They kept to the bushes and trees, avoiding the open areas like the beach and the golf course. After a while, he took the puppy from her arms and they ran farther inland, past the restaurants and shops, to the three-hundred-year-old stone tower that had once been a sugar factory. Rolling hills and grassy valleys spread out before them and in the distance a brown ribbon of road cut through the greenery.

''Over here,'' called Mac.

Jeff grabbed Caroline's hand and pulled her down the gentle slope and through a stand of trees. On the other side sat a bright red Jeep.

''Great car, lousy color,'' Jeff muttered.

''Beggars can't be choosers,'' Mac replied, pulling the keys from his pocket. ''Let's move it.''

Caroline scrambled into the back as Mac slid behind the wheel and slipped the car into gear. The Jeep was moving as Jeff handed her the puppy and climbed in after her.

"Now what?" she asked.

"We're only a couple of miles from Christiansted," Jeff explained. "But from Christiansted it's another twenty minutes to the airport or forty-five minutes to the docks at Frederiksted."

"So which way are we going?"

The words were barely out of her mouth when a single rifle shot exploded into a rear tire. Mac swore and jerked the wheel, but the Jeep ran up over a small outcropping of rocks and flipped. The next thing Jeff knew, he was airborne.

His hip crashed into the solid earth. He rolled once and came up in a low crouch, gun drawn, already knowing where everyone was.

Everyone but the sniper.

Caroline had landed about ten feet away. Mac was farther down the hill. The Jeep rolled twice more, then rocked on its right side, the two left wheels spinning slowly in the air.

Instinct took over. Scrambling to Caroline's side, Jeff covered her body with his as a second shot broke the eerie silence. It bit into the dirt just inches from their heads.

"Down here!" Mac yelled. "I'll cover you."

Jeff gauged the distance, then pushed Caroline down the hill toward the trees, as Mac returned the sniper's fire. It was a futile gesture and they both knew it. A third shot whizzed by and she screamed.

Lunging and stumbling, they ran past the Jeep and into the relative safety of the trees. A moment later, Mac joined them.

"Everybody okay?" he asked.

Jeff looked at Caroline. She had a gash on the back of her hand, but other than that, she seemed fine. "You all right, Bright Eyes?"

"I think so." She let out a long breath. "Now what do we do?"

Jeff looked from the Jeep to the surrounding countryside. "Either we take out the shooter, or we try to right the Jeep."

Mac looked up the hill to where the Jeep listed on its side. "Forget the Jeep. I don't like the way it's smoking, and besides . . . aw, shoot," he said and took off running.

"Now wha—?"

Dumbfounded, Jeff watched his brother race back up the hill. The forgotten puppy wobbled unsteadily, sniffing at the smoke. Mac scooped up the dog with one hand and was halfway back to the trees when the shot rang out.

"Roll, damn it!" Jeff shouted, firing uselessly into the distance.

Mac tucked the dog to his chest, and hit the dirt, rolling the rest of the way down the hill.

"You damn fool," Jeff roared. "You trying to get yourself killed?"

Mac shook his head and grinned, gasping for breath. "Hey, you save the girl, I save the dog. All in a day's work. But I'll tell you this much—" he drew another long breath "—you can forget the Jeep. In addition to the smoke, the oil pan is cracked and it's leaking like a sieve."

"So we go after the sniper," Caroline said. She struggled to her feet, massaging the spot on her shoulder where she had landed in the fall.

"Whoa," Jeff said, grabbing her arm. "What's this 'we' business? You're not going anywhere."

"So what am I supposed to do? Sit here while you two play Rambo? I don't think so."

"Well, you're sure as hell not going after a sniper."

"Oh, for pity's sake," Mac said. "If you're that worried about her following us, tie her to a tree and be done with it."

"She's an escape artist," Jeff said, never taking his eyes off her. "She'd be free before we got to the clearing."

Arms folded across her chest, Caroline smiled.

"Fine," Mac said. "Then you stay with her and I'll go after the shooter."

"Forget it," Jeff answered. "I'm not going to put your life on the line just because she can't be trusted. You stay here. I'll go."

"No," Caroline said, more forcefully than she intended. Mac and Jeff turned in unison to look at her. Reluctantly she slumped against a tree and slid down the trunk to the ground. She didn't want them going after the sniper any more than she wanted the sniper coming after her. But she couldn't stop them. All she could do was stack the odds in their favor. "I know the best way for you to get this guy and not get hurt is to work together." She looked away, not wanting them to see the fear that was undoubtedly written all over her face. "I'll stay here with the dog."

Jeff studied her through narrowed eyes. "You give me your word you won't try to follow us?"

She nodded. "I swear on my brothers' graves. I won't follow you."

Jeff hesitated, needing to trust her, afraid not to.

"I'll be fine," Caroline said. "Just don't take all day."

Finally, Jeff nodded. "Let's do it," he said to Mac. "And let's do it fast."

Caroline watched them work their way along the line of trees until they were nothing more than specks of color. The puppy put his front paws on her chest and licked her chin, nuzzling her and snuggling close. She wrapped her arms around him, needing desperately to keep something safe.

She wanted to believe Brian was still alive, that it really was his voice she had heard less than an hour ago. But her head dealt with the facts even as her heart absorbed the pain. She had seen Brian's face contort as the bullet ripped into him; seen the massive amount of blood soaked into the Persian rug. And she knew Jeff was right. There was very little chance Brian had survived.

A barrage of gunfire echoed in the distance and her heart stopped, then started again with a jolt. Tears stung her eyes, and she offered up a silent prayer that Jeff and Mac would return unharmed.

A little ways up the hill, the Jeep was smoking. The smoke grew steadily thicker, making it harder and harder to see.

Then a blast caught her unexpected and unprepared, a rising fireball that blossomed into a roiling black cloud.

She shuddered violently and hugged the puppy as adrenaline poured through her body. The acrid smell of burning metal and rubber filled the air, reminding her of the explosion on her father's boat. The explosion that had taken Alden's life.

They were gone. Both of them. The two brothers she loved more than life itself. And she was supposed to avenge their deaths.

"I can't," she cried. "I can't do it."

"Yes, you can, Princess," Alden said. *"You're strong and you're smart."*

"And we'll be with you every step of the way," Brian added.

For a moment, she just sat there. Listening. Crying. Remembering. Then she thought of two other brothers. Jeff and Mac. Brothers who risked their lives to save hers. They were out there right now, looking for the person or persons who wanted to make her another notch in Augie Davis's belt.

There was nothing she could do to bring back Alden and Brian.

But she could prevent it from happening again.

Her mind made up, she stood and scanned the area. She had given Jeff her word that she wouldn't follow him. And she wouldn't. But neither would she stay and wait for him or Mac to be shot down by a bullet meant for her. She would go back to her original plan. Go underground until the trial. She would do everything in her power to avoid the clutches of Augie Davis. But if he did get her, she'd die knowing Jeff and Mac were safe.

Holding the puppy close to her chest, she started running in the direction of Christiansted.

A sniper's rifle was lying in the dirt next to him, and a large red stain was spreading across the front of his shirt. Jeff knelt and put two fingers on the side of the man's neck. He looked at Mac and shook his head. Using the back of his hand to open the guy's jacket, Jeff reached inside and carefully removed the wallet. He took a quick look, then stood and showed it to Mac. "That name mean anything to you?"

Mac shook his head. "No. But then I don't keep a list of hit men on the top forty."

"I doubt he had a partner," Jeff said, holstering his gun, "or we would have known about it by now. Let's get back to Caroline and then get out of here." He handed the wallet to Mac, then started out across the hills. "Chances are someone heard the shots. And I don't want to be here when the cops arrive."

"Agreed." Mac stuffed the dead man's wallet in his back pocket and hurried to catch up with his brother. "I'll call Arthur, tell him what happened and send him this ID. He'll have to send someone down here to clean up."

"In the meantime," Jeff said, "we've got to get Caroline off the island. The cover's blown, and when Davis finds out his man is dead, he'll send another. I want to be a few hundred miles from here when—"

Whatever else he was going to say was lost in the thundering noise that rocked the valley. For a split second, Jeff froze in his tracks as a paralyzing fear swept through his body. "The Jeep," he breathed. *Please, God, don't let her be anywhere near that Jeep.*

He set off at a dead run across the fields, his heart pounding wildly in his chest. As he mounted the next rise, a stitch caught in his side, but he kept up the grueling pace. In truth, he was less than half a mile from the Jeep, but it might as well have been fifty.

Finally, he spotted it. A black cloud of ash and smoke hovered over the smoldering remains. The adrenaline surging through his bloodstream drove him on. Never breaking stride, he hurtled downhill, past the burned-out carcass of the Jeep, to the thick grove of baobab trees where he had left Caroline.

She wasn't sitting at the base of the tree or walking nearby. She wasn't anywhere. He tried to call her name, but the word stuck in his windpipe as he gulped in air.

Mac bolted back up the hill, getting as close to the Jeep as he dared. He gave Jeff a thumbs-down sign, then hustled back to join in the search.

"Caroline!" Jeff scoured the stand of trees, moving in larger and larger circles as he combed the area. "Caroline!"

His brain reeled with the possibilities. For the second time in ten hours he'd made a mistake. And this one might well cost Caroline her life. Of the anger, guilt, and fear he felt, anger was the easiest to deal with. He grabbed a large branch that had fallen to the ground and swung it against a tree, feeling it crack halfway up his arms.

"Think, man," Mac said. "That's your strength, use it."

Jeff rubbed his head with the tips of his fingers. "The dog," he said. "Call him. He might come or bark."

Obligingly, Mac pursed his lips and whistled several times. "Here, pup!" he called.

They listened for a moment. Nothing greeted them but the sound of the birds and their own heavy breathing. Jeff shook his head. "They might be too far away to hear."

Mac jammed two fingers in his mouth and let loose with a roof-rattling whistle. Still nothing. "Okay," he said. "Let's go over the other possibilities."

Jeff nodded.

"What if the shooter was a decoy to get her alone so someone else could grab her?"

"Doesn't work," Jeff said. "The sniper couldn't possibly have known we would leave her. Besides, if he had an accomplice, he wouldn't have stuck around long enough to get himself killed. As soon as he saw us come after him, he would have taken off."

Jeff raked an angry hand through his hair, remembering what she had said.

"There are no seconds, McKensie. No second chances. If anything goes wrong, I'm out of here."

"She split," Jeff said. "She's running." He thought for a moment, trying to put himself in her shoes. "The first thing she'd do is get off the island."

"And there are only two ways to do that," Mac added. "The airport and the ships at Frederiksted."

Both men took off. "I'll take the airport," Jeff shouted. "You get to the docks and call Arthur."

One way or another they would find her—of that much Jeff was sure. And once they did, he swore he would never let her out of his sight again.

At this hour and dressed as she was, Caroline looked just like any of the other joggers out for a little morning exercise in the public park in Christiansted.

Only they weren't running for their lives.

She stopped at a water fountain and washed the blood off her hand. Then, choosing a bench away from the beaten path, she sat down and took several long, cleansing breaths. By now Jeff and Mac had either caught or killed the sniper. Guilt nipped at her conscience. She knew Jeff would be angry and worried sick at her disappearance. But better for him to be a little worried, than a lot dead. She had to get off the island before he found her.

Quickly she removed one of her earrings and used the wire to remove the screws in the Walkman. The back slid off easily and she exhaled a sigh of relief when she spotted Grover Cleveland's dour face. Two faces actually. Two neatly folded one-thousand-dollar bills. She removed one of them and reassembled the radio. Then she tightened the screws, replaced her earring, and hung the radio back on her belt loop.

The next stop would be the airport or the cruise ships at Frederiksted. But they were both too far away and too obvious.

With the puppy on her heels, Caroline jogged to the Christiansted pier. She'd find a way off this island, even if she had to buy a boat and start rowing.

A small sign at one end of the harbor caught her eye. Caroline smiled. Maybe she wouldn't have to row after all.

Chapter 14

Caroline looked out the window at the waves slapping against the pontoons. The little plane skimmed the water, scooting out of the Christiansted harbor. Within minutes they were airborne, and she blessed the Puerto Rican company that had decided to revitalize the seaplane service. They couldn't take her to the mainland, but she would get as far as Charlotte Amalie on St. Thomas. From there, it was a straight shot to Miami, Atlanta, or anywhere else she wanted to go.

Sticking her fingers through the screen of the pet carrier, she comforted the frightened puppy. "Don't worry, fella. It'll all be over soon."

After landing in the harbor, Caroline took a taxi inland to the airport and hurried to the airline counter "One one-way nonstop ticket to Atlanta, please."

The attendant punched the keys on his computer terminal. "I can get you on a flight departing at 2:05 this afternoon."

That was about four hours longer than she wanted to wait, but at this point, her options were limited. "Fine,"

Caroline said. She placed the pet carrier on the baggage rack. "And I'd like to bring my puppy."

The attendant nodded. "No problem. That will be an additional fifty dollars, and I'll need to see his papers."

"Papers?"

"Veterinary certificate. There's no quarantine from the Virgin Islands to the mainland, but you must have a document signed by your vet to prove vaccination for rabies, distemper and so on."

Caroline offered him her most woeful sigh. "Oh, no, I forgot it."

"I'm sorry, miss, but I can't let him on the plane." The attendant eyed her curiously. "Do you still want the ticket?"

"Yes, please." Tucking the ticket into her pocket, she picked up the carrier and headed for a bank of telephones. "I'm sorry about this, fella, but I don't have a choice." She dropped into the seat, and opened the phone book. Animal Brokers... Animal Health Products... Animal Rescue...

"Here it is," she announced. "Animal Shelters."

Caroline looked down into a pair of soulful brown eyes. "I ought to have my head examined," she muttered. But she flipped to the back of the directory, to the section labeled "V."

Less than an hour later, she stood in the waiting room of one of the local vets. It would be a while before the vet could squeeze them in, so the receptionist had offered to take her phone number and call as soon as the puppy was ready to leave.

Caroline chewed on the end of the pen, debating what to do. The only solution was to leave Jeff's name and the number of the hotel. He'd certainly pick up the puppy—he couldn't abandon him any more than she could. And he'd also know she was safely off St. Croix. He wouldn't be happy, but maybe he'd realize she could take care of herself.

And by that time, she'd be long gone.

For the umpteenth time, Jeff checked the overhead monitor, studying flight numbers that were already burned into his brain. He had been at the St. Croix airport, waiting, watching, praying since early morning. The terminal was small. He had contacted every airline, every attendant, every custodian he could find. But no one had seen her. Mac was doing the same thing at the docks. They touched base every hour on the hour, but it was as though she had simply disappeared.

Jeff recounted again the reasons he had to be thankful. Caroline was smart, she had incredible survival skills, and she'd do anything to avenge her brothers' deaths. Any of those should have been enough to give him some comfort.

Should have . . . two words that paved the way to hell.

His heart contracted in his chest. Maybe he'd been wrong to trust his instincts, his belief that Caroline was on the run. Maybe she really was abducted or hurt. Maybe it was time to call in the authorities.

One more long shot before he notified the police. He dialed the hotel front desk. "This is Mr. McKensie, Oceanfront No. 8. Do I have any messages?"

"Only one, sir. Your vet called. He said your puppy is ready."

"My what?"

The receptionist repeated the message.

Jeff shook his head. It didn't make sense, but now wasn't the time to figure it out. "Did you get a number?" He scribbled it down, fished out another coin, and dropped it into the phone.

"Island Animal Care."

"This is Jefferson McKensie. Do you have my dog?"

"Yes, sir," the woman said. "Dr. Rogoff gave him a full exam and all his shots. I've also prepared the veterinary certificate so you and your wife can take him back to the mainland."

"My wife?" His heart did a slow roll in his chest.

"Yes, sir."

"Pretty woman, about five foot seven, dark hair, brown eyes?"

"That's right," the receptionist said slowly.

Jeff fought back an overwhelming urge to kiss the phone. "Give me your address and I'll be right there."

The woman dutifully gave him a street name and number.

"Is that in Christiansted or Frederiksted?"

The woman laughed. "Neither one. It's a few blocks from Market Square in Charlotte Amalie."

"Charlotte Amalie?"

"On St. Thomas," the woman explained, her tone slow and patient, as though she were talking to someone who didn't understand English. "Mr. McKensie, is something wrong?"

"No, I'm just confused. I thought she was taking him to a vet on St. Croix. I'll be there as quickly as I can."

Less than an hour later he and Mac were in the air.

"Now what?" Mac asked.

Jeff pulled Caroline's picture from his wallet—the same picture he'd been carrying around since the day Arthur threw it on his desk. Who would have guessed he would be needing it for this?

"You go into Charlotte Amalie and get the dog. I'll flash Caroline's picture around the airport." He turned and watched as the plane descended into the mountains of St. Thomas—half the size of St. Croix and twice the population. How Caroline got here was a mystery. But she was down there right now—in the airport, on the docks, roaming the city. Finding her was another long shot. But luck had brought them this far; he had to believe it would hold out a little longer.

Caroline closed her eyes as the plane crossed the ocean heading for Atlanta.

You're doing great, Princess.

Yeah, sure, Brian. I left a trail a blind man could follow.

It's okay, came Alden's reassurance. *You're almost home.*

Home? Caroline shook her head. That word meant something once. When she was in Europe, home was the States. When she was running across the country, home was on the East Coast. When she lived in New York, home was an apartment in Brooklyn Heights. And now? After six weeks with Jeff, home was one bedroom/one bath in a Caribbean resort hotel.

But not anymore.

The years alone had left her with an aching emptiness that nothing seemed to fill. After a while she accepted it as normal. Now she knew it was anything but. It took being in Jeff's arms to feel whole. To feel loved.

But it wasn't real. Reality was being shot at and watching Jeeps go up in smoke. Reality was that her brothers were dead. Reality was that Augie Davis wanted her dead, too.

She closed her eyes and tried to imagine where Jeff was right now. She could see him so clearly. His cheek roughened with a day's growth of beard. His face etched with worry. Her heart went out to him and she wished she could call him. Hear his voice once more. Talk with him and tell him she was fine. That she would be fine, as long as *he* was safe.

"I don't suppose she gave the vet her itinerary," Jeff said when he and Mac hooked up again at the St. Thomas airport.

"'Fraid not," Mac answered. He shifted the carrier from one hand to the other. "So, where do we go from here?"

"The question is, where did *she* go?" Jeff dropped into a chair and leaned forward with his elbows on his knees. "She can't go international," he said, more to himself than his brother. "She doesn't have a passport. So that leaves the U.S. or Puerto Rico. And a pretty American who speaks fluent boarding-school French would stick out like a sore thumb in Puerto Rico. She'd go where she could blend in."

"That narrows it down to three nonstop flights," said Mac. "Miami, Atlanta and Newark."

"Scratch Newark. It's too close to home. I don't think she'd spend the next three weeks sitting in Davis's backyard."

Mac surged to his feet. "That leaves Miami and Atlanta. You take one, I'll take the other."

They hurried to the airline counter, making plans as they waited in line.

"One one-way ticket to Atlanta on your next available flight," Jeff said, pulling his wallet out of his back pocket. "Call Arthur when you get to Miami," Jeff said to Mac. "Let him know we're back in the States."

"You got it," Mac answered.

"There's a flight leaving in forty minutes," the attendant said. "But we may have trouble getting your luggage on."

"That's mine," Mac said, picking up the pet carrier from the luggage rack. "I brought him this far, I may as well take him the rest of the way."

"Well, hi, fella," the attendant said, sticking his fingers through the wire-mesh door. "I didn't expect to see you again."

"Again?" Jeff and Mac spoke in unison, turning to stare at the young man.

"He was here this morning," the attendant replied. "Either that or it was his twin."

"Did a woman bring him?" Jeff asked. He dug Caroline's photo out of his pocket. "This woman?"

The man studied the picture. "Yeah, I think it was her."

It was all Jeff could do to keep from vaulting the counter and pulling the information out of the man's throat. "Where'd she go?"

"There's only one place on the mainland we go to from here," the man answered. "Atlanta."

The heat and humidity hit Jeff in the face as he left the air-conditioned airport in Atlanta and headed for the rental car, reminding him once again that balmy tropical breezes were a thing of the past.

As if he could forget.

Was it only twenty-four hours since he had taken her to dinner . . . taken her into his arms . . . taken her into his bed? Sometimes the past seemed irretrievably far away. What he wouldn't give to turn back the clock just one day.

Oh, he had no second thoughts about loving her. Her desire and passion matched his own. In that way, and in a dozen others, they were made for each other. But he should have waited—waited until the job was over, until he was off company time, until he knew she was safe. Because if he *had* waited, they sure as hell wouldn't be in this mess right now.

Jefferson McKensie, master planner, had a plan for every escape. He had a plane plan, a boat plan, a car plan, he even had a plan that involved escaping on horseback. But in every one of his plans, he and Caroline were together. Even if something had happened to him, he knew Mac would be there to step in and carry out the plans. Not in his wildest dreams had he considered the possibility of her getting away, of them being separated.

And that was exactly what had happened.

He pulled up to the passenger pickup and Mac tossed the empty dog carrier into the back seat, then climbed into the front, scooting the wriggling puppy out of his way. The dog promptly climbed into his lap and pressed its nose against the window.

"Did you call Arthur and have him check the bus terminal?" Jeff asked.

Mac nodded. "But what makes you so sure she hopped a bus? Maybe she took another plane."

Weaving in and out of the airport traffic, Jeff headed for the interstate. "She can't have much money, and she wouldn't waste it on airfare. Rental cars are too easy to trace, and she could get trapped on a train. That leaves bus, thumb, or grand theft auto." Jeff threw his brother a tight-lipped smile. "I'm banking on the bus."

"Well, Arthur pulled a list of all the tickets paid for with cash at the Atlanta bus station during the last four hours. But believe me, there are a boatload."

"I'm betting she went north," Jeff said. "She'll blend in better than she would in the South, and it'll be easier to get to New York for the trial."

Mac pulled a notepad from his pocket and flipped through it. "If you're right, that really narrows it down. Because everything going north stops at Chattanooga."

Jeff stepped on the accelerator... and prayed. He'd been closing the gap all day. And now she was less than two hours ahead of him. Less than two lousy hours.

But two hours could be the same as two days if he made the wrong decision.

He knew there was a chance he was chasing the wrong person. A chance that Caroline was still in Atlanta, or flown to Timbuktu, or that she had defied all his expectations and gone due south.

But he didn't think so. It didn't feel right. A harsh laugh stuck in his throat. That was rich. The last of the see 'em to believe 'em was flying on raw instinct.

But then, he'd resort to a crystal ball and a Ouija board if it meant getting Caroline back alive.

Caroline shuffled into the truck-stop diner outside of Chattanooga and climbed onto a stool at the counter. "Coffee," she said to the waitress. "And, uh, how about a bowl of chili?"

"Comin' right up," the woman said.

Caroline watched as she ladled the chili into a bowl. The waitress was small, about fifty-five, with haunted gray eyes, and a name tag that read "Maxine." Caroline turned and checked out the rest of the patrons. At a quarter of ten, the place was pretty much deserted. Just three truckers laughing at a corner table.

"Here you go, honey," the waitress said. "You eat that up. You could use a little meat on your bones."

Caroline smiled her thanks and crumbled a cracker into the chili. It was good. Good and hot. Just what she needed to keep her going for the next few hours.

The little bell over the door jangled twice. She glanced up as a man slid onto a stool at the far end of the counter. He ordered a plate of chicken-fried steak with mashed potatoes and gravy, then pulled out a newspaper and began reading.

Caroline tried to focus on her chili. She looked up, surprised to find the waitress studying her. She met the woman's cool, assessing eyes, then quickly looked back down again.

"This is good," Caroline said, lifting another spoonful.

"Thanks," Maxine replied. She wiped the counter, moving the stained cotton cloth slowly back and forth over the Formica. Finally, she leaned across the counter until her face was inches from Caroline's. "So," she said, her voice husky and low. "You're runnin'."

A knot of fear twisted in Caroline's stomach. She gripped the mug of coffee to keep her hands from shaking. "Wh-what?" she stuttered.

"Honey, I can spot a runner a mile away."

That knot of fear uncoiled and re-formed around her heart. Even her best lie wouldn't cut it here. "A runner?"

The rag never stopped moving. "Some are runnin' to. Some are runnin' from. Which are you?"

Caroline crumbled another cracker into the bowl and stirred it around with her spoon. She weighed her options again, not at all reassured by her choices. This woman wasn't going to buy anything but the truth. "A little of both," she answered.

The waitress nodded her head thoughtfully, silently...waiting for Caroline to continue.

"I left him," Caroline said simply. "And now I'm going home." That, so help her, was the God's honest truth.

"Hey, Maxine." One of the truckers at the corner table lifted his cup. "We need another round."

"Keep your shirts on, boys. I'm comin'." Lowering her voice, she added, "Sit tight, sugar. You're safe here."

Oddly enough, Caroline believed her.

Maxine carried a coffeepot to the table and filled the men's cups, pausing long enough to share in one of their jokes. By the time she returned to the counter, Caroline had finished eating.

"Thanks." Caroline pulled five dollars from her pants pocket and slid the bill across the counter.

"Hold on," Maxine said. "At least let me give you a refill."

Caroline assumed she meant the coffee, but before she could object, Maxine had ladled chili to the top of her bowl, as well. Caroline fingered the five-dollar bill. "I . . . uh."

"It's on the house," Maxine said.

"Oh, I couldn't—"

"Sit down and eat. You need the energy."

Maxine was right. She hadn't eaten anything but a bag of peanuts all day. She sat back down and dipped the spoon into the steaming bowl.

The cloth started moving again. "Where'd you dump him?"

"What?"

"The guy. Where'd you leave him?"

Caroline bit the inside of her lip. "Savannah."

"And where's home?"

The questions were coming too hard and too fast. "Fort Wayne," Caroline said casually. "Indiana."

"That's a long way." The rag stopped moving and Maxine inclined her head toward the window. "I don't see no car out there. You hitchin'?"

She nodded. "Some. And taking the bus. And walking."

The waitress's eyes narrowed. "I don't like girls hitchin'. It's dangerous. Too many crazies out there."

Raucous laughter erupted and two of the truckers pushed away from the table.

"Hey, Patch," Maxine called. "You're headin' north, ain't you?"

A man the size of a lumberjack trudged over to the counter. He was wearing something that at one time must have been a baseball jacket, but now every square inch was covered with patches. From Abilene to Zion, from the Catskills to the Rockies—the man was a walking advertisement for cities from coast to coast. Caroline looked from the jacket to the baseball cap pulled low over his face. It, too, sported a dozen patches. The trucker was well named, and, if the wearable road map was any indication, he was also very well traveled.

"I'm goin' to Scranton," he said. "Why?"

Maxine smiled. "This lady needs a ride to Indiana."

The trucker looked Caroline up and down. "I don't take no passengers," he said. "It's against the rules."

Maxine's snort was anything but ladylike. "Since when did that stop you?" Heedless of the fact that she was half the man's size, she shook the rag under his nose. "You'll take her," Maxine said. "Or you'll never show your face in my place again."

"It's okay," Caroline said. "Really. I don't mind walking." *To Indiana?* She held her breath, but no one seemed to notice the absurdity of her statement.

Finally, the man called Patch nodded. "Throw in a piece of pecan pie, Maxine, and you got a deal. But only as far as Knoxville. That's where I switch to 81."

Maxine winked. "I'll get the pie."

Caroline looked skeptically at the mountain of a man who had been so easily blackmailed into giving her a ride.

"Don't worry about him," Maxine said, reaching over the counter to hand him a wedge of pie wrapped in cellophane. "He's just a big old teddy bear."

Patch grunted. "Cab's open. It's the blue Peterbilt. I got some gear in the locker room. Be right out."

Caroline nodded, then offered her hand to the waitress. "Thank you. Very much."

Maxine's smile extended all the way to her eyes as she squeezed Caroline's hand. "You take care, honey."

Damn, this was going to be easy. He swallowed the last of the chicken-fried steak, dropped a bill on the counter, and slipped into the men's room. With his hand in his pocket, he wrapped his fingers around the grip of the gun.

The guy they called Patch stood in front of a sink. He glanced up into the mirror, offered a barely perceptible nod, then bent forward over the basin.

Easy? Hell, it was going to be a cakewalk. Whipping out the pistol, he cracked the barrel against the trucker's head. Patch crashed forward into the sink, then slumped to the floor.

Stripping Patch of his hat and jacket, he slipped into the clothes, his own jacket providing bulk under the trucker's.

Then he fished through the pockets looking for the keys. Nothing. The truck was probably still running, like most of the rigs parked out there.

Grinning, he pulled the brim of Patch's cap down low over his face and flipped up the jacket collar. He was pretty sure it was her. And if it wasn't? Well, he'd make damn sure she made the trip worth his trouble.

"Now what?" Mac asked, stroking the puppy. After inhaling three bags of French fries, the dog had finally rolled over and fallen asleep, sprawled out on the front seat between them.

"I don't know," Jeff said sullenly. They hadn't made it to the Chattanooga terminal in time to meet the bus from Atlanta, but they were there before it took off and continued its way north. Caroline wasn't on it, but several passengers recognized her from Jeff's picture.

"Come on," Mac said. "At least we know we're on the right trail. Your hunch paid off." He leaned forward and fiddled with the car radio, trying to find a decent station. "Now you have to figure out what she'd do next."

That was the problem. Jeff didn't know what she'd do next. She could be eating, sleeping, running. From here on out it was a crapshoot. And he couldn't even stack the odds in his favor.

The radio blasted and Jeff winced.

"Sorry," Mac said, reaching to turn down the volume.

"You're as bad as she is," Jeff grumbled. "You can't be in a car five minutes without listening to the—" He twisted the wheel hard right into a fast-food parking lot and slammed on the brakes. "That's it!" he shouted. "Find an oldies station."

"Say what?"

"You heard me," Jeff said. "Oldies. Fifties stuff. Rock and roll. We're only two hundred miles from Graceland. There's got to be a station somewhere in this state that plays Elvis."

And if there was, Caroline would find it.

Jeff hopped out of the car and ran to a public phone. Grabbing the Yellow Pages, he flipped to the back. R—R—R— Radios. He tore out two pages of Radio Stations and Broadcast Companies and sprinted back to the car. "Did you find it?"

"Got it," Mac called. He fingered the dial, moving it slowly back and forth until the reception was clear. Sure enough, some doo-wop group was crooning a love song.

"The call letters," Jeff muttered, eyeing the list of radio stations. "Give me the call letters." Precious minutes ticked by as two more songs came and went without interruption.

Finally the smooth, velvety voice of the deejay hit the radio waves. "That was the late, great Marvin Gaye. And this is your own Rockin' Robbie sending you the sounds of the fifties and sixties, right here on WROC, the best of rock and roll."

"WROC," Jeff repeated. "Yes!" He copied the address onto a piece of paper and handed Mac the torn Yellow Pages. "Call Arthur," he said, pointing to the phone booth. "Tell him I'll need some clout at this radio station and someone to get me an address from a phone number." He reached across Mac and opened his door. "Meet me at the station."

"How am I supposed to get there? Fly?"

"Take a taxi," Jeff said. "And here." He handed Mac the leash. "Take the dog with you."

"Is this another of your crazy plans?" Mac asked.

"You bet it is," Jeff replied. Leaving Mac and the puppy on the sidewalk, he spun off down the street, trying hard to forget that his plans had a tendency to go to hell in a hand-basket wherever Caroline was concerned.

Caroline climbed the steps on the passenger side. The cab was a lot higher off the ground than she had expected, but the inside was clean and spacious. The dashboard was a maze of instruments, reminding her more of an airplane cockpit than any road vehicle she'd ever seen. And on top of everything else, the motor was running. It was a wonder someone didn't just hop in and drive off.

Yeah, right. As if the average person knew how to drive one of these rigs.

She looked around curiously. Above the visor was posted a variety of papers—license, registration, permits. According to the ID, her chauffeur's name wasn't really Patch, but there was no doubt this was his truck. In addition to the official documents, there were a half-dozen photos—Patch and a pretty woman standing in front of the truck, the pretty woman sewing patches on a jacket, Patch proudly displaying said jacket.

The rig had been backed into the parking lot, and from her vantage point she could see the comings and goings of everything and everyone in the vicinity. Things were fairly quiet at the diner, but next door, at the convenience store and gas station, the activity was nonstop.

Caroline let out a long, slow breath. The chili had revived her some, but it was still more than twenty hours since she had last slept. She was running on empty and it was only a matter of time before she crashed. Another hour and a half, she promised herself. Once she got to Knoxville, she would find a place to sleep.

She spotted Patch coming out of the diner. She watched him in the side-view mirror and a sense of disquiet rippled through her. Something was wrong.

Definitely wrong.

His head was down, the baseball cap pulled low over his face, much as it had been in the diner. And the jacket was the same....

The gear! He'd said he had to get his gear. But, as far as she could tell, this guy was carrying nothing.

Not even a piece of Maxine's pie.

Panic ripped through her as the man turned toward the line of trucks. She lunged for the door, but sanity claimed her. If she jumped out now, he would spot her for sure. She needed to be patient, needed to wait until he was behind the truck and out of sight. She considered cracking open the door to hasten her getaway, but was afraid the dome light would come on. So, with both hands squeezing the door handle, she waited. Her heart thudded painfully in her chest as she monitored his progress in the side-view mirror, each step bringing him closer. Finally, he rounded the back of the truck and disappeared from view.

Caroline yanked on the handle, but her hands, slick with perspiration, slipped and she fell back against the seat. A heartbeat later, she heard him climb the step. Heard the driver's door open. She tugged frantically on the handle. It clicked open and she threw her weight against the door. A man appeared on the driver's side—his smile mocking, his eyes cruel, his hand leveling a gun.

She dropped out of the cab. The door bounced on its hinges and swung back. The sound of the shot was muffled by a silencer, but she heard the bullet hit the door.

And she knew for certain.

Whoever he was, he wasn't Patch.

Chapter 15

Caroline scrambled under the wheels. Crouching low, she ran toward the back of the long trailer. The entrance to the diner was less than sixty feet away. Surely she could sprint that far.

And then what? Call the police? Hide behind Maxine's apron? No one could protect her from Augie Davis and his army of assassins. If she wanted to stay alive, she'd have to do it by herself. It was that simple.

She heard the man jump from the rig. "You can't hide forever," he growled. "Easy or hard, it's up to you."

It's your choice. We can do this the easy way, or the hard way.

Dear God, had it only been a few weeks since Jeff had said those words? What she wouldn't give to be with him now, safe in his arms, on St. Croix or anywhere else in the universe. But that assumed there was someplace where Davis couldn't find them. And *that* would be one hell of a fatal assumption.

Watching the man's feet as he walked around the truck, she kept herself hidden under the trailer, behind the huge tires. When he rounded the far side of the rig, she bolted from her hiding place and ducked under the next truck . . . then the next . . . and the next. Finally she reached the end of the line. Behind her was the row of tractor trailers. To her left was the interstate. To her right was the diner. And straight ahead was the gas station.

"I'm through playing games, lady." The guy was angry, real angry, but his voice was soft. Either he was deliberately keeping it low, or he was still looking around Patch's truck.

Peeking around the tire, she could see the man's feet. Just as she had, he was crawling under the rigs. One by one. When he got to the last truck, she would be caught. She had to get out of here. Now.

She glanced again at the gas station. An old station wagon was parked in front of the last pump—with no one near the tank, and, as far as she could tell, no one inside. It was too good to be true. With a fleeting glance in the direction of the would-be attacker, she sprang across the parking lot.

The door was unlocked and she hopped inside. Reaching beneath the steering column and dashboard, she fumbled for the wires to hot-wire the car.

The man had searched the last truck and was now scanning the parking lot. Caroline slumped sideways across the seat, still struggling with the wires. It was a simple task—one she had done at least fifty times. But never like this. Never under this kind of pressure. She willed her shaking hands to calm down, letting rote memory take over.

She heard voices and looked up as a woman walked out of the gas station. Davis's man spotted her and started running toward the car. So did the woman.

With a half curse, half prayer, the old station wagon roared to life. Caroline threw it into gear and spun out of the parking lot. In the rearview mirror, she could see the woman pointing and screaming. The man was racing back to the diner. Then Caroline turned onto the entrance ramp, and the commotion faded.

Her hands shook and her heart raced like an eighteen-wheeler out of control. Reflexively, she flipped on the radio and turned the dial until she found an oldies station.

"This is your own Rockin' Robbie on WROC. Our request lines are open, so call in and let the Sandman make all your dreams come true. And now here's a little Who for all you night owls—'Tommy.'"

The familiar music had a calming effect, and as her mind cleared, Caroline began to sort through her options. There weren't many. She didn't know much about rigs, but she did know they were slow starters. If that man took Patch's truck, she would be long gone before he got it up to speed.

But he probably had a car.

And that screaming woman had surely called the police. Caroline glanced at her watch. She had ten minutes—fifteen, tops—before an A.P.B. would have every cop in the state watching for her. She'd have to get off at the next exit and ditch the car.

"It's ten after ten," the deejay crooned. "And tonight we've got a little contest to keep you listening. I'll play three songs, each containing a clue. Put the clues together and be the first person to call in with the right answer. But remember, you only have ten minutes. Call me here at 555-9762, that's 555-WROC. And here's our first song."

Caroline spotted a green interstate sign with white lettering. She pushed the car a little faster until the words came into view. Ten miles to the next exit and a town called Ooltewah. She let out a long, slow breath. Ten miles was a hell of a long way when the police were on your tail.

And a hit man.

She glanced in the rearview mirror. No flashing red lights. No car of any sort barreling down on her. She relaxed a little as Neil Diamond's soothing voice sang "Brooklyn Roads."

If only I were back in Brooklyn, instead of here...

Five more miles. Automatically her mind rehearsed the steps. Find a good-size all-night grocery store. Park the car. Casually enter the store. Purchase a candy bar or a pack of gum. Leave the store on foot.

She searched the rearview mirror again. It was too eerie. Nothing in front of her. Nothing behind her. It was if every car in the world had suddenly vanished. What had happened to the guy wearing Patch's jacket?

What had happened to Patch?

She shivered and tried not to think about it.

"No winners yet. So here's clue number two."

The velvety voice of the deejay grounded her again and her mind reached for the next song—"Total Eclipse of the Heart"—not an oldie, but still a good song.

"Turn around, Bright Eyes."

From out of nowhere two pinpoints of light appeared behind her on the horizon. Specks at first, they grew larger and larger as the car closed the distance between them.

Another highway sign. Three miles to the exit.

No flashing lights. No sirens. But the vehicle was still gaining on her. The driver had to be doing ninety.

Caroline pressed down on the gas pedal and the speedometer needle climbed slowly.

Two more miles.

The driver was coming up behind her. Fast. Staring into the headlights reflected in her rearview mirror, she couldn't tell make or model.

But she wouldn't reach the exit before he overtook her.

The small car came up beside her, slowed, then swerved into her lane. Gripping the steering wheel, her foot holding the pedal to the floor, she braced for impact.

The car rammed her. But the old wagon was built like a Sherman tank and the small car seemed to bounce off it. It picked up speed again. Preparing for another hit.

The exit loomed ahead. If she could just trick him. Make him think she was staying on the highway and at the last minute grab the exit ramp. He might not make the turn.

She veered left, straddling the centerline. The phantom car backed off momentarily, then pulled toward the center, directly behind her.

A hundred yards...fifty...thirty.

The car bore down once more. They were nearly past the exit. A scant second before impact, she whipped the wheel hard right. A spray of gravel shot across the highway as she fought to bring the heavy car back to the ramp. The small red car zigzagged wildly down the interstate, missing the exit altogether.

She ran the stop sign at the bottom of the ramp and turned in the direction of Ooltewah. Her hands shook and tears burned behind her eyes.

"Here's the third and final clue," Rockin' Robbie said. "Put it together and figure it out."

Another Neil Diamond song swirled into the night air— "Sweet Caroline."

The words struck her with a force far stronger than colliding cars. "Sweet Caroline"—her name. "Brooklyn Roads"—the place she had come from and was returning to. Bright Eyes—Jeff's own nickname for her.

This was crazy. It couldn't be. Could it?

She listened intently as caller after caller offered their best guesses.

"I'm sorry, folks. No winner tonight, which is too bad because our prize, donated by a travel agency, was a doozy— a Caribbean vacation for two on enchanted St. Croix in the U.S. Virgin Islands."

Oh, my God.

Jeff.

She abandoned the car in the first parking lot she came to, and ran down the street, looking for a pay phone. She found one at a gas station, a few blocks away. "Five-five-five-WROC," she repeated, pulling a coin from her pocket. Time expanded as she listened to the digital beeps and waited for the connection.

And then what? Tell Rockin' Robbie that *she* was the answer to tonight's song puzzle? If she was, then it could only be due to Jeff—and another of his almighty plans.

The phone rang once. Twice. She would bet her last nickel he was there. At the station. She was within the sound of his voice. But how? How had he known where to look? How had he found her?

The same way someone else had.

"WROC request line. This is Rockin' Robbie."

A lump swelled in her throat and she choked back the tears. She couldn't talk to Jeff. Couldn't let him know where she was.

"Hello? Hello?"

Caroline dropped the receiver, slumping against the booth. Tears ran down her cheeks. There was only one way to keep Jeff safe.

And that was for her to keep her distance.

* * *

Every time the phone rang, Jeff jumped. The song puzzle had been a stroke of genius, and Rockin' Robbie had played it like a pro. But so far, it had turned up zilch. The phone jangled again and as Rockin' Robbie lifted the receiver, Jeff scribbled down the number from the Caller ID. A man's voice filled the sound booth and Jeff crossed off the number.

Someone offering an answer to the puzzle. Someone calling in a request. Everyone but the right one.

The wall clock read ten-fifteen. Jeff expelled a long breath. He would stay another fifteen minutes and then he would have to admit defeat.

The phone rang again.

"WROC request line. This is Rockin' Robbie."

Jeff jotted down the number and the two words after it—"Pay Phone."

"Hello? Hello?"

The deejay looked at Jeff and shrugged. "Hung up," he said. "Must have changed his mind."

Her mind, Jeff silently corrected. He bolted into the next room. "It's a pay phone," he said, giving Mac the number. "Find out where."

"A pay phone? Jeff, that's a real long shot."

Maybe. But right now, long shots were all he had. And slim was a far sight better than none.

Jeff pulled up next to the phone booth and Mac hopped out of the car, leaving the door open behind him. "This is it," Mac said, comparing the number on the phone to the one on paper. "The call definitely came from here. And look—" He pointed to the receiver dangling from its metal cord. "Phone's off the hook."

Mac dropped the receiver into the cradle. He walked back to the car and leaned inside, one arm resting on the roof, the other propped against the door. "If it was her, she has a twenty-five-minute head start."

Before Jeff could respond, the puppy jumped over the front seat and scooted between Mac's legs. He sniffed at the sidewalk, squatted on a small patch of grass, and then sniffed some more. When he reached the phone booth, he began yapping.

"Hey," Mac said. "Look at that."

"Forget it, Mac. I know what you're thinking and it won't work."

"Says who? I'll bet you a month's salary he smells Caroline. I told you he was a smart dog. He'll lead us right to her."

Jeff sighed. "He's a puppy, Mac. And he's not even a bloodhound. He doesn't know the first thing about tracking and *you* don't have a month's salary to bet."

Mac folded his arms across his chest. "Have you got a better idea?"

Touché. Reluctantly, Jeff reached into the back seat and snagged the leash. "Lead on, Macduff."

Slipping into the shadows, Caroline surveyed the street. Quiet. Dark. No sign of a small red car. No sign of her assailant or anyone else wearing Patch's unmistakable jacket.

But then, he'd probably taken it off.

She struggled to remember the man's face, his hair, his coloring—anything that would distinguish him. But the attack had happened so fast, she never got more than a fleeting glance. Bottom line—if he ditched the car and the jacket, she wouldn't recognize him.

She shivered. Tennessee in August was hot and muggy, even at this hour. It was an internal cold that chilled her. She zipped up her jacket.

Another car drove by slowly, and she pressed against a tree. How many times in the last twenty-four hours had she felt this fear? She couldn't go on like this. She couldn't keep hiding in the shadows, always looking over her shoulder, always sneaking around. She had to get out of here before the danger to her mind became more deadly than the danger to her body.

Once again, she began to run.

Jeff sat in the car and watched the puppy run in circles with Mac calling to him and encouraging him on. Impatience and fear gnawed at him. Caroline was out there somewhere—alone, in trouble, maybe hurt—while they were chasing their tails. Literally.

After a few minutes, the dog yapped and ran off down the sidewalk, with Mac in hot pursuit. Jeff put the car in gear and followed slowly. The puppy led them out of town, into the countryside. The houses were scattered, punctuated by large fields. All dark, tucked in, and quiet. No neon lights, no traffic lights, no streetlights, no light of any kind except the moon, and that had ducked behind a cloud.

He didn't figure Caroline to be much of a country girl, but if she couldn't hide in the noise and crowds of a big city, this would be a darn good second choice.

Jeff pulled the car up even with Mac and rolled down the window. "It's a straight shot along this road," Jeff said. "I'll go on ahead. You stay with the dog."

Too winded to speak, Mac simply nodded, and Jeff pulled away. They were closing in on her, he could feel it. Now it was only a matter of time.

Caroline cast a hurried glance over her shoulder. For as far as she could see along this country road, it was pitch-dark. She tried to relax, but the unease persisted. And she'd come far enough to know the importance of trusting her instincts. Quickly, she jumped the four feet into the ditch, her sneakers squishing in the mud. Up on the road there was no cover. At least down here she wouldn't be easily spotted. She began moving again, her progress slowed by the high grass and uneven terrain. An eternity passed while she trudged and listened, hearing nothing more than crickets and the sound of her own breathing.

And then a dog barked. It was faint...far away...but unmistakable. And there was a sound like a motor. Caroline peeked out of the ditch and looked down the road. The soft purr of the motor grew louder, and out of the darkness came the shape of a car.

She crouched back down and held her breath. The vehicle was going very slowly. Without lights. It stopped. The motor switched off and she heard the click of a door opening. Heard footsteps on the gravel. Whoever it was, he was no more than a hundred feet away.

She held her breath until she thought her lungs would burst. Her leg cramped and she eased her foot back, snapping a twig. It echoed like a cannon, and an aeon passed before she felt sure she hadn't given herself away.

Then she heard footsteps running on the road and the sound of heavy wheezing.

"Well?"

That single word said it all. Jeff. It *was* him. The sound of his voice squeezed her heart and Caroline pressed her hands to her mouth to keep from crying out. He was within hearing distance... seeing distance... touching distance.

Shooting distance. Anyone coming after her might hit Jeff or Mac instead.

The puppy yapped wildly and jumped into the ditch. Caroline could hear him struggling through the undergrowth.

No, she silently cried, pressing herself against the embankment. *Please, go away.*

But it wasn't to be. Sniffing and panting, the puppy sought her out, then climbed into her lap and licked her face.

"Where did he go?" Mac asked.

"I don't know," Jeff answered. "It's too dark to see anything."

Caroline felt more than heard the thud as they jumped into the ditch, calling and whistling for the dog. She clamped a gentle hand over the puppy's muzzle to keep him quiet.

"Maybe he found a rabbit," Mac said.

The puppy squirmed in her arms, and reluctantly she released him and stood. "He didn't find a rabbit," she said. "He found me."

Jeff didn't know whether to hug her or slug her. So he did nothing. Just stood there and stared at her. She looked awful. Worn, tired, half-dead. The anger resurfaced—anger at her, anger at Davis, anger at himself.

"What the hell do you think you're doing?" he seethed.

"Hiding." She brushed the dirt and grass from her clothes.

"From *me?*" His tone was incredulous.

"At the moment, yes."

"For God's sake, why?"

She looked at him for a long moment. "You wouldn't understand," she said tiredly.

"You got that right." He grabbed her arm and spun her in the direction of the car. "What are you grinning at?" he snapped at Mac.

"My dog," Mac said proudly. "He found her."

Caroline stopped and turned to look at him. "*Your* dog? When did that happen?"

Mac shrugged. "He just kind of grew on me. You don't mind, do you?"

"Of course not. I just wanted to find him a good home. If you want him, he's yours."

"Do you two mind?" Jeff interrupted. "I'd like to get out of here before someone finds us and blows us to kingdom come."

Biting her tongue, Caroline climbed into the back seat and the puppy leaped in after her. *What a difference a day makes,* she thought ruefully, studying Jeff as he drove. This was not the man who had wined and dined her less than two days ago. This was not the man who had held her in his arms as they danced in the moonlight and made love to her with the sound of the ocean pounding on the shore.

This man was angry, explosively so. And yet, already she felt safe. Felt the tension and fear draining from her body.

But she couldn't be that selfish, couldn't put him in such danger. Somehow she would have to make him understand that she could survive on her own until the trial. Somehow she had to convince him to let her go it alone.

She looked at the stern face and rigid posture of the man driving the car. Jeff of Gibraltar. Convincing him of anything wasn't going to be easy.

"Well, did you?"

"What?" Suddenly realizing he'd spoken to her, Caroline met Jeff's gaze in the rearview mirror.

"I said, we heard on the radio that a woman matching your description had stolen a station wagon. Was it you?"

She looked away. "Yes."

"In the middle of a truck stop? With half a dozen people watching?"

"More like two or three, but yes."

"Mind telling us why?"

Caroline bit her lip. She didn't want Jeff to know just how much trouble she'd been in, but *not* telling him endangered them further. She opted for telling the truth with as much levity as possible. "It seemed the fastest way to get away from the guy who was shooting at me."

"Sheesh," Mac said. "Did he follow you here?"

She nodded. "He was in a small red car with the passenger door caved in."

Jeff had neared the northbound entrance to the interstate. At her words, he whipped the wheel and headed south instead.

"What are you doing?" Mac asked.

"We're going back to Chattanooga."

Caroline jumped up and leaned over the front seat. "Are you crazy? I just spent the last two hours trying to get out of there. That's where I ran into Davis's man."

Jeff smiled. The first smile she'd seen on him tonight. Lord, she loved that smile.

"Exactly," he said. "That's the last place they'd look for you. Now, get down and stay down."

"Wait a minute, Jeff—"

"I mean it, Caroline. Down!"

The dog obediently dropped to the seat. Reluctantly, she followed suit. There were a few problems with that caveman mentality. But now was not the best time to point them out.

Within the hour they were back in Chattanooga. The rental car was too easy to trace, so Jeff turned it in, while Mac bought an old heap from a guy in a bar. And the whole time, Jeff didn't let Caroline out of his sight.

At two in the morning they stopped for gas on the northwest side of Knoxville.

"Where are you going?" Jeff asked, as she climbed out of the car.

She pointed in the direction of the gas station. "Little girls' room. Unless that's a problem."

"Not at all." He turned the pump over to Mac and trailed behind her as she got the key from the night clerk, then followed her around to the side of the small building.

"You know," Caroline said, "I've been doing this on my own since I was four. I think I can manage."

Jeff folded his arms across his chest and leaned back against the concrete, as stiff and unyielding as a cigar-store Indian. "I'll wait."

She shrugged. "Suit yourself."

He was still standing there when she came out moments later.

Caroline passed a weary hand across her eyes. "We need to talk, Jeff."

"You got that right. But not here and not now." He took the key from her hand, then cupped her elbow. "Get back in the car."

Her jaw clenched and she tried to pry his fingers from her arm. "This macho routine is getting real old."

"Think so?" His grip tightened. "Well, get used to it."

She stopped struggling. "What's that supposed to mean?"

"It means I can't trust you to stay with me. You'll take off again the first chance you get. So, you don't get any more chances."

"I won't let you treat me like a crimi—"

"Been there, done that," Mac said, coming up on the argument. "You guys swing like a pendulum—animosity, passion, passion, animosity. Make up your minds."

Jeff scowled and Mac held up his hands.

"Look," Mac said. "I doubt any of us has had more than a few minutes' sleep in the last twenty-four hours. So before you light into me, I say we find a place to crash and pick this up in the morning. I saw a place a few miles back."

After a moment, Jeff nodded.

When they reached the motel, Caroline and Jeff went in first to get a room. Mac offered to wait a while and watch for a tail before getting a room of his own.

The gloves came off as soon as the door closed. "All right," Caroline said, "let's get this over with."

Jeff nodded and dropped into a chair. "Ladies first."

Caroline sat down on the edge of the bed facing him. She took a deep breath. "I appreciate your dedication. I really do. And I respect the fact that you are a man of your word. But I have proved time and time again that I can take care of myself." Jeff started to say something, but she held up her hand. "Please, let me finish. I got off the island, by myself. I got to the States, by myself. I went from Atlanta to Chattanooga, by myself. And I outwitted, outran, and outmaneuvered a paid assassin, by myself. What will it take to convince you I can go it alone?"

Jeff shook his head. "What will it take for you to realize you don't have to go it alone? I don't want you to be alone. What is wrong with accepting my help?"

It could get you killed.

Her voice dropped to barely a whisper. "Do you have any idea what I was thinking when that sniper started shooting and the Jeep blew up?"

Jeff shook his head.

"I was thinking about my brothers."

He reached for her, would have touched her, but she pulled back. She didn't want comfort. She wanted him to understand.

"And then I saw two other brothers—you and Mac—and I decided I would never let that happen again. I won't let Augie Davis destroy your family—the way he destroyed mine."

"That's not going to happen—"

"You want to put that in writing?"

Regret clouded his face.

"I didn't think so," Caroline said. "There are no guarantees, and we both know it. That's why I *have* to do this alone. That way, only one person can get hurt." She unzipped the backpack he had tossed on the bed and fished out a hairbrush. With an energy she didn't feel, she brushed the tangled strands. "I'm wiped out. I admit it. And I'm ready to sleep here for the next twenty-four hours if need be. But after that, I want to leave. By myself."

Jeff came nearer. He put out his hand, and for a moment she thought he was going to touch her—she would have let him—but he didn't. His hand dropped to his side. "I can't do that, Caroline."

She clutched the brush so tightly her knuckles turned white. "Why the hell not?"

"Because believe it or not, you *need* me. You can't stay awake twenty-four hours a day. You can't always watch your back. I can. *We* can. Together." He seemed to stagger under the weight of his own words. "The three of us," he amended. "You, me and Mac."

"No. I won't let you risk your life for me."

"It's my life and I'll do whatever the hell I want with it. Now, stop arguing and get some sleep."

In a burst of fury, Caroline hurled the brush across the room. It crashed against the wall, the sound echoed by the bathroom door as it slammed closed behind her. A moment later, he heard the shower run.

Jeff rubbed his forehead and temples with the tips of his fingers. Why was she so stubborn? Why was she destined to learn everything the hard way?

One way or another, he had to show her. Had to prove that she was vulnerable. She'd hate him for it, but it might be the only way to save her life.

With a flick of her wrist, Caroline turned off the water and reached for a towel. After squeezing most of the water from her hair, she wrapped the towel around it, turban-style. Then she wrapped another one around her torso, tucking the end in across her breasts.

She flipped off the bathroom light and stepped into the bedroom. Darkness surrounded her. "Jeff?" she whispered. She hadn't been in the bathroom long, but it was long enough to fall asleep when you'd been on the run for twenty-four hours. She listened for a snore, a moan, or even heavy breathing. But there was only silence.

She turned back to the bathroom, fumbling for the light switch. But before she had gone two steps, she was grabbed from behind. A hand clamped down hard over her mouth, and her scream died in her throat.

Chapter 16

Caroline stomped down hard on the man's instep. It would have been a whole lot more painful if she had been wearing heels, but it was effective enough. He staggered.

Then she jammed her elbow into his stomach. He made a woofing noise. His grip lessened and she wrenched away.

Adjusting to the darkness, she saw the outline of the furniture. She grabbed a lamp from the dresser and ripped the cord from the outlet, then spun around, the lamp raised above her head.

"No!" Whether the sound came from him or her, she couldn't tell.

She swung the lamp in a wide arc, aiming for the man's head. Steel fingers snapped around her wrists as he wrestled her for the lamp.

"Stop fighting," he grated. "It's me, Jeff."

Moonlight filtered through the thin curtains and she got her first good look at him. Coarse stubble covered his jaw, making him look dangerous. But the sharp planes of his face were familiar.

"Damn you!" she seethed, the lamp dropping from her hands. "Are you out of your mind?"

He caught the small lamp and righted it on the dresser, then flipped on the bathroom light. His eyes met hers. And in that moment, she knew. This little ambush had been a test. Her anger exploded.

"You still don't get it, do you?" she said. "Read my lips, McKensie. I can take care of myself." She jabbed his chest with a finger. "You're standing there with a sore instep, an aching gut, and you came within inches of having your skull cracked open. And me? I don't have a scratch." She stepped back and spread her arms wide. "See for yourself."

That's when the towel came undone.

His gaze remained fastened on her face. He blinked, then looked at her. All of her. His expression, if anything, became even harder.

A deafening silence filled the room. Caroline felt the blood rush to her cheeks. The towel lay on the floor. She bent to retrieve it, but he kicked it aside.

Reflexively, she backed up. His eyes were dark, dangerous. His lips drew back in an almost-savage smile. Her breath caught in her throat.

The turban that held her hair slipped, and she yanked on the second towel, pulling it off her head, holding it awkwardly in front of her. He took a single step forward and ripped it from her hands, tossing it across the room.

Excitement racked her body. Heat swept through her like the flash of a blowtorch. He would take her. Ravish her.

And she wanted him to.

Jeff stared at her. Her skin glowed with a damp, pearlized sheen. Her dark hair was wet and tangled, her breasts swollen, nipples hard, and her eyes—more tempting than ever. He wanted to strangle her. Wanted to punish her.

Hell, he just wanted her. Hard. Fast. Now.

Somewhere, in the back of his mind, he recognized the feelings as madness. Anger, or maybe frustration born of fear. Whatever it was, wherever it came from, damned if he could stop it. He grabbed her wrist and wrenched her into his arms.

Caroline winced as his fingers dug into her flesh. His mouth crushed down on hers, and she tasted rage mixed with desire. She met his violent demand with one of her own. With a low, hungry growl, she pressed her naked body against him, her teeth raking his tongue.

He buried his hands in her thick, wet hair, and inhaled her scent. The fragrance of soap and shampoo swirled around him like a whirlpool, drawing him in deeper. Her mouth added fuel to a fire that was already raging out of control. Again and again his tongue slipped between her lips, savoring the taste of her.

He grabbed her hand and pushed it down between their bodies to the hard ridge straining against his pants. Never in his life had he been so painfully hard. She unzipped his fly and stroked him slowly with her palm. Up, down, then up again. A hand dipped in fire, igniting flames with every touch.

He threw her onto the bed, and blanketed her with his body, his weight wedged between her thighs. He took her mouth again, claiming her, savagely branding her.

Reaching down, he brushed past the soft mound of hair, his fingers seeking her warm center. She was hot, slick. He probed and stroked, deeper and deeper, with bruising caresses, her long, throaty moan reverberating against his mouth.

Her hips arched against his, seeking him, fighting to bring him closer. His shirt bunched in her hands. She clutched his shoulders and moved beneath him in suggestive invitation. She was seductive. She was daring. She was his.

Triumphantly, he rose over her, the muscles in his back and arms trembling as they supported his weight. For a second he hesitated, but her eyes—those damned eyes that tempted him beyond endurance—were open and locked on to his. He drove into her, burying himself with one desperate stroke.

Caroline cried out, then relaxed, trying to draw him in deeper. Nameless sensations battered her and tears dampened her cheeks. She was so full, so complete. Her fingers dug into his shoulders, urging him on.

He thrust powerfully again, his teeth clenched in a grimace of exhilaration and torment. Perfect pleasure. Perfect pain. His mind raced his body for control. But there was no control. His heart pounded and his body shuddered with every ragged breath.

Her neck arched and her head pressed into the mattress as she tried to gulp air into her lungs. His body slid over hers again and again until every nerve screamed for release. She clung to him, wrapping her arms around his neck, locking her ankles over his—entangling their limbs, entwining their needs.

He felt the helpless quiver that took her body—felt it to the depths of his soul. She wanted him. And that fact alone drove him to a summit of pleasure he had never known. He rode her like fury, and she matched his surging rhythm.

She came with a wicked shudder and a final cry of stunned release that echoed through the room and sang in his blood. He felt the sudden surge of her body, and then her fingers lessened their grip on his clothing. He held her, shaking and shivering, tightly against his body and drove once more deep inside her pulsating warmth. He exploded, shattered, clutched her close and held on as the vicious ecstasy caught him. Strength sapped, he called her name and collapsed onto her while the whole world drifted away.

Moments later, with his heart still pounding and his lungs gasping for breath, he considered moving off her. But he couldn't summon the energy. The truth was, sex with this woman was unlike anything he had ever known. Glorious, overpowering, mind-shattering. A union he hadn't thought possible.

And thoughts like that could get them both killed.

Sanity returned, and with it came a host of recriminations. He'd done it again. Compromised her safety. He'd always been able to plan everything down to the last detail. But one look at her, and every one of his well-laid plans had gone up in smoke. Not to mention any idea of careful, responsible, safe sex.

She could have pulled away, he reminded himself. Resisted, slapped his face. But the fact that she wanted it as much as he did, did little to absolve his conscience. He'd behaved recklessly, foolishly. That wasn't like him.

And it scared him to death.

Her eyes closed, Caroline tried to comprehend the imponderable. They had come together like thunder and lightning—a noisy, turbulent energy that was terrifyingly wild. Even through the clothing, his body radiated heat, and she could feel his heartbeat, still far from steady. Serenity and calmness enveloped her now, like the quiet after a storm. She had never felt such peace...contentment...love.

Then she felt him slip away. Felt cool air move across her body. Heard the rasp of a zipper as he adjusted his clothes.

"Caroline."

The bed shifted under his weight as he sat down beside her. She opened her eyes and saw a mix of emotions darken his face—shock, confusion, and, God help her, regret.

"Caroline, I'm—"

She pressed her fingers against his mouth. "Don't say it, Jeff," she warned. "Don't tell me you're sorry. I can handle anything else you have to say, but not that."

"I—" He looked into her eyes and his heart stopped cold. There was no pain, no anger, no bitter resentment. Just a smoldering passion that even their lovemaking had not doused.

He hadn't the words to describe what he was feeling, so he said the first thing that popped into his head. "I still don't know how you got off the island. You didn't have a penny to your name."

Caroline smiled. "We're even. I don't know how you managed to follow me from a field in St. Croix to a field in Tennessee."

She sat up on the bed, unembarrassed, uninhibited... still naked. She looked like a Botticelli nude—elegant, unassuming, beautiful. He felt himself hardening again. He stood and walked across the small room, as far away from her as he could get.

"We can compare notes later. I think right now, we'd better get some sleep."

She nodded and rose from the bed. "My clothes are in there," she said, pointing toward the bathroom. "I don't have a spare set." She smiled. "I travel light."

Jeff waited until she'd disappeared in the bathroom before stooping down to retrieve the discarded towels. His hands were finally steady, but his insides were still shaking. He dropped down into the chair and held the towels to his face, inhaling the fragrance of her shampoo, her soap, *her*.

He looked up when she came into the room. Her hair was brushed and she was wearing a light blue T-shirt that barely covered her bottom. When she walked, a hint of white showed from beneath. She peeled back the covers on the bed and slid between the sheets.

He stretched out in the chair. "It's probably better if I stay here."

She laughed and the sound was as warm as sunshine. "Isn't that a bit like locking the barn door after the horse ran away?"

Her smile was infectious and he returned it easily. "Yeah, I guess you're right."

She patted the bed beside her. "You'll be better off if you sleep here. And if it puts your mind at rest, I give you my solemn word I won't be running out on you tonight. I don't have the energy." With her back to the center of the bed, she lay down and tucked a hand under her pillow.

Slowly, Jeff stood and turned out the bathroom light. He undressed in the dark, stripping to his underwear, then crawled in next to her. The bed was only a double; much smaller than the king-size bed they'd had on St. Croix. But size didn't matter. Being away from her did—whether it was a few feet or a thousand miles.

He wrapped his arms around her, pulling her close. She turned, sighing as she snuggled against his chest. Like it or not, accept it or not, she was part of him. The best part. And finding her again was like finding the other half of himself.

Sleep clung to her like wet wool, thick and heavy, and Caroline struggled to force it aside. She rolled onto her stomach and stared at her watch. Almost seven—she lifted the window curtain above the bed—in the evening. She'd slept through the entire day. And if her growling stomach hadn't wakened her, she might have slept right through the . . .

Trial.

She glanced from the empty spot beside her to the bathroom. The door was ajar and the shower was running. She staggered out of bed and into her clothes as the flood of memories washed away the dregs of sleep. Last night had meant everything—and had changed nothing.

More than ever, she was determined to finish this alone. Davis wanted her dead. Davis would kill anyone who got in the way. It was as simple as that. And she couldn't . . . wouldn't risk Jeff's life.

She grabbed her nylon jacket and slipped out the door.

"Good morning." Mac looked up at the moon. "Or is it good night?" He tossed a small stick to the puppy.

"Whatever," Caroline muttered, cursing herself and fate and just about everything else.

"You hungry?" He didn't wait for an answer. "When Jeff gets out of the shower, we ought to get some breakfast . . . or dinner."

She spun around. "How did you know he was in the shower? No," she said, "don't answer that." As he'd promised, Jeff wasn't going to give her any opportunity to slip away.

"Looks like I'm the last one," Jeff said, sauntering out of the room. A smug smile danced across his face. "I'll turn in the keys and then we'll hit the road."

Half an hour later, they stopped to eat. The place was billed as a family restaurant—nice but not fancy. A waitress showed them to their table. "Here you go," she said, handing each of them a menu. "I'll be back in a few minutes to take your order."

Caroline leaned back in her chair and opened the menu. Breakfast items on the first page, lunch on the second, dinner on the—

She stared at the small white paper clipped to the top of the third page.

GO TO THE PHONE. NOW.

She closed the menu and looked around the restaurant. A few late diners, but nothing out of the ordinary.

"Get a load of these specials," Mac said. He tapped the small white paper clipped to his menu. "Meat loaf, liver and onions, turkey and dressing. That's what I call real food. None of that tofu bean-sprout stuff."

Caroline opened her menu and looked again. No meat loaf. No liver. No turkey. She swallowed hard.

"Are you ready to order?" the waitress asked. She put three cups of coffee on the table and pulled a pad and pencil from the pocket of her apron.

"Meat loaf with the works," Mac said, "and Dutch apple pie for dessert."

"I'll have a ham-and-cheese omelet, pancakes, and hash browns," Jeff said.

"And you, miss? Miss?"

Caroline stared at the waitress. She was perfectly composed, calm, her face revealing nothing as she waited for Caroline to place an order.

"Caroline?" Jeff nudged her arm.

"Sorry," Caroline said. "What's your soup today?"

"Bean with bacon and clam chowder."

"I'll have the chowder and an avocado-and-tomato sandwich." She closed the menu and held it out to the waitress. The woman finished scribbling on her pad, then tucked all three menus under her arm.

"By the way," Caroline said. "Where's the ladies' room?"

The waitress pointed to two doors at the far end of the restaurant. A waist-high partition stood in front, dotted with potted plants. "Right behind that half wall. The one on the right." She turned to leave, but Jeff grabbed her arm.

"Are there windows in there?"

The woman's brows drew together. "No. Why?"

Jeff grinned. "Just curious."

The waitress left, and Caroline looked scathingly at Jeff. "Do I have your permission?"

Jeff nodded. "Be my guest."

Taking her time, she pushed away from the table and walked slowly toward the back of the restaurant, looking for the phone. It could be a trap, an ambush. But if something was going down, she didn't want Jeff or Mac anywhere near it. She had rounded the half wall before she spotted the phone, in an alcove at the far end of the hall. She could feel Jeff's eyes on her back, watching her every move. Wiping the smile from her face, she leaned into the ladies'-room door, pushing it open as far as it could go. The room turned sharply to the right.

Caroline let go of the door, took one step around the corner, dropped to her knees, and scooted back out the door before it closed. Crouching below the wall she hurried to the pay phone. It rang the moment she stood.

She reached for it, then stopped. What if it was Brian's voice? Or Alden's? She steeled herself, prepared for the worst.

"Hello?"

"Hello, Caroline. This is Augie Davis."

Of all the voices she expected to hear, his was the last.

"How did you know I was here?" she asked. Her voice cracked and she cursed the fear that made it happen.

"I know many things," he said. In contrast to her squeak, his voice was a smooth purr. The same purr she'd heard in the library. The purr of a tiger before it strikes.

"What do you want?"

"I want to talk."

"I have nothing to say to you."

"Oh, but I have a great deal to say to you."

"Then you may say it in court, Mr. Davis. Goodbye."

"I wouldn't be so hasty to end our conversation, Caroline. Or should I call you... Mrs. McKensie?"

Her insides started shaking like a leaf blowing in the wind.

"Yes." He chuckled. "I thought that would get your attention. It's wonderful to be married. It's even more wonderful when you're in love. Your father loved your mother very much. Did you know that? And love makes people do all sorts of... unpredictable things."

"I asked you before, I'll ask you again," Caroline said. "What do you want?"

"Nothing," Davis answered. "Literally, I want nothing from you. Not a statement. Not a deposition. Not a testimony. Nothing."

The light began to dawn. "Or what?" she countered. "You'll kill me? You've already tried that—three times. What makes you think you'll be any more successful this time?"

"You misunderstand, my dear. I have no desire to hurt you. Killing *you* would only attract more attention to *me*. No, I give you my word, a solemn oath, that I will not harm you in any way. In fact, if anyone even crosses your path, they will have me to deal with."

"Get to the point," Caroline said, feigning more bravado than she felt.

"The point. Ah, yes. Well, simply put, if you say so much as one word against me, Jefferson McKensie is a dead man."

"No!" Anger, hot and flowing, surged through her body. Never had she hated anyone as much as she hated this one man. She wanted to reach into the phone and grab him by the throat. "No," she said again. "This is between you and me. Leave him out of it."

"But he's already in it, my dear. The minute he became involved with you, he became involved with me. If you keep your mouth shut, no one will get hurt. Do I make myself clear?"

She could barely summon the strength to speak. "Yes," she half whispered.

"Good. I was sure we could come to an understanding." A smug satisfaction laced his words. "Goodbye, Mrs. McKensie."

Chapter 17

The line went dead before she could answer. She spun around looking for someone, anyone who might be watching her. But she was alone in the telephone alcove.

That didn't mean anything. Davis had contacts everywhere. The waitress, the busboy, the cook—any one of them could be in his employ. The thought was staggering. And what was worse, he knew about her feelings for Jeff. She felt violated, having him know anything at all about her, let alone the fact that she was in love.

In love?

She turned the words over in her mind. For days she had danced around it. But there was no denying the truth. She was in love. And the man she loved would die if she testified.

Minutes ticked by as Caroline stood there, frozen. She didn't know what to do about Davis, but she had to get away from the phone before Jeff or Mac came looking for her.

A woman turned the corner around the half wall and entered the ladies' room. Crouching low, Caroline sneaked into the bathroom before the door closed. Then she stood and opened it again.

"I will not harm you...will not harm you...will not harm you...." Davis's words echoed in her head as she walked back to the table and dropped into her seat.

"Are you okay?" Jeff asked.

Caroline stared at him, memorizing every feature. His tousled blond hair. Eyes the deepest blue she'd ever seen. The square jaw with just a hint of a dimple.

"Jefferson McKensie is a dead man...a dead man...a dead man...." Her anger returned, and with it came a sense of powerlessness. Augie Davis would make good his threat.

There was no way on earth she could testify.

"I'm fine," she stammered. "Just need some coffee to wake me up." She wrapped her hands around the mug and took several quick sips. The scalding liquid seared her throat, and she welcomed the pain that chased away the numbness.

All through the meal she felt unseen eyes watching her. There was no getting away from Jeff, and no chance of them getting away from Davis. He knew everywhere they went and everything they did. She wouldn't risk Jeff's life by testifying—but she had to make Davis pay for killing her brothers.

But how?

"I want to go to my father's house," she announced as they climbed into the car.

"Forget it," Jeff said.

Caroline shook her head. "I've given this a lot of thought, and I'm convinced there are more ledgers. Duplicate sets or photocopies, computer disks, something."

"We've been over this before, Caroline. Davis wouldn't leave incriminating evidence lying around. And you said yourself there were no ledgers in the library when the police arrived. Face it, Bright Eyes, they're gone."

"But what if they're not?" she persisted. "Davis didn't actually shoot Brian. He just ordered his goon to do it. They never found a body, and it's my word against his that he was even in my father's house that night. If I can't convince the jury, Davis could walk."

"That's not going to happen," Jeff said. "They're going to believe you and they're going to convict him."

"Fine," she said. "So Davis is convicted of conspiracy or accessory or whatever the heck you call it. Tell me, counselor, what's the sentence on something like that?"

Jeff hedged. "It varies from state to state."

"But it's short. Too damn short. In a few years, Davis will be out and free to destroy someone else's life." The memories gnawed on a corner of her soul, and she turned away. When she spoke again, it was more to herself than anyone else. "Brian wasn't stupid. If he had something on Davis, he wouldn't have given it away. It's somewhere in that house—proof that will put Davis away forever. And I'm going to find it."

Jeff shook his head. "We're staying out of the city until the trial starts. And I've got plans about where to stay and how to keep you safe during the trial."

"Damn it, Jeff. You're not listening to me. I need these last few weeks to find the ledgers."

"And you're not listening to me. There's no way I can check out that house in time for us to use it. It's not a good plan."

"You trust Mac," Caroline insisted. "Send him on ahead."

"I'm with her," Mac said. "If there *are* records, and if we find them, she could put Davis away permanently. I don't know about you, but I don't want to be looking over my shoulder in a few years when Davis gets out."

Jeff turned the problem over and over in his mind, examining it from every angle. For a pastry chef, Caroline sure knew a lot about the law. She was absolutely right about the charges. A few years' jail time, a few years' parole, and Davis would be back before anybody missed him.

Remembering how close he'd come to losing her—how he could *still* lose her—made the decision no decision at all. If there was any chance of putting that bastard away for good, he had to take it.

* * *

A sense of melancholy covered the house like a shroud. Even the lights shining from the windows didn't dispel the gloom. Jeff parked the car across the street, and they sat there, just looking. He didn't know what Caroline was thinking, but the thoughts couldn't have been very pleasant. Nothing associated with this house was pleasant. He squeezed her hand. "You sure you want to do this?"

"I'm sure," Caroline said. She fingered one of her earrings. "I don't have a key, but I can always use this," she quipped.

Jeff smiled. "You don't need a key or a lock pick. Mac's expecting us."

Sure enough, by the time they'd climbed the steps of the brownstone stoop, Mac had the door open. "You're late," he grumbled. "I was beginning to think you'd changed your minds."

Caroline stood in the hall. Stood in the house that had been purchased with her father's ill-gotten gains. Stood in the building where she had last seen her brothers. She tried to speak, but the words stuck in her throat. She swallowed and tried again. "You checked it out?" she asked Mac.

"Sure did. I contacted the electricity, phone, and gas companies and had the service restored. And, with Arthur's help, I had a new security system installed. I didn't touch anything but the fridge." He made a face. "Believe me, after four months, nothing in there was worth keeping."

Caroline inclined her head toward the staircase. "Okay if I go down?"

Mac nodded. "I checked for bugs, taps, and stuff like that, but Caroline..." He waited until she looked him full in the face. "I left everything else just the way I found it."

"I understand." She crossed the hall. When Jeff moved to follow her, she laid a hand on his arm. "Please, don't. I need to be alone. Just a for a little while."

Jeff hesitated, then finally nodded. He watched her descend the stairs, trailing fingers along the handrail. He didn't want to let her go, not for a single second, but he had no choice. She needed time and space to face her demons, to grieve for her loss, to heal. He wanted to take her in his arms and hold her and kiss her and make all her problems go away. But he couldn't. This was something she had to do alone.

"What's the layout?" he asked Mac, when Caroline was out of earshot.

"It's a five-floor brownstone," Mac explained. "The fifth floor is actually an attic that was converted into a huge playroom. Floors three and four are bedrooms. Three bedrooms on each. Floor two, where we are now, has a kitchen, dining room and living room. And the first floor, below us, has a music room, billiard room, and—" he glanced toward the stairs "—the library."

Jeff looked around, noting the twelve-foot ceilings of hand-pounded tin held in place by plaster cornices. It was a grand old house that spoke of years gone by. He whistled softly. If these walls could talk . . .

"There's more," Mac said. "According to Arthur, the contracts on Caroline's life have been canceled. Apparently Davis changed his mind. He doesn't want her dead anymore."

Jeff scoffed. "And you believe him?"

"Not for a minute. But face it, bro, we haven't had a bit of trouble since Tennessee. Something weird is going on."

"I know," Jeff said soberly. "And I don't like it."

Caroline lit a single candle on the small Chinese tile table then turned off the lights and sat down on the sofa. The room looked exactly the way it did the last time she was here. Papers and files everywhere. Blood on the carpet.

The French had an expression—*plus ça change, plus c'est la même chose*—the more things change, the more they stay the same.

Her life had changed so very much in the last few months. And yet, here she was, right back where it all started. As soon as the trial was over, she would sell this place, and then she'd never have to step foot inside this room again.

Her head swam with the magnitude of all she had to do. Her father's estate was still unsettled. Probate had been put on hold until after the trial. She laughed bitterly. Her whole life had been put on hold. But soon she would change that. Would start living again. She would see to it that Alden's share went to his wife in Switzerland. But Brian... She didn't even know if he had a will.

The candle flickered and Caroline watched the hot wax pool around the wick. The flame threatened to extinguish itself, drowned in its own liquid. But a single drop gathered strength, poised on the rim of the candle, then trickled down the side. Behind it, a torrent of drops, unleased, unchecked, followed the carved path.

A single tear gathered strength, poised on the rim of her eyelid, then trickled down her cheek. Behind it, a torrent of tears, unleased, unchecked, followed suit.

And like the flame, Caroline knew she would burn brighter again in the morning.

Jeff stopped inside the library door. The single candle barely lit the corner of the room, but it was enough for him to see Caroline. She lay on the sofa, deep in sleep. He crossed the room and knelt beside her. Her arm was tucked under her head and her hair fell across her face. Gently, so as not to wake her, he brushed back the silky strands. The eyes beneath seemed sunken and ringed with dark circles. Her cheeks were streaked with dried tears. His soul cried out and again he was at a loss to understand how she could impact him so.

Even in sleep, she touched him, arousing emotions he couldn't define. His feelings went beyond gut-wrenching desire or fevered lust or a force waiting to be appeased. This was something deeper, richer, infinitely more special.

He wanted to share it with her. All of it—his thoughts, his feelings...his life. There was so much he wanted to tell her. But this wasn't the time to throw her another crazy, emotional curve.

He blew out the candle, lifted her into his arms and carried her upstairs to bed.

* * *

Caroline rolled up the sleeves of the flannel shirt to about the elbows—or rather, to where the elbows would have been on either of her brothers. On her, it was just above the wrist. Worn over a T-shirt, it wasn't haute couture, but for the work she had planned, it didn't matter. She pulled the edges of the shirt over her nose and inhaled deeply. It was faint, but it was still there. Beyond the detergent and fabric softener, she could smell Brian's own special scent. Or maybe it was simply her imagination fervently wishing it so.

Wearing a man's shirt somehow brought you closer to him, and today she needed to be closer to Brian than ever before. She needed access to his thoughts, wanted to crawl inside his mind, had to put herself in his shoes—she chuckled—or at least, in his shirt.

She heard movement in the hall outside the bathroom, and knew Jeff had passed by. She wasn't ready to face him yet. She had awakened this morning in her own bed and vaguely remembered Jeff carrying her there. She wasn't used to that kind of compassion and tenderness. There were a lot of things she wasn't used to. A lot of things she was beginning to enjoy.

And wouldn't she love to have a chance to wrap herself in some of *his* clothes—a shirt or a robe or even a pair of... Her imagination was off and running, and reluctantly she reined it in.

Her number-one priority had to be keeping Jeff safe. Her second priority was seeing Augie Davis put away. Both objectives could be accomplished with one solution—finding the ledgers.

Snatching up a rubber band, she pulled her hair into a ponytail. With her head down, she hurried into the hall and promptly collided with Jeff.

"Whoa," he said, his hands catching her shoulders, steadying her. "Where's the fire?"

Caught in his embrace, she felt the fire the moment he touched her. She tried to look away, but he cupped her chin in one hand and looked deeply into her eyes. His smoldering gaze was so focused, so intense that her throat closed up and it hurt to breathe. He traced a finger along her jaw, lightly, gently, drawing her closer to his heat.

He lowered his head until his lips softly brushed hers, teasing, tempting. His arms tightened around her and he deepened the kiss, scorching her nerves, branding her soul.

"Wow," he said, when they drew apart. "I've kissed a lot of women in my life, but you're the only one whose kiss knocked the world out from under me."

"Did you want something?" she asked, then blushed at the innuendo.

"The D.A. called. He said he'd call back."

Caroline shook her head. "When he does, tell him I'm not here."

Jeff's forehead furrowed. "Honey, the trial starts in ten days. He needs to go over your testimony."

"No," Caroline said flatly.

"It's routine," Jeff explained. "Trial prep is something every witness goes through. I'll sit with you the whole time. Trust me, it will make the actual testifying a lot easier."

She looked him square in the eye. Her voice was deathly calm. "Neither the D.A. nor anyone from his office is going to step foot in this house."

Jeff offered her a conciliatory smile. "He thought you'd be more comfortable here. But if you'd rather, we can go there."

"No," she said again. She pushed past him and ran down the stairs.

"What do you mean, no?" Jeff followed her into the kitchen. "You've got to have someone prepare you, especially for the cross-examination. If you don't, Davis's lawyers could destroy you on the stand."

Caroline took a deep breath. "I'm not going to testify."

"Excuse me?"

"I've given it considerable thought, and without proof of Davis's activities, I don't stand a chance of convicting him. I'm not going to put myself through the pain of reliving that night. Instead," she said, "I will find those ledgers or whatever it was Brian had on Davis, and I will turn them over to the D.A." She picked up a coffee cup, but he wrenched it out of her hands.

"I don't buy it. You've faced your memories before. You know they can't hurt you. What are you really afraid of?"

She ignored him; concentrated on finding a box of cereal, a bowl, a spoon.

He grabbed her arm and spun her around, the spoon clattering to the floor. "The first time I talked to you, in the limo, I thought you were the most courageous person I'd ever met."

"Well, that just goes to show you how wrong first impressions can be."

"I wasn't wrong, dammit. You're hiding something."

Caroline wrenched her arm away. Tears stung the backs of her eyes. "What business is it of yours, anyway? You were hired to keep me alive. You did your job. Now collect your money and go home."

"I told you months ago, I wasn't in this for the money. I'm still not. So give me one good reason why you're quitting."

"Because of what it's cost me, Jeff. That man has already cost me far too much."

"And what about the other people he's destroyed—the addicts, the hookers, the kids? Think of what it cost them, their families. You can stop him if you testify."

"I can stop him by finding the real proof."

"And what if you don't? What if you don't find a damn thing? What then? If you let this man walk all over you, everything you've been through will be for nothing. What will your life be about, then? Just getting by?"

"Yes, just getting by. Which will put me way ahead of Brian and Alden."

Jeff's eyes narrowed and he slammed his fist on the counter. "He got to you, didn't he? Answer me, Caroline. Somehow Davis got to you."

"Leave me alone, Jeff. I don't have time to argue with you. I have to find those ledgers."

* * *

"Well, make her change it again!" Arthur roared, his voice bouncing off the office walls. "I want her on that stand."

"And you think I don't?" Jeff retorted. "She needs to go through this. She needs a sense of justice. She'll never have closure on her brothers' death if she doesn't."

"Closure?" The veins on the old man's neck stood out against his pale skin. "Closure? You were hired as her bodyguard. Not her shrink. Three months ago she would have walked through hell and back to put Davis away. Now the D.A. is threatening to subpoena her as a hostile witness. You want to explain that, doctor?"

"Davis got to her," Jeff said. "Somehow, someway, that bastard got to her."

"And what? Paid her off?"

"No way. She'd never take his money. She'd rather see him rot in hell."

"Then he's got something on her. He's blackmailing her."

"With what?" Jeff countered. "She's got nothing. You've got her business partner in protective custody, and she doesn't have another soul in the world."

Arthur stroked his chin. "Except you."

"That's crazy."

"Is it?" He looked Jeff slowly up and down. "Exactly what's going on between you two?"

Jeff spoke through clenched teeth. "That, Arthur, is none of your business."

Arthur surged to his feet. "The hell it isn't. I've been working too many years to nail this guy. This case is on the line, and I'll be damned if I'll let you blow it. Now, I'm asking you straight out. Are you involved with her?"

Jeff dropped into a chair. The final piece clicked into place. He already knew how Caroline felt about brothers getting hurt. And he had ample reason to believe her feelings for him went a whole lot further than that. It wouldn't take much for Davis to capitalize on it.

"Yes," Jeff said quietly. "We're involved."

Arthur leaned back in his chair. "Then the only way she'll get on that stand is if *you're* out of the picture."

Apprehension coiled in Jeff's stomach. "Meaning what?"

"Meaning, if Caroline thinks you're...gone...she'll get on that stand and tell the whole world everything she knows."

"Are you crazy? If anything happens to me, Davis loses his leverage. He'll come after her for sure."

Arthur grinned. "She'll take the stand in forty-eight hours. Davis doesn't have time to make a move, and even if he did, Mac and an army of handpicked men will be there to protect her." Arthur rubbed his hands together. "Her testimony will break the jury's heart."

"And what about *her* heart?" Jeff asked. "Do you have any idea what this will do to her? What you're asking *me* to do to her? I won't be a part of it and that's final."

Arthur looked fondly at Jeff. "I'm sorry, son, but you don't have a choice." He punched a button on his phone and three armed men entered the room. "Take him out," Arthur ordered. "The Lazarus Plan begins now."

Caroline rubbed her eyes and looked at her watch. Time was slipping away and still she'd found nothing. She sat on the floor in the middle of her parents' room, surrounded by photos and mementos and memories. Her father had kept everything her mother ever touched, ever wore, ever admired.

She traced her mother's face in a worn photo taken of the family when Caroline was about six. Father, mother, brothers—all gone. She was totally and completely alone.

"You're not, you know." Mac lounged against the doorjamb, watching her.

"Not what?" she asked. She pulled the puppy out of a box and put the photo inside.

"Alone. You got us. Me and the dog...Arthur and Gran...Jeff."

She cast him a sideways glance. "You psychic or something?"

"Nah." He grinned. "You're just an easy read."

"Gee, thanks." She finished packing the box and taped it closed. If she was that easy a read, no doubt Mac would see right through her question, but she asked it anyway. "Where's Jeff? I haven't seen him all day."

"He had a meeting with Arthur. He left right after breakfast. Told me to keep an eye on you." Mac winked broadly. "Nice change of pace. Usually I get all the grunt work."

The phone on the night table rang and Mac picked it up. "Hello?"

Caroline jumped to her feet. "Is it Jeff?"

Mac shook his head and mouthed the word "Arthur." "What's up, boss?" he said into the phone. A moment later his face and voice sobered. "Let me write it down." Caroline dug out a scrap of paper and a pencil and handed them to him. "Go ahead," Mac said. She watched as he jotted something on the paper. "Got it," Mac said. "I'll be there as fast as I can." He hung up the phone and raced downstairs.

"It's about Jeff, isn't it?" Caroline asked, right on his heels.

"Lock the doors," Mac said. "All of them. Set the alarm. Stay away from the windows. I'll be back as soon as I can."

"Forget it," she told him, her hand on the knob of the front door. "I'm going with you."

"You can't," Mac insisted. "You have to stay here."

"Something's wrong," Caroline said. "Don't insult my intelligence by trying to deny it. I know this city inside and out." She pointed to the paper in Mac's hand. "I can be there before you figure out whether you want the Holland Tunnel or the Brooklyn Bridge."

Mac fingered the paper. "Okay," he finally said. "Here."

She read the address. "This is in Jersey—the warehouse district. What's he doing there?"

Mac shrugged. "Only one way to find out."

Fighting the traffic and a growing sense of fear, Caroline maneuvered the car through the city. On the east side of the Hudson, in Manhattan, real estate was at such a premium that the old warehouses had been torn down or converted to residences. But on the west side, in Jersey, from Liberty

State Park to Bayonne, the waterfront was dotted with warehouses—some in use, many abandoned.

They pulled up in front of a seedy, run-down brick building about three stories high. Some of the windows and doors had been boarded up, others had been ripped open again. Weeds grew around the outside and spray-painted graffiti covered much of it.

Mac let out a long, slow whistle. "Not the safest place in town."

Caroline forced a smile. "Not the worst, either. Believe me." She set the brake, then double-checked the address. "They don't exactly mark the buildings, but by the process of elimination, I'm pretty sure this is it." She reached for the door handle, but Mac grabbed her arm.

"Stay here. Lock the doors and wait for me. Anyone bothers you, put it in gear and go."

She laughed. "Not a chance and you know it."

Mac returned her grin. "Hey, it was worth a try." He checked his gun, then squeezed her hand. "C'mon, then, let's go."

They hadn't gone more than a few steps, when a figure waved to them from a half-boarded window upstairs.

"It's Jeff," Caroline said. She waved back, then cupped her hands around her mouth to shout to him. Her words were drowned by a booming explosion that shook the ground. Smoke billowed from the windows. Two more explosions went off in rapid succession, sending fire and flaming debris into the air. The old building trembled and she watched in helpless terror as Jeff disappeared from view.

"No!" she screamed. "No-o-o-o-o!"

Chapter 18

Dear God, no!

"Jeff!" she screamed. "Jeff!" She raced for the door, but Mac's strong arms held her back. "Let me go! Let me go!"

"No, Caroline." His voice was thick. "We'd never make it."

She turned on him, beating his chest with her fists. "We've got to get him out. You can't just let him die!"

Sirens echoed in the distance, offering help that was too far away and too late in coming.

"We'd better get out of here," Mac said.

"No!" Caroline cried. Scratching and clawing, she tried to break free, tried to get into the inferno that had once been a warehouse.

A fire truck arrived, sealing off the area, pushing them back to the street.

"Jeff's in there," she sobbed. "Please, get him out. Please!" Hysteria set in. She could feel it take control of her mind, turning her tears into near laughter.

"Look at me, Caroline." Mac grabbed her by the forearms and shook her hard. "Look at me! The police will be here any minute. They'll want answers. Answers we don't have. We've got to leave."

A crowd had gathered—street kids, transients, the media. Someone stuck a microphone in Caroline's face.

"Do you know who was in there? Is this one of Augie Davis's warehouses? Does this have something to do with Davis's trial?"

Mac shoved the reporter aside and put his arm around Caroline, pulling her close. Pushing through the growing crowd, he ushered her into the car and drove away.

Caroline stood in the middle of the attic playroom. Her mother had never made it into this room. She'd lived in the house only six months, and was confined to her bed the entire time.

But for those six months, the attic had been Caroline's refuge.

A place to run to when she was all alone. A place to hide when the doctors came. A place so high up that no one could hear her cry.

She walked around the room picking up pieces of her life. A doll given to her by her mother. A book of poems from Alden. A stuffed animal from Brian. She sat in the old rocking chair and held the items in her arms. Rocking them back and forth. Gifts from the ones she loved.

Jeff hadn't given her anything tangible. No trinket to hold and caress and keep safe. But he'd given her the happiest days she had ever known. Would ever know.

Tears bathed her soul as she wrapped herself in the memories. She loved him. More than she had ever thought possible. And he was gone.

Mac rapped softly on the open door. "Caroline?" He flipped on a light, pulling her out of the darkness. "I brought you some tea." He set a little breakfast tray on the floor next to her chair, then stooped in front of her.

Caroline looked down at him. "Did they...did they find anything?"

Mac shook his head. "Not yet."

"Then there's still hope. Maybe he got out."

Mac forced a smile. "Maybe." He squeezed her shoulder. "I'll be downstairs. If you want anything, just . . ."

She didn't try to stop the tears that flowed down her face. "I just want him."

"I know, kiddo. I know."

The tea grew cold as she rocked and rocked. Back and forth, trying to make sense of a senseless tragedy.

What was it Davis had said? *"Your father loved your mother very much."*

Through the murky haze of pain, she finally understood. Understood that her father's actions were born of love. Love for her mother. How desperately he must have wanted to help her, make her well, keep her safe. And so he became involved with a monster.

Just as she had.

Love makes people do all sorts of unpredictable things.

Like keeping the truth from the one you love.

All the things she'd never told Jeff echoed inside her head like a Greek chorus gone mad. She loved him more than life itself. All she had ever wanted was to keep him safe.

And she had played right into Augie Davis's hands.

Davis understood the power of love. He had twisted and warped the most blessed emotion to his own advantage. But she would see to it that he never did it again.

She would start by testifying tomorrow and put Davis away for whatever length of time the court would allow. And then she'd spend the rest of her life looking for evidence to put him away forever. But that was tomorrow.

Today, all she could do was cry.

Laying aside the childhood toys, she pulled a huge book from the bookshelf and carried it reverently back to the rocking chair. It had been Brian's. She rubbed her fingers over the gold lettering on the cover—"Photo Album."

She remembered clearly the day Brian had gotten a camera. He had run around the house snapping away, shooting three rolls of film in ten minutes, then was furious to discover it would take days to develop his pictures.

When the photos arrived, their father gave Brian a special antique album to keep them in. There were no self-adhesive plastic pages that you pulled apart and slapped together. These pages were large and cream-colored, like in a scrapbook, and Brian had used little gold tricornered pieces to affix the pictures to the page, and then had scribbled a caption under each of them in his own childish hand.

Caroline opened the book and smiled. On the front page was a picture of her and Alden—from the neck down. There were lots of pictures like that, cropped off or out of focus. The memories resurfaced as she turned page after page. An embarrassed Alden running in his underwear. Caroline doing a "Look, Ma, no hands!" on her bicycle. A listing Christmas tree that had crashed in the middle of the night, convincing Caroline there really was a Santa Claus—albeit a clumsy one.

She laughed and turned another page. A pure white accounting sheet stared back at her. It was covered with entries and numbers, all in the meticulous handwriting of a bookkeeper—her father.

Her lip quivered and her fingers trembled as she touched the paper. Quickly she turned the page. Once again Brian's ridiculous photography greeted her. She looked back, thinking she had been dreaming, but *no,* it was there. A white ledger sheet buried among the cream ones.

She turned the pages as fast as her shaking hands would allow. Photos, photos, photos—numbers. Photos, photos, photos, photos, photos—numbers.

She screamed and laughed and cried all at the same time. Mac burst into the room, his face drained of color. She knew he feared for her sanity. But she couldn't speak. Instead, she thrust the book into his hands.

Comprehension flooded his features. "My God, Caroline, you did it! You found it!"

They sat on the floor and inspected the sheets. Six pages. Six precious pages detailing Davis's connections to members of a drug cartel. Money that passed through a dozen hands, a dozen dummy companies before reaching South America.

"A scrapbook," Mac said. "Who would have thought to look in a damn scrapbook? The color and size of the pages are so close, you'd never notice it."

Caroline looked from the book in Mac's lap to the bookcase. "Mac..."

He followed her gaze to the top shelf where another dozen photo albums sat—all identical. Their eyes met and held, then they scrambled to their feet and began yanking the books off the shelf.

Minutes later they sat sprawled in a sea of ledger sheets—thin pieces of paper that connected Augie Davis to gunrunners, racketeers, prostitution, and gambling.

"It's over," Caroline said, tears running down her cheeks. And soon their souls would be laid to rest—Alden's, Brian's... and Jeff's.

She was on the stand for four grueling days. Although Caroline was worn down to the point of collapsing, her testimony was nothing short of stirring. The defense would spend the next week or two presenting its case, but everyone in the D.A.'s office and the police department said a conviction would be sure and swift. And armed with Donald Southeby's account sheets, police and prosecutors brought a host of new charges against the mob boss and dozens of his acquaintances, including the cop who had been on Davis's payroll. Facing lengthy jail terms, a few turned state's evidence, further incriminating the kingpin. Davis's entire empire lay in shambles.

Caroline sat in the stripped-down library of her father's home. She hadn't been near her own apartment or The Coffee Café in months. Now it was time. Time to put the For Sale sign in the yard, lock the front door, and walk away. It was time to return to her old life—her life before Augie Davis.

And before Jeff McKensie.

The brownstone was cold and empty and Caroline drew her jacket around her shoulders. Cold and empty. A fitting description of the way she felt.

Trailing her fingers along her father's desk, she moved to the window. The day was gray and rainy, weather that mimicked her mood. Fall was coming. The leaves were dying, becoming brown and shriveled. Another sentiment that suited her just fine.

Somewhere down the street, a dog barked and she thought of Mac and the puppy. Mac had been a pillar of strength, never leaving her side. She had tried to convince him to go to his grandmother, that she needed him far more than Caroline did. But he refused, saying only that this was what Jeff would have wanted.

And now Mac was gone, too. He had left for the airport about an hour ago, taking the dog with him.

A shiver racked her body. Maybe someday she'd feel warm again. But she doubted it. The cold was too deep, the emptiness too vast.

A single tear ran down her cheek and plopped on the windowsill. "Goodbye, Jeff," Caroline whispered. "I love you."

"I love you, too, Bright Eyes."

"Oh, please, God, no."

A sob tore from her soul and she clamped her hands over her ears. Not this. Not *his* voice. For months she had lived with her brothers' voices echoing in her head, hearing them when she least expected it. Sometimes they were a guiding force, but more often than not, they simply deepened her pain. She didn't think she could bear the torment of hearing Jeff's voice day after day.

"I'm here, Caroline, really here."

She shook her head, her hands still covering her ears. "No," she cried. "Go away. Please, just leave me alone."

"Caroline."

A hand touched her shoulder.

"Look at me," the voice said.

Slowly she turned around. Like an apparition, he stood before her. His thick blond hair fell across his forehead—just as she remembered. His deep blue eyes were filled with promise—just as she'd dreamed. With one shaky hand, she reached out and touched the solid wall of his chest. A small cry escaped her lips. Her fingers moved of their own accord, touching, exploring his face, his neck, his arms. Tears streamed down her cheeks. "This isn't a dream," she sobbed. "You're alive. You're really alive."

"Guilty as charged," Jeff said, smiling the smile that she knew so well.

"But how? The fire...the explosion...I saw you...." Her voice trailed off, and she grabbed his hand, afraid that he might yet disappear.

"Ah, that." Jeff brushed a strand of hair away from her face. "Maybe you'd better sit down." He led her to the couch, still clinging to his arm. "The explosion in the warehouse was—" he swallowed, knowing there was no easy way to say it "—staged."

"What?" A bubble of hysteria caught in her throat. "What do you mean, 'staged'?"

"It was all part of the plan."

"The plan?" A feeling of dread swept down her spine.

Jeff turned to face her on the couch, taking both of her hands in his. "Arthur figured out that Davis was using me to prevent you from testifying. He knew the only way you would testify against him was if I was out of the picture."

"So you faked your own death?"

Jeff nodded. "Arthur arranged it, but, yes." He reached for her, but she pulled back.

She clenched her fists as the anger grew. "Tell me, Jeff. How many people were in on this little drama?"

"It wasn't like that—"

"Mac?"

"Well, yes," Jeff admitted. "Arthur needed him to take care of you—"

"And your grandmother, did she know?"

"We couldn't very well let her think I was really dead."

Caroline lost it. "Why the hell not? You let *me* think you were really dead." She paused, choking back the tears, the anger that he could have been so cruel, so heartless. When she spoke again, her voice was barely audible. "Do you have any idea what you put me through these past five days? *Five days,* Jeff. For five days I couldn't eat, couldn't sleep. All I did was cry."

"I know, Caroline. I'm sorry. I never wanted to hurt you." Jeff tried to take her into his arms, but again she backed away. "I swear, it wasn't my idea. Arthur forced me into it. It was the only way he could get you to testify. And he wouldn't let me out until your testimony was over."

Caroline laughed hysterically. "So you finally got a taste of your own medicine. Tell me, how does it feel to lose control of your life? To have someone else planning and masterminding and exploiting you?"

"Caroline, listen to me. You're upset—"

"'Upset'? This is not about being upset, Jeff. This is about being betrayed. About having my heart ripped to shreds. How many times over the last few months did you tell me to trust you? 'I won't let them hurt you,'" she mimicked. "'Trust me.'" She wrapped her arms across her chest. "Well, *they* didn't hurt me, Jeff. *You* did."

Jeff raked a hand through his hair. "I'm sorry, Caroline. I'm really, really sorry. But don't you see? Now that Davis is gone, we can get on with our lives. I'll make it up to you. We can make plans for the future—"

"No!" Caroline shouted. "You and your damn plans! You don't know when to stop. Preparing is one thing, but you're light-years beyond that. What you do isn't planning. It's scheming, manipulating, conspiring. And I won't be part of it."

"Bright Eyes, I—"

Caroline's laugh was harsh and laced with pain. "My eyes aren't bright anymore, Jeff. They're red and bloodshot and sore from all the jagged bouts of crying. But I'll tell you this much, they're wide open."

"Let me explain. I thought—"

"No, Jeff, you didn't think. You and Arthur planned. You planned what was going to happen to me without ever considering how it would make me feel."

Jeff fisted his hands. He had envisioned this scene a hundred times, and not once had it played out like this. She was supposed to be in his arms showering him with kisses. Instead, she was on the opposite side of the room, shooting daggers from her deep brown eyes.

"I can't live my life according to your blueprint." Her hands moved aimlessly in front of her, as if searching for the right words. "That's not living. Real life is exuberant and spontaneous and impetuous." Her hands dropped to her sides. "I don't know if I'll ever find that. But I know it can't be that way with you." She turned her back to him and faced the window. "Please go."

Jeff paused in the library doorway, his hand on the door-knob. His voice was as thick as hers. "Maybe I did plan out my whole life, Caroline. But you know what? I never planned on falling in love with you."

He closed the door behind him. The pain of her words tore at his heart. Slowly he climbed the basement stairs. Maybe he was a bit too...methodical. Maybe he could afford to be a tad more laid-back and impetuous. He could do that—with a little practice.

But he wouldn't give up. One thing he was sure of, he would never give up on the woman he loved.

Jeff nearly laughed out loud as he sprinted out the door and down the street. If she needed a life that was impulsive and spontaneous, that was exactly what she'd get.

And he'd plan it for her.

Right down to the last detail.

Wearing her oldest, baggiest, most comfortable sweats and a pair of worn slippers, Caroline slopped around her apart-ment, randomly tossing things into a box. She couldn't live in this city any longer, couldn't go back to working in The Coffee Café, couldn't look at a croquembouche without re-membering. So, this morning she had met with her attorney and deeded over her half of the business to Johanna, leaving her friend enough cash to hire the best pastry chef in the city. The attorney called Caroline impulsive and reckless, but that only strengthened her resolve.

With the trial over, the house sold, and probate done, she was ready to move on. She didn't have a clue where that was, but Paris seemed like a good place to start. A good place to try to forget.

As if she could.

She had thought about Jeff nonstop since the day he'd walked out on her.

The day you threw him out, her conscience corrected.

Whatever.

But he was probably off planning his career, mapping out his life, charting his very existence.

"It's better this way," she said aloud. "I need surprise and excitement in my life. I can't live, knowing every mundane step that lies ahead."

Like your days are now? Each one a carbon copy of the one before. Each one emptier than the last.

Okay, so maybe he wasn't Mr. Impetuous. The truth was, a planned day with Jeff was better than a spontaneous day alone.

She understood a lot of things now. Understood that sometimes people do all the wrong things for all the right reasons. But it was too late. She hadn't seen or heard from Jeff in weeks. Not a call. Not a letter. Nothing.

Feeling lost and dejected, she dropped a tape into the cassette player. Sam Cooke's mellow voice filled the tiny apartment, bemoaning the fact that it was Saturday night and he didn't have "no-o-o-body."

"Shows what you know," Caroline muttered. "It's only Friday."

Then came the Righteous Brothers, lamenting the loss of their loving feelings. And by the time Paul McCartney finished singing about yesterday, Caroline was ready to crawl into what was left of her heart and never come out again.

The phone jangled and she jumped for it, grateful for any excuse to break out of her growing depression. "Hello?"

"Caroline? It's Mac McKensie."

"Mac." The name alone was enough to send hope surging through her system.

"I'm sorry to bother you—"

"No bother. I was just listening to some music." She took a deep breath. "What's up?"

"I...uh...Arthur asked me to call you. He was afraid you'd hang up on him."

"He's right," Caroline said. "I would." Arthur had called her a couple of times in the past few weeks—presumably to apologize for his actions. She never gave him the chance.

"Yeah...well...apparently there's some kind of glitch with this marriage thing. Papers got recorded that weren't supposed to, something like that.... I don't know the details."

Caroline sucked in a quick breath. "Are you saying I'm really married?"

"No, of course not," Mac answered quickly. "But they need you here to help untangle the mess. You and Jeff have to appear before a judge."

The air whooshed out of her lungs. "I see."

"Arthur will pick up the tab for the airfare. It's the least he can do," Mac muttered. "And I'll meet you at the airport and drive you to the...courthouse. Will you come?"

You and Jeff have to appear. You and Jeff. You and Jeff.

It took less than a heartbeat for her to make up her mind. "Yes, I'll come."

Mac's sigh of relief was clearly audible. "That's great. I'll tell Arthur. He'll make the arrangements. He's good at that sort of thing."

"Yeah, I know," Caroline said dryly.

An awkward silence stretched over the wires.

"Look, Caroline, I'm sorry about my part in that stupid plan. About lying to you—"

"It wasn't your fault, Mac. It certainly wasn't your idea." Quickly she changed the subject. "How's the puppy?"

"Fine. Getting big. I named him Clouseau—since he turned out to be such a great detective."

Caroline laughed. "I can't wait to see him."

"Yeah...well, I'd better go. Thanks, Caroline. See you soon."

Mac was waiting for her—alone—when she stepped off the plane. Bitter disappointment crept into her heart, but she tried not to show it.

"Good flight?" Mac asked as they headed up the concourse back to the terminal.

"Fine," Caroline answered.

"Do you have any luggage?"

"Just my carryon," Caroline said. She forced a laugh. "Old habits are hard to break. I still travel light."

Mac managed a gruff smile. "Right. My truck's in the lot. Not too far."

After a few halfhearted attempts at small talk, they resigned themselves to riding in silence. Mac gripped the wheel, staring straight ahead. Caroline looked out the window, vaguely noting the passing scenery. When they entered a park, she sat up straighter.

"Isn't this the park where—"

"Shortcut," Mac announced. But minutes later he pulled to a stop in front of the Whiteside Chapel.

"What's going on, Mac?"

"Don't look at me," he said, holding up his hands in surrender. "This wasn't my idea, either."

Before she could object, Jeff wrenched open the truck door. One minute she was in the cab, the next she was in his arms. His mouth zeroed in on her lips and her protests dissolved in the heat of his kiss.

When he finally released her, she gulped air into her lungs. "What's going on?" she gasped.

Jeff grinned. "We are being reckless, my love. Impulsive, impetuous, spontaneous... We're getting married."

Sleepless nights and a long, tiring flight had clearly dulled her brain. She could have sworn he said they were getting married. "What?"

Jeff pointed to the chapel behind him. There on the steps stood his grandmother... and Johanna... and Arthur, all beaming from ear to ear.

Caroline turned her disbelieving eyes to Jeff. "You planned this? A wedding?"

Jeff grinned. "Flowers, organ music, a *real* minister, reception, wedding cake, dance band—the whole shebang."

"Without mentioning it to me?"

"Right again."

The shock wore off and anger bubbled like hot lava ready to explode. "You idiot! You moron! You...bozo!" Caroline clenched her fists, resisting the urge to plant one of them in his stomach. "You've done it again. This is exactly what happened last time—exactly what I told you I couldn't...*wouldn't* tolerate."

"No, Caroline. This is *not* like last time. It will never again be like last time. I swear it." He grabbed her fists and pressed them to his lips, kissing first one, then the other. "Hear me out, and then if you still want to leave, I promise I'll let you go and never bother you again."

Caroline gritted her teeth and glanced at her watch. "You've got exactly thirty seconds."

Jeff flashed her a wicked smile and lowered his voice. "Do you remember our last countdown?"

"Twenty-five seconds."

"Okay, okay. Caroline, I'm a planner. I was born that way. I can't change it even if I wanted to. It's part of who I am, part of my charm."

Caroline frowned, but said nothing.

"And you're who you are," Jeff explained. "Irreverent, impetuous, impertinent, exasperating—"

"Nineteen, eighteen—"

"We're a team, Bright Eyes. We complement each other perfectly. And if you'll let me—"

He stopped. His voice lost the light, teasing tone, and his eyes reflected the depth of his passion.

In the middle of the park, in front of the little chapel, Jefferson McKensie knelt before the woman he loved. "Marry me, Caroline. And I promise to plan a lifetime of surprises for you—all of them wonderful."

Caroline looked at the errant tuxedoed knight kneeling at her feet. His incessant plans would probably drive her crazy. But on the other hand, she would have something new and different to look forward to every day of her life.

And what could be better than that?

"I suppose you've also planned a honeymoon," Caroline said.

Jeff stood and calmly brushed the knees of his trousers. "Of course. And believe me, it's a humdinger. One of my more spectacular plans, if I do say so myself."

"Really?" She looped her arm through his as they headed up the stone walkway. "Exactly where are we going?"

Jeff looked aghast. "I can't tell you that." He winked. "It would spoil the surprise."

Epilogue

Jeff stood at the front of the chapel and looked out over the sea of faces. The tiny church was filled with the fragrance of autumn flowers and the soft, low strains of organ music. Sunshine poured in through the stained-glass window above the altar, spilling pools of emerald, ruby and sapphire light across the altar steps. Jeff smiled at Mac, and reluctantly his brother acknowledged it. Clearly, Mac had not quite forgiven Jeff for making him lie to Caroline.

He watched his grandmother walk down the carpeted aisle and take her place in the wooden pew decorated with a white satin bow. After a moment, Johanna, Caroline's maid of honor, began to glide down the aisle.

The music swelled and the familiar strains of the wedding march rose to the vaulted ceiling. In one fluid motion, the congregation stood and turned in unison to face the vestibule.

Jeff's breath caught in his throat as he watched Arthur offer his arm to a vision in white lace. Her bearing was regal. She walked with the grace and elegance of a princess, seeming to float down the aisle. She carried a bouquet of white roses and yellow freesia and wore a crown woven of the same flowers. A gossamer veil, attached to the crown, covered her face.

Jeff watched, spellbound, as the distance closed between them. She lifted the skirts of her dress and ascended the stairs to stand next to him.

He offered her his hand and she took it, accepting his protection and allegiance . . . and love. And then she raised her eyes—large and dark, to meet his.

And smiled.

* * * * *

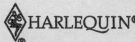

The Calhoun Saga continues...

in November
New York Times bestselling author

NORA ROBERTS

takes us back to the Towers and introduces us to
the newest addition to the Calhoun household,
sister-in-law Megan O'Riley in

MEGAN'S MATE
(Intimate Moments #745)

And in December
look in retail stores for the special collectors'
trade-size edition of

THE
Calhoun
Women

containing all four fabulous Calhoun series books:
COURTING CATHERINE,
A MAN FOR AMANDA, FOR THE LOVE OF LILAH
and *SUZANNA'S SURRENDER.*
Available wherever books are sold.

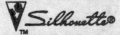

In February, Silhouette Books is proud
to present the sweeping, sensual new novel
by bestselling author

CAIT LONDON

about her unforgettable family—*The Tallchiefs*.

TALLCHIEF
FOR KEEPS

Everyone in Amen Flats, Wyoming, was talking about
Elspeth Tallchief. How she wasn't a thirty-three-year-old
virgin, after all. How she'd been keeping herself warm at
night all these years with a couple of secrets. And now one
of those secrets had walked right into town, sending
everyone into a frenzy. But Elspeth knew he'd come for
the *other* secret....

"Cait London is an irresistible storyteller..."
—*Romantic Times*

Don't miss TALLCHIEF FOR KEEPS by Cait London, available
at your favorite retail outlet in February from

COMING NEXT MONTH

THE COUSINS

Olivia Okrent and her cousins grew up spending their summers at
the family's country estate, unaware that dark secrets and haunting
betrayals would one day be their legacy.

Now the cousins have lives and families of their own, getting together
only for special occasions. But when lies and infidelities threaten her
comfortable life, Olivia is faced with a choice that may separate her
from her family, once and for all.

by

RONA JAFFE

Available this December at your favorite retail outlet.